PRAISE FOR STEWART FOSTER

'A wonderful book about ov
event and the remarka
Lisa Thompson, author of *The Goldfish Boy*

'Powerful, moving and uplifting. This beautifully-
told story highlights the gift of perseverance.'
Polly Ho-Yen, author of *Boy in the Tower*

'A moving, empathy-boosting, and hopeful story
about a young musician navigating hearing loss.'
Rashmi Sirdeshpande, author of *Think Like a Boss*

'A sensitive and brilliant story of hearing
loss, full of humour and hope.'
A. M. Howell, author of *The Garden of Lost Secrets*

'A gripping and deeply moving book.'
Jamila Gavin, author of *Coram Boy*

'Poignant, hopeful and heartbreaking.'
The Bookseller

'An uplifting, positively life-affirming story
with a very memorable hero.'
Parents in Touch

Also by Stewart Foster

CAN YOU FEEL
THE
NOISE?

STEWART FOSTER

SIMON & SCHUSTER

Mum

First published in Great Britain in 2022 by Simon & Schuster UK Ltd

1 3 5 7 9 10 8 6 4 2

Simon & Schuster UK Ltd
1st Floor, 222 Gray's Inn Road
London
WC1X 8HB

www.simonandschuster.co.uk
www.simonandschuster.com.au
www.simonandschuster.co.in

Simon & Schuster Australia, Sydney
Simon & Schuster India, New Delhi

A CIP catalogue record for this book is available from the British Library.

PB ISBN 978-1-4711-9127-5
eBook ISBN 978-1-4711-9128-2
eAudio ISBN 978-1-3985-0010-5

WHITE CORRIDORS AND BRIGHT LIGHTS

'Will it grow back . . . ? They said it would grow back . . .'

A nurse smiles, then she smooths my hair.

'Yes, it will grow back,' she says.

Smiley face. Her blurred, smiley face.

'My friend Rocco said I should have a Mohican.'

'What's that, Sophie?'

'My friend . . . Rocco . . . He said you should shave both sides of my head so I have a Mohican.'

Another sting in my hand. *Was I supposed to feel that?*

'It's okay, Sophie. You're going to feel a little drowsy now. We're just going to take you down to the operating theatre.'

Dark shadow. A doorway, then a white corridor, with bright lights passing over my head.

My eyes start to flicker.

'My friend Rocco . . .'

Smiling face. Warm, smiling face – lips moving, but too blurry to read.

I feel sleepy. I feel so sleepy. Warm hand on mine.

'Your mum said you like to play guitar?'

I smile.

'Yeah.' My eyes flicker again. 'My friend . . . Rocco said I should have a Mohican.' The nurse's face fades away. So sleepy. So sleepy. 'My friend Rocco . . . He said . . . He said . . . I should have . . . a . . . Mo . . . a . . . Mo . . . hi . . . can.'

CHAPTER 1

SIX WEEKS EARLIER

THE NOISE

It started as a distant hum. A low drilling noise, like roadworks had begun on my street one Sunday morning. It was so real I kept checking out of my bedroom window for white vans and workers digging in reflective clothing. But there was no one there, except for a boy from the house four doors down, kicking his football against a wall.

The hum was still there in the afternoon.

'Perhaps it's the fridge,' my mum suggested. 'It's on its way out.'

'Or maybe it's the electricity pylon down the road,' said my dad.

'No,' I said. 'The fridge is more of a drone, and the pylon is a buzz – this is as irritating as both but is neither.'

They shrugged because they couldn't hear a noise anything like the one I was describing, but they could tell how annoyed I was, because Dad was still trying to help identify what it was during tea.

'Are you sure it's not the pylon?' he said. 'Only, you know I'm fairly sure it causes my psoriasis.'

'Dad,' I snapped, and put my knife and fork down. 'It's not the pylon. You blame everything on it – your psoriasis, your bald patch, the grass not growing.'

'Only trying to help, Soph,' he said, like I'd upset him.

'I know,' I said. 'I'm sorry – it's just the noise has been there all day, like a million midges, midging away at my brain.'

'Midging?' Mum chuckled.

'Well,' I said, 'whatever it is that midges do.'

We all laughed, then Mum put her hand on mine.

'Perhaps it's wax, Soph,' she said gently. 'I'll put some olive oil in your ears before you go to bed.'

That night I went to bed, ears so greasy I felt like my head was slipping off the pillow. But the noise was still there. For a while, I thought it was my stepbrother, Liam, outside with his friends revving their motorbikes, even though I was sure I'd heard him come in at eleven. I was doubly sure it was him when I sniffed the smell of burnt toast wafting under my door.

But that didn't stop me getting up and checking three more times during the night. My alarm clock said 2.05 a.m. the next time I got up.

2.26 a.m. the next.

3.09 a.m. the time after that.

It had to be something, somewhere – a truck, or a bus idling – but each time I looked, all I saw was the neighbourhood cats stalking each other under the village street lights.

That day in May was the first time I had the noise, but it wasn't the first problem I'd had with my ears.

I'd noticed it first in the final term at my primary school, six months ago, whenever Mrs Santo turned her back and wrote a sum on the whiteboard. As she spoke, all I could hear was the mumble of her voice, just loud enough that I could make out how many syllables she was saying. Most times I could see what she'd written, and would be able to answer, but if she asked another question after that, I wouldn't be able to work out what she'd said. I'd sit still, feeling dumb, while other kids in the class were waving their hands in the air.

The first person I told was Mum, and it turned out she wasn't surprised. She'd noticed how every day it felt like she was having to shout louder up the stairs to tell me when tea was ready. She'd thought that I'd been ignoring her, or maybe I had been too immersed in playing my songs on my guitar.

She took me to see a hearing consultant, Dr Cowans. He gave me a test and said my hearing wasn't as good as it could be, and that we should monitor it for a while. A month later, I didn't need another test to know my hearing was getting worse. I could still hear, but I was now sometimes missing questions, even when Mrs Santo was facing the class, and I'd have to ask my friend Mia what she'd said. And over the summer holidays, Mum and Dad had noticed that I'd started turning the TV up louder.

I began to notice it more when I started at Cromwell High. It might have been because the classes were bigger and the students noisier, but I had to sit near the front to hear the teachers. Luckily at my last appointment with Dr Cowans a few months ago, he said my hearing seemed to have stabilized; while it wasn't getting better, it didn't seem to be getting any worse. Which made me feel great – it finally felt like things were starting to look up.

But the morning the noise started, it didn't feel like things were looking up; it felt like they were getting worse.

It was still with me when I got on the bus to school with Mia the next morning. My noise was irritating me so much that I didn't want to talk about it; I thought Mia might think it was weird. Besides, she seemed more preoccupied with how I smelt.

'What is it?' she said, sniffing the air as she looked at me.

'Maybe it's my deodorant,' I said.

'No.' Mia leaned close. 'It's not that.'

'Maybe Mum's changed our fabric conditioner.' I held out my arm for her to smell.

'No.' She screwed up her face.

'What is it, then?' I asked. 'Because you're making me feel gross.'

Mia didn't answer, and we hardly talked as the bus drove out of our village. I just stared out of the window because I'd gone to bed with the noise, woken up with the noise, eaten breakfast with the noise, and now it was still there, whining away above the rumble of the bus wheels. I closed my eyes, took deep breaths to try to calm down, but it was still there like an alarm clock, ringing in my head. I just wished I could reach up with my hand, slam the button and turn it off.

Mia didn't say much in registration either, but then sometimes we're like that. Being friends for five years, we don't have to talk to know how the other is feeling. She knew I was irritable in the same way I knew she was upset when Lotto, her dog, died. We just don't have to spend all day reminding each other what's on our minds. She's in the band with me. In fact, we were the ones who started it in the second week after winter break.

We were sat together at lunch, playing our guitars, when two boys from our year came and joined us – Ty and Rocco. They often came to the music room, but we'd never spoken to them before. They said they'd heard us playing songs that they liked, like 'Fade Away' and 'Dying Sun', and Ty showed us his rucksack where he'd painted the band name BURNOUT in big yellow letters on to the back of it.

That's the moment I knew we'd get along, and we decided to form a band, with Ty on keyboard and Rocco as our lead singer. We played for fun more than anything else and hadn't even come up with a name when our music teacher, Mrs Hopkirk, said we should enter the Battle of the Bands competition to find the best school band in our area. We've already got through the first round with HiFi Dad from Year Nine and a group of sixth-formers called the Longshots, and we're all playing in the semi-finals in three weeks' time. The final is at Rock City, the biggest music venue in town, two weeks after that. We spend most of our lunchtimes practising in the music room, and today was like any other. Except this time, I had my noise, and all anyone could talk about was the weird smell.

'Chips!' Rocco said. 'That's what it is! You smell of chips.'

'What?' I sniffed my arms again.

'Chips!' He seemed almost happy about it. 'But don't worry, sometimes I know I stink of my dad's homemade beer. It's not your clothes; it's your hair.'

'No, it's not,' I said. 'Is it?' I pulled a band out of my hair. 'Oh no, it is,' I said, lifting my hair up to my nose. 'It's everywhere.'

'What is?' asked Mia.

'Olive oil,' I said.

'Olive oil?' they all said at the same time.

'Yeah,' I said. 'I've got this noise in my head. A high-pitched whine. My mum thought it might be trapped wax, so she put olive oil in my ear to loosen it.'

'Gross,' said Rocco, scrunching up his nose.

'Thanks, Rocco,' I said. 'I know it makes it look like I haven't washed it for week.'

'True.'

'You're not supposed to agree with me,' I said irritably.

'Just saying.' Rocco smirked.

I turned to Ty, who had cranked his amp up so loud it hummed. 'And can you at least keep that down until we're ready to play?'

'Haven't touched it,' said Ty.

'You have,' I snapped at him like I had at Dad the night before. 'I can hear it.'

'Soph, it's not.' Ty lifted up his keyboard lead. 'It's not even plugged in.'

'Then what is it? That hum.'

The band looked at each other.

'Can't you hear it?' I said, panicking. 'Please tell me you can hear it.'

'There's no noise, Soph,' said Mia. 'You know we've not turned the amps up loud since your doctor said not to.'

I suddenly felt hot and like I was trapped in a box. The noise was in my head, and it had followed me from home to school. But it was changing: one minute it was a rumbling truck engine, the next it was like I was being followed by a screeching alien. Now it was like a thousand bees stuck in a jar. At first it was annoying, but now I'd started to freak out.

I put my guitar down beside me and sat on a desk. I wanted to leave, but we'd just got through the first round of Battle of the Bands and needed to practise as much as we could. We had the semi-finals coming up, then if we got through, the finals were at Rock City, in the centre of town.

Rocco came over to me like he could tell I was worried.

'It's okay, Soph,' he said. 'Maybe just sit here quietly and write some lyrics instead.' Then he went off, bouncing around while pretending he was singing into a microphone. He could be an idiot sometimes, but he could almost always make me smile. I couldn't smile then, though, and I definitely couldn't think of any lyrics, not with the noise *buzz*, *buzz*, *buzzing* in my head.

When I got home from school, I went straight to my room. Mum came in and asked if I was okay. I told her the noise was still there. She told me she'd call Dr Cowans in the morning to make an appointment. I knew I had to go. I'd been six times in the last year, but still I hated having the cold metal probe in my ear, like a tiny telescope with a light shining through. And I hated having my ears tested, which might have been why Mum let me eat my tea in my bedroom ... or maybe she knew I didn't want to hear Dad going on about the pylons.

That evening, I tried to do my history homework, but the harder

I concentrated, the worse the noise got. I turned on the TV to try to cover it, but it was still there, like a pack of hyenas, screaming in the middle of my head. I tried playing music, I tried putting my hands over my ears, I tried wrapping my head in my pillow, but there was no escape.

After two hours, my phone buzzed beside me.

A message from Rocco.

Rocco: Hey, Soph are you okay?
Still got the 🐿️?

Sophie: Yes. Still there.

Rocco: Hope it goes. I got a song for next round of Battle of the Bands.

I smiled even though my noise had made me so tired.

Sophie: How does it go? It better not be about a 🐿️

Rocco: It's not 😊 Hang on . . .

I looked at my phone, imagined Rocco in his garage recording his song idea. He couldn't play drums, but when we were together, he'd play me simple beats he'd find on the internet and then we'd sit side by side and he'd sing the tune and I'd add the melody and the lyrics.

My screen lit up as a file from Rocco arrived.

I opened it up.

A simple drumbeat played, then Rocco began to sing '*la-la-la*' over the top of it. I smiled. Rocco had a good voice, but it was weird without lyrics.

Rocco: What do you think?

Sophie: It's a good tune.

Rocco: Cool. We could work on it tomorrow?

Sophie: Could do, but I might have to go to hospital as Mum's calling them in the morning.

Rocco: About the 🦟?
Just swat it 🏸

Sophie: I'll try.

Rocco: Maybe that's what we should call the band. The Bees ☺ Or the Swats ☺

My phone kept vibrating as Rocco sent more names, but my noise was wearing me out.

I put the phone down on my bedside table and switched off the light. For a moment I thought about Battle of the Bands, imagining us all at Rock City, with me and Mia playing guitars and Ty standing behind the keyboard, while Rocco jumped around onstage like Tigger from *Winnie the Pooh*. I smiled, but that soon disappeared as the noise came back again – the hyenas had gone, but the bees were back. Like they were stuck in the corner of a window trying to get out.

It didn't matter which way I tried to sleep – it was always there. So bad, I felt like swatting it with one of my music books, just like Rocco had said. The next minute it didn't sound like a bee at all. It was like I was watching a monster in a scary film, creeping and crawling. If it *had* been a film, I would've jumped up and turned it off before it got to the scary bit, but this noise didn't have a switch – it was in the middle of my head.

CHAPTER 2

THE DAY MY WORLD WENT DEAD

It was three whole days before I got to see Dr Cowans. I still went to school and met the band at lunchtimes, but it was impossible to concentrate on lessons or even think of writing a song when my noise seemed to be changing in tone and loudness all time.

'Tinnitus.' That's what Dr Cowans said when I sat down in his office with Mum and Dad. 'It can be linked to hearing loss, but it can also be caused by loud music ... You have been playing music acoustically, like I asked?'

'Yes,' I said, 'I have.' Which was true, but every once in a while, Rocco had turned the drum machine up loud.

'Or maybe it's stress,' Dr Cowans continued, tapping the side of his head. 'That noise is actually blood rushing to your nerve ends and back again. Have you changed your routine, or is anything _____ at school?'

13

I glanced at Mum and Dad because Dr Cowans had momentarily turned away towards his screen.

'*Stressful*, Soph,' said Mum, filling in the word I'd not been able to catch.

I hadn't realized it when I first started doing it, but as my hearing had got worse, I had automatically begun to lip-read the words I couldn't make out, or I'd ask my friends or Mum to repeat them. They'd also started tapping me on my shoulder to get my attention if they had started talking while I had my back turned.

I didn't feel like it was linked to being stressy.

'No,' I said. 'Nothing I can think of.'

Mum and Dad looked as lost as I was, but at least Mum looked relieved when Dr Cowans said that her home remedy of the olive oil wouldn't have made the noise any worse.

'So –' Dr Cowans tapped his pen on his desk, like he knew I wasn't going to like what he was going to say next – 'shall we take another test, Sophie?' He nodded at the hearing cubicle in the corner of the room.

I glanced at Mum. She knew I hated going in there.

'Do I have to?' I said. 'We did it last time?'

'I know.' Dr Cowans held out the headphones. 'But things seem to have changed now that you're hearing noises.'

I took the headphones and I sat down on the chair in the cubicle.

'You know what to do.' Dr Cowans smiled as he handed me the clicker. 'Just press the button with your thumb whenever you hear a sound. Just once.'

I looked down at the buzzer as Dr Cowans closed the cubicle

14

door. This was the bit I hated, the bit where I felt like I was trapped in an upright coffin.

Dr Cowans looked in through a small window.

'*Ready?*' he mouthed.

I nodded, but already I could feel the buzzer slipping as my palms began to sweat.

A high-pitched whine started, then another, and another. It seemed to come and go like toothache – sometimes it was loud, sometimes it was soft – but I always knew it was there. And it was there now, not through the headphones, but between my ears. My noise, not his noise. I reached up to take the headphones off. Dr Cowans shook his head, held two fingers up.

'*Two minutes,*' he mouthed.

I took a deep breath, tried to keep myself calm, but it felt like the headphones were squeezing my head like it was a grape in a vice. I winced as the noises pierced through my brain.

I needed to get out. I needed to escape. Because if Dr Cowans's computer was making sounds, I couldn't hear them. All I had was my own noise, which had started like the wind, but now it had turned into a hurricane.

I fidgeted restlessly in my seat.

'*One minute,*' mouthed Dr Cowans as he moved the mouse. Normally this would make the sounds the computer generated louder, but I still couldn't hear them.

I shook my head as my frustration built inside me.

The headphone cable grew taut as I stood up. I pulled the headphones off my ears and dropped them on the floor.

Air – I needed air.

I pushed the cubicle door open.

Mum and Dad were standing in front of me.

'Soph,' said Dad. 'You need to finish the test.'

'I know, but I hate it in there. All I can hear is the noise.'

Dr Cowans must have said something, because both Mum and Dad looked at him. He was only trying to help, but I just wanted to leave.

Mum put her hand on my arm.

'It's okay, Soph,' she said.

She held my hand and I sat down beside her.

Dr Cowans gave me a concerned look. 'I know it's not easy, Sophie,' he said. 'But we are going to need to do some more tests.'

I sighed.

'How about we stop for today –' Dr Cowans smiled – 'but I'll need you back in soon. In the meantime, maybe don't play guitar at all, and you could try listening to a noise app on your phone. Sometimes playing something soothing will calm the noise down. I've given your mum and dad the details. Perhaps get some good headphones.'

'Well, that should make you happy, at least,' said Dad. 'She's been after a pair of those BigBeat things for ages.'

Dad was right. I had been after a pair of BigBeats, but I wanted them so I didn't disturb anyone when I played guitar, not for covering up a noise in my head.

And that's what I was thinking as me and Mum stayed in the car while Dad ran across the car park towards the electrical store in the rain. Normally Mum chatted like mad, but this time she looked out of the window and pointed at random dogs coming out of a pet store, saying they were cute, and then wondering aloud if Liam was working in McDonald's when we both knew he wasn't working that day. It was like she was trying to avoid talking about the appointment until she said, 'Don't worry, Soph, you'll soon be able to play your guitar again.'

It was bad enough that I was scared about what was happening, but Mum acting like my noise was just a little bump in the road only made me feel even worse. I stared out of the window as the shop signs glowed bright in the rain. I wanted Mum to turn the radio on, or at least speak about something normal. Anything to help disguise the buzz that seemed to be getting louder again.

I jumped out of my thoughts as Dad opened the car door and got in.

'God, I'm soaked,' is what I think Dad said. I'd heard the 'God' and 'I'm' and I guessed the 'soaked' because he'd wiped his hand through his wet hair and I'd counted one syllable. I'd got used to piecing together bits of what I heard with actions and the situations people were in. Like Dad wouldn't have said, 'God, I'm boiling,' when the rain was hammering down. It was like putting pieces of a puzzle together, and most of the time I got it right. Some numbers were hard because the lip movements looked the same, like forty and fourteen, but I didn't have any trouble hearing Dad say, 'Hundred and twenty blimmin' quid,' as he handed the headphone box to me between the seats.

'Don't be so mean,' Mum said. She seemed to be stuck on 'worry mode', but Dad was carrying on like normal because I could see his eyes smiling at me in the rear-view mirror.

'Don't worry about it, Soph,' he said, extra clear. 'I'll just work a

17

few extra shifts.' Which did make me feel bad as he already got up to deliver letters at four a.m. every day.

I took the headphones out of the box and hung them round my neck. As Dad pulled away, I caught my reflection in the car window.

They were wireless.

They were cool.

I smiled as I imagined getting a medical exemption certificate and being able to walk around wearing them at school.

I took a selfie on my phone and sent it to the band. They replied instantly.

Mia: 🖤

Ty: 👍

Rocco: WAAAANT!

I pulled the headphones over my ears. I wanted to try them straight away, but they needed to charge, which meant that all the way home, the squeak of Dad's windscreen wipers fought with the buzz in my head.

When I got in I went straight upstairs to my room and looked up tinnitus on my laptop. It said that the sounds could be interchangeable and sometimes they could mimic the last thing you could hear, especially high-pitched noises, like seagulls squawking, church bells or the whine of a vacuum cleaner. Which is why my head was *wow-wow*-ing now because a car alarm was going off outside our house.

At first I thought my head had created the noise on its own, until I looked out of my bedroom window and saw the lights flashing on one of Liam's friend's cars as he walked around it, pointing his key fob. But when the lights stopped, the *wow-wow-wow*-ing continued in my head, and I wished my headphones were already charged so I could drown it out.

The car alarm was still in my head as I got changed for bed, and it was still there as I searched the tinnitus sound app on my phone that Dr Cowans had mentioned. *Gentle Breeze ... Blowing Leaves ... Soothing Birds* – I scrolled down. The alarm was so loud I thought I needed more than 'gentle' or 'soothing' to drown it out. But that wasn't the point, the app blurb said; the aim was to soothe, to calm.

I selected *Summer Sounds of Our Great Oceans*. I put the headphones on, lay back on my pillow and pressed play. I took a deep breath, then another. I closed my eyes, let the water wash over me, just like I did when we went to the beach with friends and we made barriers with our bodies to protect our sandcastles from the waves.

A wave washed over me, then faded away.

Another wave washed over me, faded.

A wave washed over me.

A wave washed.

A wave.

This is nice, I thought to myself.

This

is

nice.

*

19

I don't remember falling asleep, only waking up, with the sun shining a light through my curtains, cutting a line like a lightsabre across my bed.

I blinked, rubbed my eyes. The house was quiet. My room was still, except for particles of dust flying in the beams. I took a deep breath. *It must be the weekend*, I thought. Mum and Dad were lying in. I rolled over, pulled my duvet up to my neck, felt something hard under my pillow. I reached under and pulled my headphones out. Wait! No noise. No noise! I smiled. No noise . . . For the first time in three days, no noise. I smiled with relief. It was like I'd been stuck in a heatwave and someone had turned the air conditioning on.

I put my headphones round my neck, looked up at the ceiling.

'No noise,' I said to myself. I clenched my fist and smiled.

'No noise.' I said it so quietly, I couldn't hear my own voice.

'No noise,' I said a little louder.

'No noise,' I said even louder, but I couldn't hear a thing, just felt the rumble of my voice in my chest.

I sat up and looked around. My alarm clock was flashing like it did when it went off – Friday 7.04 a.m. The radio should be playing. I pressed the volume control button – the red numbers flashed from eight to nine to ten. As loud as it could go. No voices, no music. Nothing. I sat up quickly, clicked my fingers by my right ear, then left. Still nothing – just my fingers rubbing together in silence. I clicked them again in panic. 'It can't be . . .' I said to myself. 'I can't hear anything.' I clapped my hands together, twice. No sound. I clapped again, so hard it made my hands sting. It was like I was wearing gloves stuffed with cotton wool. *This can't be real*, I thought to myself, my stomach a knot of pure fear. *I'm not awake; I'm stuck in a silent dream.*

I shook my head.

Wake up. Please let me wake up!

The flashing figures on my alarm clock changed to 7.05 a.m. I felt my heart thud on every flash.

This is real; this is happening.

I pushed back my duvet and swung my legs over the side of my bed. No rustle. I stood up. No creaking floorboard.

'No,' I shouted. 'No!' I cried. 'No. No. No!'

I ran out on to the landing. Mum was at the top of the stairs in her dressing gown.

'Sophie. What's wrong?' her mouth moved, but no words came out.

'Mum . . . Mum . . .' I pointed at my ears, even though my hands were shaking. 'I can't hear you.'

'What? No!' Mum held out her arms, pulled me towards her.

I felt her say my name as it rumbled through her chest.

I felt her hand on the side of my face.

I felt her kiss on my head.

I felt all of this. But I couldn't hear a thing. I couldn't even hear my own cry.

CHAPTER 3

ALIEN SPACESHIPS

The light switch in the hall didn't click.

The front door didn't bang.

The car doors didn't slam.

The letters on Mum's car radio said Radio Universe was playing, but I couldn't hear a sound.

She turned it off, tried to smile. But I couldn't smile back. All I could do was stare ahead as we drove through the village with cars passing us in silence, like alien spaceships had landed on Earth.

Dad met us at the accident and emergency reception. He must have already walked ten kilometres posting letters, but that didn't stop him pacing up and down the waiting room. I hadn't had an accident, but it definitely felt like an emergency as my heart thudded in my chest. I felt alone and lost as nurses and doctors walked by. Every once in a while, Mum smiled at me and mouthed, *'Don't worry, Soph. It will be fine.'*

Each time, I'd give her a nervous smile, then look at the ground, as Dad went by again. Two minutes later, she squeezed my hand, and that's when my tears came pouring out. She hugged me so tightly I didn't want her to let go.

I didn't hear the nurse call my name.

I just got up when Mum did, and I followed her and Dad. I'd been to A&E before when I'd broken my arm. That day the ward was full of nurses and doctors talking and the sound of their clicking footsteps, but now it felt like they had been muted and were wearing slippers.

We were shown into a cubicle and a green curtain was pulled round us. A nurse started talking to Mum and Dad. I tried to read her lips, but now my hearing had totally gone, there were no syllables to piece together with actions for me to make sense of.

'Okay, can you _____?'

I looked at Mum.

'Well, she's been _____.' Mum pointed at her ears.

'And when did _____?'

I was so cut off I was on the verge of crying again.

'And had she been _____?' The nurse looked down at her notepad. I lost sight of her lips, just saw Mum nodding, then Dad.

Had I been what?

'No,' said Mum.

The nurse shook her head.

Why was she shaking her head?

'And any _____?'

Any what?

I reached out and tugged Dad's arm.

'Dad,' I said. 'What's going on?' I don't know how loud I said it; all I could feel was a rumble in my chest like I was talking from inside a cardboard box, but it may have come out more as a cry because Mum gave me a look like she was going to cry too.

The nurse slid her chair closer to me as tears fell down my cheeks. I felt like I was locked inside the hearing booth, shouting in silence, trying to find a way out. I looked around the room at all the concerned faces. *Please help me! Please help me!*

The nurse handed me a tissue, then pointed at her lips. 'Are-you-able-to-lip-read, Sophie?' she said slowly.

I nodded.

'A bit,' I sniffed. 'But it's harder . . .'

'It's-okay. Take-your-time.'

I looked at Mum and Dad

'It's hard . . .' I swallowed. 'I can't hear anything . . . and I hate talking when I can't even hear my own voice.'

'*I-know,*' Mum mouthed as she reached for my hand. '*But just go slow-ly, Soph. I will help.*'

'So, So-phie,' the nurse said. 'I-just-asked-Mum-if-you'd-had-_____ or _____ where-you've-just-not-been _____ well.'

I shook my head. I couldn't make out words when they were more than a single syllable.

'No.' Mum turned and looked at me. 'No fee-ver, Soph? You've been okay?'

I nodded.

The nurse made a note on her pad, then said, 'Sophie,

I-won't-be-gone-long.' She pointed to a gap in the curtain. 'I-will-be-back-with-a _____ soon.'

For nearly all the time she was gone, all me, Mum and Dad could do was look at each other, at the floor, at each other, at the floor, and seeing how worried they looked made me feel even worse. Every now and then, Mum reached over and rubbed my hand, but I could tell she was as scared and worried as I was.

It felt like hours before two doctors came and asked the same questions the nurse had asked – had I had a fever, or headache? Was there anyone else in my family with hearing problems? Had I poked anything in my ear?

No, I hadn't. No, there wasn't, and the only thing that had been poked in my ear was their cold metal instruments for the hundredth time. They were trying their best to help, but the probing and silence was making me hot and anxious. I was beginning to wish I had a cut on my head, or a bruise on my ankle, something they could look at and send me for an X-ray. They mentioned I could have a CT scan, which is basically another type of X-ray on a computer, but that wasn't something they would consider straight away. Meanwhile, they made an appointment for me to see Dr Cowans on Monday.

We went home in the car, with Dad checking on me in his rear-view mirror, while Mum sat next to me holding my hand. All I could do was look out of the window as we passed people, cars and buses, all moving in a silent world, and all I wanted was for my hearing to suddenly come back so I could hear them all again.

CHAPTER 4
SEARCHING FOR ANSWERS

'She's what?' Liam had been looking at me like he'd trodden in dog poo ever since we'd got back from the hospital. 'Deaf? What, like _____ sure? She's not _____ so she can get off school?'

'Liam!' That was my mum. 'How could you?'

'Just saying, _____ be the first time, like with her _____.'
I couldn't work out his words, but when he pointed at my arm, I knew.

'IT WAS BROKEN,' I snapped. 'And why are you even here anyway? You should be in college.'

'Home study afternoon,' said Liam, giving me one of his annoying smirks.

Normally I'd have said something back, like he stank of burgers, or his spots were as big as volcanoes because he ate as much of the food as he served in McDonald's, but I was so upset that I pushed past him and rushed upstairs to my room.

*

That evening was scary and weird, with Mum and Dad taking it in turns to pop their head round the bedroom door, like they were checking on a baby sleeping. Each time they'd try to get me to eat something, and each time I would be staring out of the window at the darkness outside, wondering if my hearing would ever come back.

On one of the times, Mum brought me up some tea; she said I had to eat something. She handed me a plate with a ham sandwich and some carrot sticks, and gave me a packet of crisps. I ate the sandwich okay, but I noticed the crisp packet didn't rustle when I opened it, and I couldn't hear the crisps crunch. Then every time I bit on raw carrot it felt like all the bones were shattering in my head, so bad I decided I would never eat them again.

As we couldn't find out what might have happened until we saw Dr Cowans on Monday, I decided to see if I could google it. Mum was always saying how dangerous it was to try to self-diagnose. One of her colleagues at the paper suppliers had started eating mints at work for a pain in his chest. He swore it was heartburn as he'd looked up the symptoms online, but two weeks later Mum heard he'd had a heart attack. I knew I wasn't having one of those, but I was desperate to find out what could be wrong.

I typed in *sudden deafness* and *fever*. (I still didn't have one, but they'd checked so many times at the hospital I thought I'd add it, just in case.)

Meningitis came up as the top result – the symptoms listed were a rapid onset of fever, headaches, hypersensitivity to light – all the things the doctors had asked me about. It was like they'd thought I was turning into a vampire. I kept reading. Right at the end it said: *Can result in hearing loss.*

I put my hand on my forehead, but my hands were so sweaty

I couldn't tell if I had a fever or not. I went to read the rest of the article – I wanted to know what was wrong with me, but I was too scared to look. I closed my laptop lid. Mum was right. Google diagnosis wasn't the right thing to do.

I stayed in my room all evening, not wanting to talk to anyone or do anything but lie in my bed. Mia messaged, asked why I wasn't at school, because she was sure she'd seen me in the car with Mum when she went by on the bus. I thought about replying, but every time I went to type *I've gone deaf,* my heart dropped into my stomach. I couldn't tell myself I was deaf, let alone find the words to tell my best friend. And if I did press send, I knew she would call me and I wouldn't be able to hear a word she said.

I put my phone down by my side and stared up at the ceiling.

The doctors at the hospital had said they'd hoped it was temporary, that things like this happen to people all the time, but that didn't stop me thinking about the things I was already missing, like Mum and Dad's voices, and their laughs, even though, like me, they hadn't had anything to laugh at all day.

I couldn't hear the floorboard creak on the landing.

I couldn't hear the click of the shower.

I couldn't hear the water trickle down the drain.

I couldn't hear the rub of my towel against my skin.

I couldn't hear my mattress ping as I got into bed.

And I couldn't hear Mum when she walked into my room and asked, 'Are you okay?' And I tried to speak, but all I did was cry, and she opened her arms and she hugged me so tight I thought she was never going to let go.

CHAPTER 5

'THINGS HAVE CHANGED'

I stayed in my room all weekend in silence, except for my noise. It always seemed to be there, although sometimes I would forget about it, until it changed pitch, or volume, and it would hit me again, like a monster gnawing away in the dark corners of my brain.

Mum and Dad kept coming up and checking on me, and by then I knew things were really bad because even Liam was being extra nice. Every time he went down the shop, he'd ask me if I wanted anything, and when I said no, he'd still come back with a bag of Haribo and a Coke. He could be the most irritating stepbrother – we were always falling out about whose turn it was on the PlayStation, or how long he took in the bathroom, but whenever things got serious, like when Laura Pearce picked on me in primary school, or when he got expelled in Year Eleven, we always stuck up for each other. But I wasn't used to him being as concerned as this.

Even Liam kept out of my way on Sunday evening. It was like everyone knew how nervous I was feeling about seeing Dr Cowans and was best left alone. I was so scared that my hearing would be gone for the rest of my life that I went to sleep hoping my ears were like a human amplifier and all Dr Cowans had to do was flick a switch and the sound would come back, belting through.

I couldn't stop myself shaking when I sat with Mum in Dr Cowans's office the next morning.

'So, So-phie,' Dr Cowans said, slowly. 'Things-have _____ since-you-were-last _____.' He held his hand up in front of his chest and pointed at the floor.

Things have something, since I was last something.

Mum caught sight of my confusion and leaned in front of me. 'CHANGED, SOPH,' she said, opening her mouth wide so I could catch eh-ver-ree syll-a-ble. 'THINGS-HAVE-CHANGED-SINCE-YOU-WERE-LAST-HERE.'

'Yes.' I nodded. 'They have.' I looked back at Dr Cowans, feeling frustrated because if he didn't have a beard, it would make his lips much easier to read.

He pointed at the chair beside his desk, like he knew I needed more clues.

'Let's-just-have-a-look-So-phie,' he said.

He picked up a tiny metal instrument. I'd had that probe in my ears so many times it felt like the doctors were drilling a hole. But now I was deaf, I would do anything to get my hearing back, even if it meant having that probe stuck in my ear every day for the rest of my life.

I leaned forward, felt the cold of the metal in my right ear.

Dr Cowans turned my head like a hairdresser wanting to cut the other side.

Cold metal in my left ear. Cold metal in my right.

Dr Cowans made a note on his computer, then picked up a tuning fork on the edge of his desk to make it vibrate. It's like having a giant big pair of tweezers held against the top of my head, and I have to say if I can hear it or not.

'Any-thing, So-phie?'

'No,' I said.

Dr Cowans moved the tuning fork to one side then the other, then back to the front, back to the middle.

'Still-no-thing?'

'No.' I could hear nothing, but I could feel the marks where the metal had touched my skin, like heavy pinpricks on my scalp.

'And-what-about-the _____, Sophie? The-noise. Is-it-still-there?'

'Yes,' I said. 'It's there, but I get used to it until it changes tone. Like, one minute it can sound like a rumbling truck; the next it sounds like a washing machine; then it just whines.'

'Okay.' Dr Cowans made another note. 'And is it something you feel gets worse at night?'

'Yes,' I said. 'And when I'm stressed.'

I wanted to add, '*Like now*,' as Dr Cowans made a note on his computer, then turned and pointed at the cubicle. My heart sank.

'Do I have to?' I said. 'I hate it in there.'

'I know,' said Dr Cowans. 'But it's the only way we can check.'

I fidgeted anxiously in my chair.

'Soph.' Mum rubbed my hand to try to calm me down, but the thought of going back in that cubicle again was making my noise screech like out-of-tune violins.

31

'No,' I said, standing up. 'I'm not going in there.'

Dr Cowans turned to his computer and started to type, his bearded jaw moving like he was saying what he was typing out loud.

Then Mum's mouth moved, too quickly.

Then Dr Cowans's jaw moved again.

I wanted to tell them to stop, that I couldn't understand them. I wanted them to unmute.

I was there – they should be talking *to* me, not *about* me. I wanted to tell them, but I was trying to avoid speaking because the vibration of my voice in my chest was like being buried alive in a coffin.

Still, their mouths moved. I picked out the odd words – 'quiet', 'room' and the phrase 'not the same'.

I leaned forward, tried to get Mum's attention. She smiled, but went back to talking.

No! Stop talking about me.

My stomach flipped like I was going to be sick. They were my ears; this was my hearing. I wanted to know if I was going to be stuck deaf for a few days, or was I going to be like this for ever.

'Let's see _____,' Dr Cowans continued.

'Of course.' Mum nodded.

'She might_____.'

No! Stop! Stop!

My heart thudded in my chest. I was so annoyed I wanted to scream.

I stood up.

'Sophie, where are you going?' Mum said, finally noticing me.

'Stop talking about me,' I said. 'I'm here – I'm not dead!'

32

Mum stood up, tried to put her arm round me. 'Soph,' she said. 'We're only trying to help.' She looked at Dr Cowans. 'Sorry, she's—'

'No,' I snapped. 'Don't apologize. Of course I'm not the same. Of course I'm quiet. Wouldn't you be if you woke up deaf?'

'Soph!'

'And it might help if he shaved off his silly pointy beard so I could actually read his lips.' I burst between them. I don't know if they shouted anything after me because I was already headed out of the door.

I rushed down the corridor – crying with no cry, running with no footsteps – just a horrible whine inside my body as I ran on a sponge.

They don't know what it's like. No one knows what it's like.

I pushed through the main doors out into the light – people talking, people walking, cars turning, buses stopping, ambulances passing by with flashing lights. It was like being in a horror movie stuck on mute.

I slowed to a walk, felt people looking at me – *Don't look at me.*

Another bus passed.

Another ambulance.

Another accident.

Another emergency.

I sat down on a bench and held my head in my hands.

This is horrible, I thought to myself. *So horrible.*

My body began to shake like it was winter.

All I wanted was someone to come and tell me everything

would be okay. But no one could say that, not Dr Cowans, not Mum and Dad.

I began to sob, uncontrollably with no sound, no sound at all, just shakes and the wetness of tears pouring down my face.

CHAPTER 6
RED LINES

I didn't need to look at the screen to know the results when Mum came out and took me back inside to see Dr Cowans.

'This is an auditory graph,' he said. 'On this side is the hearing level, and across the top is the frequency, and this jagged blue line represents the average healthy hearing capabilities for your age.' He was speaking slowly, so I could pick out his words, but they still took a while to sink in. Mum replied first.

'And where's Sophie's line?' she asked.

'Well.' Dr Cowans clicked on his keyboard. A red line started in the middle of the page, then dropped like a mountain pass to the bottom corner of the graph. 'This is Sophie's line.'

I turned away from the screen. I hadn't heard a thing when they put the headphones on me. I didn't need a red line to tell me I was totally deaf.

'But we'll run more tests,' Dr Cowans said, still speaking deliberately but looking upbeat, 'and we'll give you some steroid tablets, Sophie. It's often the best hope of recovering hearing if you start them within the first two weeks.'

'So, _____ chance Sophie will recover?' Mum said, suddenly smiling in hope, like she'd been drowning and suddenly spotted a life raft in the sea.

'Well, _____ always hope,' said Dr Cowans. 'But let's try to see if we can give Sophie more than that. _____ arrange a city for next week.'

'City?' I asked.

'Sorry, Sophie. C – T. It's a type of scan,' Dr Cowans explained, clearly having seen the worried look on my face. 'But don't worry, it doesn't hurt.' He reached over to the edge of his desk and picked up a leaflet. 'This explains everything.' He pointed at a photograph of a huge white machine with a hole in the middle. 'Just think of it as a huge camera,' he said, holding up his hands. 'But instead of taking pictures of your face, it takes hundreds of images of the inside of your head.'

I took the leaflet, looked at the machine and smiling face of a nurse looking down at a patient as he was about to be slid into the hole. While I was looking, Dr Cowans had stood up and was shaking Mum's hand.

'Don't worry _____,' he said. 'We'll just wait for _____ and then take it from there.'

I kept looking at the leaflet as me and Mum walked out to the car in the sunshine. Dr Cowans had said there was nothing to worry about, but I couldn't help it. I'd got used to the hearing test, and having probes stuck in my ears, but now having a scan seemed even more serious. I know they had to look inside my head to work out what had gone wrong. My hearing hadn't stopped like someone had cut the power, or the batteries had run out on a radio. There had to be a reason, but all I wanted to do was bury my head under a pillow and forget about it.

By the time I got home, my phone was vibrating with messages on our band group chat.

Mia: Soph, you didn't miss much today.

Rocco: Except Ryan Harris getting sent out of maths for fighting.

Ty: Again 😑

Rocco: Oh, and Mrs Hopkirk got new microphones. So I'll sound even better ☺

Ty: Hope you're back soon.

Rocco: Yeah, soon. If you don't come back this week, maybe write a song at my place on Saturday.

Ty: 👍 Great practice today.

Rocco: Yeah ☺ But, Soph, we need you. Only thirteen days till the semi-final.

I stared at the messages. I didn't know how to reply, and when I did eventually type *I've gone deaf,* I started to cry and deleted it. It was bad enough not being able to hear, let alone trying to talk about it. It wasn't like telling them I had a sore throat and could be back in a few days. Part of me wondered whether they knew, because news would always spread through my village and be passed on to the next.

My phone vibrated in my hand.

A message from Mia, direct, not on the group chat.

Mia: Soph, I didn't want to say on the group chat, but I'm outside.

I walked over to the window. The sun was going down behind the houses across the road. Mia was standing at the end of our path waving up at me. I shook my head, then typed on my phone.

Sophie: I'm sorry, Mia. I just want to be alone.

Mia: Okay. I'll come back tomorrow.

Sophie: No. I think I need longer than that.

Mia: Okay 🖤

Sophie: 🖤

I felt tears welling up in my eyes as Mia waved then walked away. I felt bad for not letting her in, but I'd hardly been able to speak to Mum and Dad, so I doubted I'd be able to with my best friend. It'd be better to sit in my room with no TV or music and avoid everyone, like I had done since Friday, even though that had made the days feel twice as dead, and twice as long.

It was great the band was practising and that they wanted me to play. Rocco seemed to be acting like it would be easy for me, but my heart sank every time I looked at my guitar on its stand beside my bedroom window. I wished I could play it. I wished I could have tunes in my head to play with the band. But there was nothing, just the whine of my noise.

CHAPTER 7
LIFE FROM A WINDOW

I didn't feel any better when I woke up the next morning. Normally I'd be getting ready for school, but all I could do was watch as the younger children walked by to the village primary, and the older ones made their way to the bus stop where I should have been. It was like the world was a roundabout, spinning without me, but I was too scared to go outside and jump on. And, of course, Mum had noticed because she was always asking me if I was okay whenever she came into my room, but I'd been up there for three and a half days, since I'd lost my hearing, and it was like she thought that was long enough.

'Soph,' she said, as she sat down on the edge of my bed. 'I know it's very hard, but you can't lock yourself away up here for the rest of your life.' She was speaking slowly, and using words with few syllables. It meant I could understand her, but it also meant that her words hit home harder.

'I know,' I said. 'But I'm scared. I hate being in here, but at least I can control what happens.' I still hated the rumble of my voice in my chest, but if I didn't try to talk, Mum wouldn't know how I was feeling.

'I know what you're saying,' she said. 'But it'll do you good to get out.'

'Or I just wait here until my hearing comes back,' I said, even though I didn't know if or when that would be.

'I've taken a few days off work,' Mum said, trying to brighten my gloom. 'So I can be with you. Dad wanted to, too, but we thought he should save a few days, just in case.'

'Just in case, what?' I asked.

'Well –' Mum smiled awkwardly – 'like you said, we don't know how long this could last. Anyway . . . just have a think about going out.'

She stood up.

'Oh,' she said. 'Forgot the very thing I came in here for . . . Maybe read this first.'

Mum held up an envelope.

'It's from Mrs Hopkirk. I chatted with her on the phone. She wanted to see you, but I said you hadn't felt like seeing anyone. So she popped this in earlier.'

I took the envelope.

'I'll leave you to read it.' Mum smiled as she went out of the door. That was another thing Mum was doing, smiling whenever she left me, when, really, she couldn't have felt like smiling at all.

I slid my finger under the seal and took out the piece of paper inside.

Dear Sophie,

I am so sorry to hear what has happened, but of all the people I know, I am sure you are the one person who can cope with it. Your mum called and told me you have not picked up your guitar

41

since it happened. I can understand that, as it must be very strange, but I wanted you to know that this does not mean the end of your music.

Did you know, after Beethoven lost his hearing he learned to compose through the vibration of his piano? Search him up on the internet, and these too: Ian Dury, Stevie Wonder, Django Reinhardt. They didn't lose their hearing, but they overcame lots of hurdles to become brilliant musicians. I think you will find them interesting and inspiring.

Do hope we see you back at school soon. We need someone to keep Rocco in place!

But, most importantly, please come round and chat when you are ready.

Mrs Hopkirk

I smiled as I read. Mrs Hopkirk was my favourite teacher. I knew her before I went to secondary school because she used to teach me and Mia guitar after school when we were in primary, and it was nice that she was looking out for me now. But she wasn't to know how I was feeling. Beethoven was already famous when he went deaf, and he was so brilliant at music that he must have been full of confidence to have played in front of thousands of people. I was an eleven-year-old girl who'd just passed grade seven guitar. I played in a band, and even though we had played in front of maybe thirty people at school, now I didn't feel like I could play in front of one. I didn't feel like I had the confidence to even meet the band.

CHAPTER 8

GETTING TO KNOW MY BEST FRIEND AGAIN

I didn't hear a ring, or a knock; I just saw Mia standing in my doorway when she stopped by after school.

'I know you said not to,' she said. 'But I couldn't stop thinking about you all—'

I couldn't make out the rest of her words because I'd jumped up and wrapped my arms round her.

'I'm so happy to see you,' I said. My tears came flooding out.

'Soph,' she said, pulling away. 'I'm so sorry, it must be _____, but _____ it'll come _____.'

I couldn't catch all her words, but I was sure she must have said 'horrible' from the worried look on her face.

'It is, I . . .' I felt my voice crack. I waited for Mia to say something, but all she did was look at me and pull me into another hug.

'I'm sorry, Soph,' she said again, when we went to my room and sat on my bed.

I forced a smile. We'd been friends since primary school, but now for the first time ever, it was like we didn't know what to say.

'Ty said to say hello,' Mia said eventually. 'And we're sorry about the messages – we knew, but we didn't know how to say.'

'It's okay,' I said.

Mia smiled awkwardly. 'But Rocco did get you some _____.' She reached into her bag.

'Mia,' I said. 'You'll have to keep looking at me. I can lip-read, but now that I can't count syllables, I need to see your face.'

'Sorry,' she said. 'I wasn't thinking. It's just . . .' She slowly pulled a box of Maltesers out of her bag. 'He says sorry he _____ them, but he got _____.'

I didn't feel like laughing, but I couldn't help grinning at the hole in the box where Rocco had poked his finger through.

'Tell him . . .' I stopped myself. 'Tell him . . .' My throat ached as tears built behind my eyes.

'It's okay,' said Mia. 'Take your time.'

I nodded as my tears trickled down the side of my nose.

'It's horrible,' I said. 'I want to talk, but I hate that I can't hear my own voice.'

Mia put one arm round me, and we rested our backs against my giant poster of *London Calling* by the Clash on the wall. Stupidly I waited for the rustle, but all I felt was the lumps of Blu Tack digging into my back. We stared across my room, towards the window, at my guitar resting against the frame. Normally we'd pick it up and take it in turns playing if Mia hadn't brought hers with her. Now all I could do was stare at it. The thought of never being able to hear it made all of my insides ache. I just had to hope it was temporary, because I couldn't bear the idea of not being able to play music again.

The mattress moved. I didn't know if Mia had said anything, but she had reached into her bag for her phone. She started to text. I wondered who she was messaging – what could be so important?

My phone vibrated on my bed, beside me.

I picked it up. A message from Mia.

Mia: Thought maybe we could chat on here?

I smiled.

Sophie: Yeah. That's a good idea.

I grabbed my pillows and put them behind our heads. Mia put the box of Maltesers on my lap. I dipped my hand in.

Mia: Think Rocco ate most of them.

Sophie: Yeah.

I put a Malteser in my mouth and sucked it so I didn't feel the crunch of my bones in my head.

Sophie: Guess it's the thought that counts.

Mia: Hmmm or just plain greedy ☺

My bed shook as Mia giggled beside me. She typed again.

Mia: I know it's the last thing you are thinking about, but Rocco can't wait for you to come back to band practice.

Sophie: You're right. I don't want to think about that.

Mia: Sorry, Soph, didn't mean to upset you.

A high-pitched whine started in my head, merged with others, and grew to a hoot. How could I be in a band when I couldn't hear a thing except the noises inside my own head? We'd already been playing acoustically with the drums down low, and now I wouldn't even be able to hear that. Who has a deaf guitarist in a band anyway?

It was like Rocco thought nothing had happened, but I should have been used to him not being serious. He was always cracking jokes, or bouncing around his garage and the music room. Sometimes it's good to have someone to cheer you up when you are feeling down, but this was like Rocco didn't even care.

Mia's thumbs pressed on her phone.

I looked down and read the message.

Mia: Powell Stevens was still singing and dancing at the back of the school bus this afternoon.

I laughed as I pictured Powell Stevens dancing. She was a sixth-former at our school, who had been on *Banned-It* the TV Talent show the year before. I watched it with Mum, and every week we couldn't believe Powell kept making it through each round because she was so bad. When she did get voted off, she smashed a vase in one of the judges' houses. But that didn't stop Mrs Hopkirk making her one of the judges for the first round of Battle of the Bands. Powell was supposed to sit at a table with Mrs Hopkirk and Mr Davids, our drama teacher, but she spent most of the time in the middle of the hall flicking her hair off her shoulders and doing an annoying dance that put a lot of the bands off.

Mia: Everyone is asking about you at school.

I read it, but suddenly I felt so tired that it didn't really sink in.

Mia: Soph?

Mia turned and looked at me.

Sophie: Feeling pretty exhausted. Think I need some sleep.

Mia: You sure? Did I say something wrong?

Sophie: No, I'm just tired.

Mia stood up.
'I'll come back soon,' she said, giving me a hug.
'Sorry,' I said.
'Don't be silly,' she replied, then turned to go out of my room.

I walked over to the window and watched her walk down the path as the street lights flickered on. I felt bad for sending her away, because she hadn't done anything wrong. Neither had Rocco, really. All he was trying to do was make me feel better, like everything would continue as it was before. The only thing I wanted was for my hearing to come back and to get back with the band, but as Mia turned the corner towards the village high street, I didn't feel like I'd be doing that any time soon.

CHAPTER 9

WALKING ON THE MOON

It turned out that when Mum suggested I should go outside, she meant the very next day. I was watching TV in the lounge with the subtitles on when she came in.

'Are you ready?' she said.

I stared ahead, pretending not to see her. She'd already asked when I got up, then again during breakfast. I was hoping she would give up or forget. It wasn't just the idea of not being able to hear anything that frightened me; it was the fact that we were bound to bump into people we knew, and I'd know that they would know what had happened.

'Just a little walk, Soph.' Mum stepped forward between the TV and me. 'And you just say when it's too much and we'll turn back.'

'What? Now, Mum?' I said. 'I've not had time to prepare.'

'But wouldn't that just make it worse?' she said. 'I know what you're like – you'd worry about it all day and not be able to sleep all night.' She picked up the TV remote. 'Besides, since when have you been interested in the news?'

49

I sighed.

'Come on.' Mum smiled. 'We'll take it in small steps, just down the road, then gradually build it up. I'll even let you wear those trackies.'

I knew she must have been desperate when she said that, because she thought they were too scruffy to wear to bed.

I was shaking as I put my trainers and hoody on in the hall. So far I'd only walked to the car for hospital appointments, and all the while I'd kept my head down so no one would see me and I couldn't see them.

'You'll be okay, Soph,' said Mum as she opened the door.

I held my breath as cold air and bright light hit me. For a moment I stood still. It was just our front path ahead of me. I walked down it every day, but suddenly I was frozen like an alien getting ready to step off a spaceship.

'Come on, it's a lovely day.' Mum beckoned.

I took a deep breath and pulled my hood up over my head. I didn't want to go, but I also didn't want to stay in my room for the rest of my life.

I stepped out on to the path and pulled the door shut behind me. Mum walked ahead to our gate, then looked back. It was only four steps, but it felt like a mile. Mum smiled, like she was willing me on.

The gate didn't click or squeak when she opened it, and as I walked my trainers didn't slap or scuff – they just made a deep dead *thud*, *thud*, *thud*, all the way from my feet up into my body.

Out of the corner of my eye I spotted one of our neighbours, Mrs

Lau, walking her dog down the opposite side of the street. *Please don't wave,* I thought. *Please don't shout out. Please don't ask how I am. I hardly ever talk to you, anyway. Why start now?*

Mrs Lau crossed over the road.

No! She's coming!

I pulled up my hood tight, stopped and scuffed the path like I'd dropped and lost a pound coin in the weeds. In my peripheral vision, I saw Mum fiddling with the latch on the gate, even though it had opened okay.

Mrs Lau ambled on.

Mum walked over to me and linked her arm into mine.

'Come on.' She grinned. 'I didn't want to talk to her, either. She'd only go on about her new car.'

I laughed and as we walked down the pavement, I thought about how I'd been snapping at Mum a lot recently, but despite that, she was still on my side.

I looked ahead. The sky was clear blue, stretching on for miles until it hit the hills in the distance, and the road weaved its way across the bridge into the village. Nothing had changed, except for the silence. The horrible, eerie silence, and my feet, moving but not making a noise – no noise, like I was walking alone on the moon.

I stopped.

'Mum,' I said. 'Can we go back?'

She squeezed my arm. I buried my head in her coat and felt her arms wrap tightly round me.

'It's horrible,' I mumbled. 'It's horrible.'

She rubbed my back. I felt the rumble of her voice. I didn't want her to say anything. All I wanted was for her to hold me and take me back home.

She put her hands on my shoulders.

'Soph,' she said, looking right at me. 'I know it's horrible, but we have to do this.' She nodded back at our house.

I looked up at my bedroom window. For days I'd been up there, looking out at people, wishing I could be them, carrying on with life as normal as they went by. Now I was out, I wanted to go back in straight away.

'Come on.' Mum slid my hoody off, patted it down. 'That's better,' she said. 'Now the world can see that lovely face.'

'I really don't think so.' I laughed as I wiped my tears on my sleeve.

'It is,' said Mum. 'You just don't always like to show it when you scowl all the time.'

'That's my resting face!' I grinned.

Mum laughed. 'I'm going to have to remember that one for your dad.'

I smiled.

'Come on,' she said, linking her arm back into mine. 'Just to the shop and back, and if you don't want to, you don't have to come in.'

I walked with Mum along the pavement until it ran out at the end of our row of cottages. Then we crossed over. All the time she kept checking on me like I was a toddler. I didn't hear the bus coming, only the waft of air as it passed, and I couldn't hear the clatter of bottles in crates as the truck driver made his delivery to the pub. I just smiled as he stepped aside, and I guessed Mum might have said something like, 'Lovely day,' because he replied, 'Yes, it is.' And I kept on walking, thinking that when you can't hear birds singing, or dogs barking, it didn't feel like a lovely day at all.

I stayed outside while Mum went into the shop. I had made it down the street, but I wasn't ready to talk to the shop assistant, and whenever anyone came out, I pretended I was reading the *For Sale* messages that people from our village had placed in the shop window.

Mum pointed at random things on the way back, like a cat sat on a wall, and a plane leaving a trail of white in the sky. I'd normally have stroked the cat or made conversation about where the plane might be going, but when you can't hear the cat purr, or the plane roar, all you really want to do is go home.

I went straight up to my room when I got in. Just walking to the shops and back had felt like running a marathon.

I reached over to my bedside cupboard and picked up Mrs Hopkirk's letter. As I read, I imagined her soft voice in my head. She was always kind, always trying to help, even when I know she would've been annoyed at me, like that time when it got hard to hold the frets because I'd over-bitten my nails and made my fingers raw.

I skipped to the bottom of her letter. I'd known that Beethoven had gone deaf, but I hadn't heard anything about how he composed his music after. I picked my laptop up and typed in his name and the word *deaf*. Four pictures came up at the top of my screen. Two of Beethoven with grey wavy hair with a quill in his hand, one with a hearing trumpet held up to his ear, and then one of him sitting at a piano.

I scrolled down. Beethoven had started to go deaf when he was twenty-eight, totally deaf by the time he was forty-six. By that time he had sawn the legs off his piano so he could feel the vibrations through a sounding board on the floor. And to feel the vibrations of the high notes, he held a long ruler in his mouth, held it against the strings and felt the vibrations through his teeth. It was so amazing that I couldn't help smiling when I read it.

I looked at the other names Mrs Hopkirk had mentioned. Stevie Wonder played the piano even though he was blind, Django Reinhardt played the guitar despite losing the use of two fingers on his left hand after they got burned in a fire, and Ian Dury had polio as a child, but that didn't stop him from becoming a singer-songwriter in a famous band. They even got to number one in the charts.

On every page I found someone who had become a musician even though they were disabled. I peered over the top of my screen at my guitar on the stand. I'd been so scared about playing it that I'd barely been able to look at it for five days. If all these people could overcome their disabilities, why couldn't I? I guess that's what Mrs Hopkirk was trying to say.

I slid my laptop off my lap and walked over to my guitar. I'd missed playing so much and I hated the thought of not being able to play again. It went everywhere with me. Dad used to say whenever I took it to school, I was like a snail carrying its house on its back. Now here I was in my bedroom, heart thudding, too scared to pick it up.

But I had to make myself – I didn't want to lose another part of me.

I put my right hand on its neck, my left hand on its body and slowly picked it up. I caught my reflection in the window. I used to practise in it, trying to look like a famous rock guitarist. One time I borrowed Mum's leather jacket and I played *my guitar* and I thought I looked cool until Liam saw me and said I looked ridiculous, which made me more embarrassed than when Dad caught me singing into my hairbrush in the bathroom mirror.

I moved my left hand on to the frets and held my right hand over the strings. *Here we go.* I strummed C major, once, then again. I looked down at my guitar. I expected to hear nothing, but I didn't expect my fingers to feel numb like they were covered in cotton wool. I strummed again, again and again. No noise, just a faint vibration through my hands and against my hip. I changed to G major, played it five times. Beethoven could tell the difference between twelve chords and eighty-eight notes. I was playing two chords and they felt exactly the same, but I wasn't going to give up. Chopping the neck off my guitar wasn't an option, but maybe if I held my ear against the back of the guitar, I would feel something.

I sat down on my bed, held my guitar across my lap, then pressed my head against its back, like Mum doing one of her weird yoga positions. It was so awkward that my right hand slipped off the frets. I repositioned them, played C major, then G major, again. My fingers switched between them. It was like trying to play in the dark, which might explain why I closed my eyes, or maybe it was because I was having to concentrate so hard.

My heart sank to my stomach. It was useless. All I could feel was a faint vibration, like a fly walking across my cheek. I kept strumming, but the more I strummed, the further my heart sank, until it felt like it had reached the floor of the ocean. And it stayed there for a minute or two. I was frustrated and confused. *Why me?* I thought. My frustration began to turn to anger.

I lifted my head, squeezed my guitar so tight the strings cut like knives into my fingers. I've seen some guitarists smash their guitars on the stage at the end of the show; I felt like smashing mine against my bedroom wall.

I sensed a shadow in the doorway and spun round.

'What are you doing?'

Liam was standing in my room, shoving crisps into his mouth.

'Nothing,' I said.

'Funny nothing,' he said. 'I heard you playing.'

'It was rubbish,' I said.

'Yeah.' Liam grinned. 'Not like you were any good before anyway. Want some?' He held out his crisp packet.

'No,' I said, trying not to turn up my nose.

'Suit yourself,' he said. 'So, how's it going?' Liam circled a finger by his ear.

'Why does everyone do that?' I snapped as I put my guitar back on its stand.

'What?' said Liam.

'Point at their ears,' I said.

'Don't know.' Liam shrugged. 'Was only asking how you were. Will you be learning sign language and stuff?'

'No,' I said.

'You should,' he said. 'Learn loads of swear words and no one will know you're saying stuff about them. A kid signs when he comes into McDonald's at the weekend.' He threw his crisp bag in the direction of my bin, then held up his hands in front of his face and started to sign. 'Know what this means?' he said, holding his hands together to form an oval shape.

'No idea,' I said.

'A Big Mac.' He laughed.

I shook my head.

'And this?' he said. He cupped one hand then dipped the other into it.

'No idea,' I said.

'French fries,' he said.

'Go away,' I said, trying not to laugh. 'That's not even a thing.'

'It is.' He grinned and went out of my room.

The silence suddenly hit me. There was no in between; people were either in front of me or they were gone, and that made me feel so alone.

I reached over for my notepad and wrote these thoughts down for a song. For a second I thought of messaging them to Rocco and I imagined him getting all excited and replying: *Do you have any more? How does the tune go? How about if we added this?*

I missed Rocco's smile, and I missed him bouncing around with his microphone, but what was the point in writing songs with him if I couldn't play them? I'd be getting excited over nothing, and that would make me feel even worse. Liam had said he thought my guitar playing sounded okay, but the more I sat and thought about it, the more I thought he was just being kind.

CHAPTER 10

MY HEARING BUDDY

Mum had called the school the day I lost my hearing, and I'd been off for nearly a week since then. I knew I would have to go back some time, but I'd only just been down to the village shop – I was nowhere near ready for a thousand kids at school. I couldn't even imagine being sat at my desk again. All I could picture were the teachers' silent open mouths, like goldfish swimming around in a giant bowl. which is why my stomach flipped when Mum said Miss Urbanski, my form tutor, had telephoned this morning.

Miss Urbanski had offered to come to the house, but I thought that would be like having parents' evening in the living room, so Mum sat me down on the sofa and told me all the things they had discussed, like arranging for me to have classwork sent home.

I'd expected that, but not what came next.

'She said they would put special things in place for you, Soph, like making sure you sit at the front of the class.'

'I already do that,' I said.

'Of course,' Mum said, like she could tell I was annoyed that we

59

were talking about school so soon. 'But there's other things, like giving you a hearing buddy.'

'A hearing buddy?'

'Yes,' said Mum. 'It doesn't have to be the same person in every lesson, but just someone who you can turn to if you've not picked up every word. I thought maybe Mia?'

I nodded because I knew Mia would do it.

'And there's a possibility for you to have a note-taker for some of the lessons, maybe a student from the university.'

'No,' I said, getting frustrated. 'I don't want that. Everyone will be looking at me. It'll be bad enough me thinking that they all know I'm deaf, but that will be like having a huge sign saying I am.'

'Okay,' Mum said. 'Maybe I'll tell Miss Urbanski it'll just be Mia for now. It's all about making you comfortable, Soph. She said she'd call again next week.' Mum looked at me like she was waiting for a reply, but my chest suddenly felt like an elephant had stepped on it. Plans were being made behind my back and then I wasn't being given enough warning – school, hospital and Battle of the Bands. It was like everyone knew there was a meteor coming but they weren't going to tell me until it had already smashed into Earth.

That evening, my noise screeched like a thousand out-of-tune violins. While Mum and Dad were out in the garden, I tried to watch TV to take my mind off of it, but concentrating on reading subtitles seemed to make it worse. I looked up ways of coping with tinnitus on my laptop, hoping that someone might have posted something that had worked since I last looked.

- Avoid irritants (that would be school and Rocco).
- Cover up the noise with something else, like a fan, music or something soothing, like special tinnitus music (couldn't do that any more because I couldn't hear ANYthing).
- Manage stress. Stress can make things worse.

Just reading that made me stress, and the best way for me to cope with that used to be by playing my guitar. I puffed out my cheeks. I was stuck in a maze with my noise and there didn't seem to be any way out. But I was desperate to find one. I couldn't hear any notes, and it had upset me last time when I'd tried to play, but I was missing how calm I'd feel when I held my guitar in my hands. Perhaps I'd given up too easily the night before? I thought about the lessons I'd had with Mrs Hopkirk, how she'd said I had a natural rhythm. She'd not want me to give up now.

I walked over to my window and picked the guitar up. My noise was still raging as I sat back down on my bed.

I put the guitar across my lap, held my hands over the frets, then took deep breaths as I closed my eyes and tried to calm my noise.

A tune came into my head as I strummed. It was 'Reasons', the song we'd played to get to the semi-finals. I'd played it a thousand times, every chord and every note, and as I played now, I imagined the rest of the band playing in my head and Rocco singing on the stage.

I opened my eyes, looked down at my guitar. I couldn't hear or feel a thing, but my fingers were dancing all by themselves across the strings.

I smiled as my noise started to subside. I didn't care if I was playing out of time or out of tune, or that I'd never be able to play in the band; I was just happy to have my guitar in my hands again.

Mia couldn't stop smiling when I told her the next day. After being in for so long, I was glad she suggested we get out for some fresh air when she came by my house after school. As we walked together, she agreed I'd always had natural timing, and that I should try to be more confident, but I wasn't sure that just those two things would be enough for me to play again. My favourite teacher and best friend were doing their best to help, but I had a lot of things to catch up on with Mia, so I told her about Miss Urbanski's telephone call and the things they might do to help me at school.

'Well, that's okay.' Mia beamed. 'I'll be your hearing buddy.'

'I didn't think you'd mind.'

'Oh, I don't,' said Mia. 'I mean, we don't have to always talk about schoolwork. We can talk about anything.'

'Yeah,' I said, suddenly positive. 'I suppose we could.'

'Imagine that in geography,' Mia continued. 'Mr Bryant won't be able to say anything.'

'Or, even better, Mrs Drew,' I said. 'You know what she's like if anyone even drops a pen. You and me talking will make her explode.'

We both laughed. The sound of laughter was still the thing I missed most, but seeing the happy tears in Mia's eyes just made me want to laugh more.

'I wonder how it'll work in PE, though,' said Mia.

'You'll have to run alongside me,' I said.

'I'll never keep up. Watch out, Soph.' Mia put her hand on my arm and pulled me towards one side of the lane. I looked behind and followed a car as it drove by.

'Thanks,' I said to Mia as we walked on.

'Oh,' she said, pointing at me and making me stop. 'You'll never guess what happened. Georgina Humphries got suspended.'

'What?' I said. 'Wait, tell me everything.'

Mia started to laugh, so much that I couldn't read her lips, but, for once, I wasn't thinking about anything else other than what she was trying to say – not my hearing, not the doctor appointments, not my noise. It was all lost as Mia giggled her way through the story. I made out the words – 'toilet roll', 'flooded' and 'boys' toilets' – and that was all I needed to know. And as we kept walking Mia tapped my arm whenever there was a car, and when we saw Mrs Lau coming with her dog, Mia was the first to jump over a gate and hide in the field.

We'd been talking for so long that it was teatime when we got back. We stood outside my house for another five minutes, talking, until my phone vibrated in my pocket. Mia kept talking and I wondered who it could be, because Mum and Dad were in the house, and I was already with her.

It vibrated again.

'You know who that is, don't you?' said Mia.

'Can you hear it?' I said.

'Yeah, but it's not just that.' She reached into her pocket. 'Mine's going off too.'

'Rocco,' I said.

Mia nodded. 'Can only be. There.' She showed me Rocco's message on our group chat:

Rocco: Practice, my place, tomorrow. Soph, Dad wants to know if you'll be coming because he's making pizza.

'What do you think?' said Mia.

'I don't know,' I said, taking a deep breath. 'Sounds like he's expecting me to play, and I'm not sure if I can, not with the band. Especially when there's only a week to the semi-finals.'

'Just don't take your guitar.' Mia smiled like she could sense my stress. 'You don't have to worry about it, then.'

'True,' I said. 'And it would be great for us all to be together again.'

'So I'll tell him yes?' Mia held up her phone.

'Yes.' I grinned. 'But tell him the pizza better be good!

CHAPTER 11

AIR GUITAR

The band had been together since January, and we'd practised a hundred times, but still my stomach was full of nerves as Dad drove me and Mia to Rocco's house. For once I wasn't just worried about playing guitar; my anxiety was about meeting people I already knew and wondering how they would react to me. Apart from Mia and the doctors, I'd been with Mum, Dad and Liam all the time. They knew when and how to talk to me most of the time, but meeting Rocco and Ty was going to be something new.

Before we'd left, Mum had tried to reassure me by saying things like, 'I'm sure it'll be fine – you're with friends,' and, 'Just remember it's going to be different for them too, so try to go easy on them.' And I think Dad could tell I was nervous because he said it was like I was trying to make the car stop as I tapped my feet in the footwell.

It wasn't just meeting up with the band that made me more and more nervous the closer we got to Rocco's house. It was the fact that he had a brother and two sisters, and I wasn't sure I could cope with that many people.

Luckily it was just Rocco's dad standing on the driveway washing his car when we got there, and I could see Ty and Rocco setting up the keyboard behind him in the garage.

'Hi, Sophie,' he said, holding a sponge in his hand. 'How are you?'

'I'm good, thanks,' I said.

'And you, Mia?'

Mia answered too quickly for me to catch her reply, but she must have asked Rocco's dad how he was, because he said, 'Can't complain. Well, I could, but I won't.' Then he nodded into the garage. 'I think George and Ringo are waiting for you both.' He always said the same joke about us being the Beatles. I smiled and wondered if he was going to ask about my hearing, but he just dropped his sponge in his bucket and stepped round us to talk to Dad.

Me and Mia walked into the garage. Rocco was now kneeling down, sorting through a box of cables, while Ty crouched in front of his amp. They must have heard us coming, but they were acting like I wasn't there.

'Well, thanks for the welcome,' said Mia.

'Yes,' I said. 'Hi, Soph! How are you? Missed you. Welcome back.'

Rocco stood up and smiled nervously.

'Sorry,' he said, twisting the cable in his hand. 'But all of that.'

Ty turned round and waved. 'Yeah, hi,' he said. 'Same.' Then went back to his amp.

I looked at Mia.

'Don't worry about him,' she said. 'You know what he's like – nothing gets in the way of his keyboard and amp.'

66

Rocco edged towards me, his eyes darting left and right, like he was unsure of how to speak to me.

'So, how are you?' he said eventually. 'I mean, I know you can't hear and stuff.'

'It's okay, Rocco,' I said. 'You can say the word *deaf*.'

'Yeah, I know ... I know.' Rocco looked at Mia like he needed her to help. But he'd never had any trouble talking before.

I remembered what Mum had said about my deafness being hard for other people, too.

'Rocco,' I said, trying to help him relax. 'It's still me. I'm still the same Sophie; it's just I can't hear.'

'Of course,' said Rocco, pulling the lead taut between his hands. 'But it's temporary, right?' Then he pointed at his mouth. 'And you can still lip-read and stuff?'

'I hope it's temporary,' I said. 'At least that's what the doctors hope. And yes, I can lip-read, but don't turn away from me or I can't.'

'No,' said Rocco. 'I won't. But that's cool ... that you can lip-read.'

This time it was me who glanced at Mia for help, because Rocco was acting so weird it was beginning to freak me out. I just wanted him to know I was the same, and I wanted him to be the annoying Rocco he always was.

I glanced out into the drive, where Dad seemed to be having a more successful time talking to Rocco's dad. Part of me wanted to go home with him, but if I couldn't get past talking to Rocco and Ty, there was no way I could ever get back in the band. At the moment it was like we were strangers not knowing what to say.

Ty walked over.

'Maybe we should just play,' he said.

'Yeah.' Rocco nodded. 'Let's do that. Did you bring your guitar, Soph?' He peered behind me. 'Did you want me to get it out of your dad's car?'

'No,' I said. 'I didn't bring it. I just wanted to meet.'

'But we're through to the semi-final,' said Rocco. 'We need to practise – that's what I said in my message. It's only a week away.'

'I know,' I said. 'But I'm not ready. I've hardly picked up my guitar.'

'Oh, sorry,' he said, glancing at the others. 'I thought maybe you'd still been practising. I just really want us to get through to the finals, that's all.'

Ty started to say something, but I couldn't make out what as he'd looked at the floor.

'She said she's not ready,' Mia jumped in. She was sticking up for me, but from the way they had all looked at each other, it was like they had been talking about it and had expected me to just turn up and play. I wanted to play and win Battle of the Bands as much as they did, but they didn't seem to understand.

I looked out on to the road for Dad. Even if I had wanted to go back with him, it was too late because he'd finished talking to Rocco's dad and was pulling away in his car.

'It's okay,' I said, looking back at them. 'I'll just sit here while you play.'

'You sure?' asked Mia.

'Yes,' I said. 'I'm sure. Just tell me what songs you're playing,

68

and I'll play the guitar lines in my head. Just don't turn the amps up loud,' I added, trying to stay calm.

'Good idea, Soph,' said Rocco, looking like he was relieved he hadn't upset me. 'Sit here.'

I smiled as Rocco unfolded a garden chair. He was looking after me like my dad did with my nan.

I sat down and pulled my headphones up over my ears.

Rocco gave me a weird look.

'Still got to protect my ears,' I said. 'Even if they don't work.'

'Right.' He nodded. 'Sorry, Soph.'

'And stop saying sorry,' I said. 'It's annoying.'

'Yep,' said Rocco. 'Got it. No more sorrys.'

I leaned back against the wall as Ty turned the amps down and Mia plugged her bass in. They all glanced at each other nervously, like when we played together for the first time. I wanted to be back in the band, but it was never going to work if they were scared of upsetting me all the time.

Mia put her hands over her strings, Ty hovered his over the keyboard, while at the back, Rocco was figuring out which buttons to press on the drum machine. Before, this would have taken a few seconds to get ready, but now it was like they were afraid to start. All because I was here.

I pushed myself away from the wall.

'Everyone,' I said. 'Just play like we always do. Stop worrying about me.'

They all looked at each other.

'Sorry,' they said at the same time.

'And I told you, stop saying sorry!' I laughed.

They all smiled with relief, and now I had said what I had, I finally felt like I could breathe.

'So, we'll start,' said Rocco.

I nodded as Rocco counted them in.

'One. Two. Three.'

Ty turned a knob on his keyboard. Mia had her head down over her guitar. Rocco was looking right at me, and the drum machine must have started because he was nodding his head in time. He started to sing 'Reasons', the song that I had written one night in my bedroom. I watched his mouth as he sang the words:

Living on a blind circular street
(Circular people live on a repeat)

Rocco nodded at me because this was the part where I would normally sing backing vocals. It was my song, and our band, but now all I could do was mime in case I sounded like a cat. Rocco sang the next line. Mia plucked her bass. I imagined my guitar was in front of me and pictured my fingers over the frets and strings. The song was coming up to the bridge that linked the second chorus to the final verse.

'Play air guitar, Soph,' Rocco said, as if he knew I was playing the notes in my head. I used to feel embarrassed if anyone caught me playing air guitar, but not if it was one of the band. When we first got together, we told each other how we would all practise in the mirror, pretending we were rock stars in our bedrooms – me and Mia

70

with our guitars, even Ty with his keyboard, and Rocco admitted he jumped around with one of his mum's hairbrushes for a microphone.

I held out my hands like my guitar was hanging from my neck, and Rocco lifted up the mic ready to sing again. The band had reached the end of the bridge and was going into the chorus. I placed my hands over the imaginary frets and strings – I nodded at Rocco, counted the beats as he nodded back at me. It was like I was watching a merry-go-round, waiting to jump on.

Now, I said to myself. *Now.*

The band smiled as I played the 'Reasons' riff on air guitar. My heart beat fast with excitement. The band kept playing. I kept playing. It was great to be back with them, even if I was miming. For over two weeks I'd been trapped in my room with my chest feeling like it had been tied tight with rope. Now I was back in Rocco's garage, and it was like I'd undone all the knots and could play free.

'You'll soon be back playing properly,' Rocco said when we'd finished.

'I'm not so sure,' I said. 'Anyone can play air guitar.'

'But you were doing the right chords and everything,' Rocco continued. 'I was watching you. You'll make the semi-final, easy.'

I sighed and glanced at Mia. Rocco was still going on like I'd been away from school with a cold and it was beginning to stress me out.

'Rocco,' said Mia, like she knew how I was feeling. 'It's not as simple as you think.'

'I know,' said Rocco, 'Look, I'm sorry. It's just that I really want to win. I know we can do it, Soph.'

'But I've not even gone back to school,' I said. I held my hand against my head as a sharp hooting sound shot through it.

They all stopped what they were doing to look at me.

'Soph,' said Mia, looking concerned. 'Are you okay?'

'Yeah,' I said, walking out of the garage into the light. 'I just need some time.'

Mia followed me. 'Is he too much?' she asked.

'Yes,' I said, glancing back at Rocco. 'Just a bit.'

Mia stood close to me, like she didn't want Rocco to hear. 'But that's him,' she said. 'You know he cares loads, but sometimes he speaks without thinking.'

'I know,' I replied. 'It's just—' I stopped talking as Rocco walked out.

'I'm sorry, Soph,' he said. 'It's just me and my big mouth. I'm just so glad to have you back.'

Rocco was really trying, but he still didn't seem to get it. Just because I was back in body, didn't mean I was back to play.

'I've barely picked up my guitar, Rocco,' I said. 'I'm not sure you get what *this* is like.' I pointed to my ears. 'I might be back, but I'm not *back*, back. That was just air guitar. In my head it was perfect, but I won't know how it sounds when it's connected to an amp.'

'But we'll help,' he said, glancing at Ty then at Mia, who had joined us outside. 'There must be stuff we can do,' he continued. 'I've got one idea. We could—'

'No, Rocco. I don't want—' I winced as the noise hooted sharper and louder. For a while it had felt like it was sleeping, but all the talk of being back in the band had suddenly shaken it awake.

72

Rocco put his hand on my shoulder.

'I'm sorry, Soph,' he said. 'Am I getting on your nerves?'

'You always get on my nerves, Rocco.' I chuckled, even though I felt like crying. 'But it's not all your fault; it's my noise. I'm anxious because I have my scan on Monday then I have to think about going back to school.'

I took my hand down as the noise started to fade. Rocco still had a concerned look on his face. Mia was right, he did care; he just didn't always know how to show it.

'It's okay,' I said, trying to reassure him. 'I'm glad I came today. I just don't want to be rushed.'

'Yeah.' Rocco let out a long breath. 'I'm sorry.'

'And stop saying sorry.'

'Okay, sorry.' Rocco grinned.

'Rocco!' said Mia.

'What? Soph knows I'm joking.'

I shook my head slowly.

'Still friends?' Rocco asked.

'Course,' I said, as the noise faded a little more.

'Maybe the scan and going back to school will be the same as today,' he said. 'It'll be better once you get them out of the way.'

'I hope so.'

Rocco glanced back at Ty, like he wanted to get back to playing.

'It's okay, Rocco,' I said. 'You can go if you like.'

'No,' he said. 'I'm okay.'

'Then what is it?' I said. 'You're making me nervous.'

'I don't know. It's hard to say.'

Mia walked away, like she thought Rocco wouldn't speak while she was there.

'Just blurt it out, Rocco.' I said. 'Like you usually do.'

'Okay.' Rocco took a deep breath. 'I just wondered if you've thought about what you'll do if it doesn't come back?'

'Most of the time,' I said. 'Everything feels dead and broken.'

'That's a good lyric.' Rocco grinned. 'You should write it down. But don't give up, Soph. Maybe you could have one of those implant things? One of my mum's friends has one. Kind of looks like a hearing aid, except it's stuck like a magnet to the side of her head.'

'Yeah –' I sighed – 'I've seen them, but I don't want to think about that now. I'd rather my hearing came back than have a piece of plastic on the side of my head.'

'Sorry,' said Rocco. 'But there is one good thing about this.' He smiled brightly.

'What's that?'

Rocco pointed at my neck. 'Those headphones are dead cool.'

We both laughed as we went back into the garage. Mum was right: losing my hearing wasn't just about how I coped; it was about how my friends reacted too. Out of everyone, Rocco was the person I'd been most anxious about seeing, but I hadn't realized it would be like getting to know each other all over again. It was great being back with the band, but I just hoped Rocco would let me move at my own pace.

CHAPTER 12

PICTURES OF ME

'Nothing to worry about.'

'You'll be fine.'

'It doesn't hurt at all.'

The words of Dr Cowans, Mum and Dad were going through my head as I lay on a hospital trolley staring up at the bright lights. Behind me was the huge CT scanner. It was like a giant white mint with a hole in the middle that I was about to go into.

'Okay, Sophie.' Myna, the nurse, smiled down at me. 'All that will happen is that you'll slide gently back, and the scan will begin. And, like I told you – any problems, just press this button.'

'Okay.' I smiled nervously. 'But it doesn't hurt?'

'No, it doesn't hurt. You might feel a thudding sensation, but that's nothing to worry about. It's perfectly normal; it's just the camera taking pictures as it moves over your head.'

'Can I keep my eyes open?'

'Yes, you can keep your eyes open, but try not to move. If you do, don't worry too much; it just means it might take a little longer if we need to go back and take more pictures again. Okay?'

'Okay.'

I put the headphones on and rested my head back into a soft cradle that had been wrapped round my neck to hold me in place.

I must not move, I thought to myself. *I must not turn my head. I must not scratch the itch on my nose.*

I felt a gentle jolt as I slid on the conveyor belt towards the hole.

I must not move. I must not move.

The nurse had told me the scan would take about thirty-five minutes and it wouldn't hurt, but I was so anxious I could feel the button she had given me slipping in my hands.

My head slid into the machine and the smooth white surface surrounded me.

Another gentle jolt.

The conveyor belt had stopped, the top half of my body in the machine, the other half out. I stared up at the white curved surface. On the way here, in the car, Dad had told me that when he'd had a scan for his back there were speakers inside so the nurse could tell him when the scan was about to begin. And that when it did, there was a loud thudding sound that went on for ages, just like the nurse had just told me there would be. But I couldn't hear the nurse, and I couldn't hear the thud; I could just feel a gentle vibration, like someone was knocking a pole into the ground in another room.

THUD.

THUD.

THUD.

I must not move. I must not move.

I must not scratch the itch that feels like an ant crawling across my eyebrow.

I must not. I must not.

I closed my eyes.

In the waiting room, Mum and Dad had told me to think of nice things to take my mind off what was happening. Dad said he'd imagined Rovers winning the cup when he'd had his, and Mum said she'd think of lying on a beach in the sun, but all I could think of was the rhythm of the machine. I imagined the camera above me taking hundreds of pictures of my brain and ears as it scanned across my head.

THUD.

THUD.

THUD.

Do not move. Do not move.

What part was it scanning now?

What would it find?

The nurse said I wouldn't find out today, but I'd have another appointment with Dr Cowans in the next couple of days.

THUD.

THUD.

THUD.

The machine kept to the rhythm and my head kept to that rhythm, and then words popped into my head.

THUD.

We're taking pictures ...

THUD.

We're taking pictures ...

THUD.

We're taking pictures of you.

It felt like the clouds had lifted when I walked through the car park with Mum and Dad.

'It wasn't as bad as I thought,' I said. 'Bit scary when I first went in, but once I closed my eyes and relaxed, I was fine.'

'Well done, Soph,' Mum said, putting her arm round me. 'I knew you'd be okay.'

'Better than okay.' I grinned. 'I got an idea for a song too.'

'Well done.' The lights on our car flashed as Mum pressed the key fob. 'The nurse told us the results should be with Dr Cowans in a couple of days. Meantime, let's go to Mollie's Diner on the way home. My treat.'

'Wish I could come,' said Dad. Then he started to walk towards his red work van. He turned back to look at me. 'But perhaps you can write your lyric down on a napkin like the Beatles?'

I ran over and gave him a hug. Rocco was right; I did feel loads better now the scan was out of the way.

As I climbed into the passenger seat next to Mum, I thought about how having the scan and meeting the band had marked two things off the list. Now all I had to think about was going back to school, but that felt like the biggest thing of all. I didn't want to think about it now, anyway. I'd just got rid of one elephant on my chest; I didn't want another. But what would I gain if I delayed going back?

78

Another week sat at home in my room doing classwork? Another week hoping that the steroids and Mum's herbal tablets would make my hearing come back? Putting school off would mean I gained nothing at all.

'I'll go back to school tomorrow, Mum.' I must have blurted it out, because Mum turned to me with a shocked expression on her face.

'What?' she said. 'Where did that come from? Are you sure?'

'Yes.' I nodded. 'I'm sure. I had a chat with Rocco, and I think sitting at home worrying will just make it worse.'

'Wow!' Mum puffed out her cheeks. 'Well, I didn't see that coming.'

'No.' I laughed nervously. 'Neither did I.'

'You are sure, Soph?' Mum said. 'I mean, I was going to chat to you about it when we got to Mollie's, but I was going to suggest you go back next week, and maybe start with half days.'

'Like infants?' I said. 'No, thanks.'

I waited for Mum to say something else, but she just looked at me with tears welling up in her eyes.

'What's wrong, Mum?' I asked.

'Nothing.' She smiled as she put her hand on the side of my face. 'I was just thinking that you're amazing.'

'Thanks,' I said. 'I guess I am.'

We both laughed, then Mum turned the key in the ignition.

I'm amazing, I thought to myself as the car pulled away. I had done the right thing, but now the decision had been made, I felt amazingly nervous again.

*

My noise was like a thousand bees as I tried to play my guitar that evening. Miss Urbanski had told Mum that everyone in school would help me out, but that didn't stop me worrying about where I would sit or how the rest of my class would react. I thought of going downstairs and telling Mum and Dad that maybe I should wait another week after all. But then I realized I had to do it, even if my stomach flipped with nerves. Instead, I finished practising and got up to go to the loo.

As I walked out of my room, I saw that Mum had left a pile of Liam's clothes neatly folded on the floor outside his bedroom door ready for him to put away. I felt queasy. Mum never went into Liam's room and neither did I. Things died in that room – at least that's what it smelt like. But that wasn't why I was suddenly felt sick. It was because my school uniform was hanging on the banister outside my room – blue sweatshirt, white shirt, blue skirt, then my white socks rolled into a ball on top of my shoes.

Liam's bedroom door opened. He looked at me like he'd just woken up and I was the first person he'd seen all day.

'What are you doing?' he said, rubbing his eyes.

'Nothing,' I said.

He looked at my uniform on the banister.

'Oh,' he said. 'Are they making you go back?'

'No,' I said. 'It was my idea.'

'What? YOU decided to go back? What an idiot. I couldn't wait to get out of that place.'

'More like they couldn't wait to get rid of you.' I chuckled.

'Well, yeah.' Liam grinned. 'That too.'

80

He stepped over his clothes and headed towards the bathroom.

I stared at my uniform. All set out in order. The only thing it needed was a body to go in it. My body. Suddenly I was so nervous I could feel myself shaking.

Liam turned round in the bathroom doorway.

'You'll be fine,' he said. 'And if you're not, just come home. Or bunk off down the fields or town.'

'Thanks,' I said. 'But it's bad enough being deaf, without getting into trouble too.'

'Just saying.' He shrugged. 'No matter how bad things are, there's always a way out. I hated school, but I'm good with college. Just because things change, doesn't mean you can't adjust.'

'Crikey, Liam!' I laughed. 'Steady! You are actually starting to make sense.'

'Not me.' He grinned. 'My careers advisor at college. Anyway,' he said, closing the door. 'Gotta go, I'm bursting for a pee.'

I turned and went back into my bedroom. What Liam had said was true. I was scared of going to school, but if I got there in the morning and felt I had to come back, all I had to do was try again.

My phone vibrated beside me on my bed. I'd messaged the band after practice saying I was coming back to school the next day. Rocco had already replied, *Great*. Ty sent a thumb. Now Mia was messaging me directly.

Mia: Saw your message. Can't wait to have you back. I'll meet you at the bus stop. No, wait. I'll call for you. Or whatever you want 😊

I might have been having second thoughts about going back, but I was so glad that I wouldn't be doing it alone.

Sophie: I'll meet you at the bus stop. But I'm so nervous.

Mia: I would be too. But we'll be together. You just tell me as soon as you think anything is wrong. I don't know what, but just anything. Mrs Hopkirk will be pleased.

I smiled at my phone.

Sophie: Thanks. I feel better knowing that 😊

Mia: 😊 Oh, and message me whenever, like if you can't sleep.

Sophie: I will.

I put my phone back down on my bed, took a deep breath, then another. I had to go to school. I had to, but the thought scared me to death. I had to get rid of that feeling, otherwise I'd get no sleep and that would only make the thought of school and my noise worse. Maybe it would help to write my feelings down.

I reached over to my bedside table and picked up the lyrics I'd started on the napkin in Mollie's, to make Mum laugh.

I copied them into my notebook and thought about the appointment again and how I'd felt as I slid towards the scanner.

Bright lights

Black hole

Bright lights

Black hole

Sliding

Sliding

Press the button if you panic

Press the button if you panic

Thud. Thud

Boom. Boom

We're taking pictures

We're taking pictures

We're taking pictures of you.

I held my pen over the page and tried to think of another line, but suddenly I felt so tired all I wanted to do was sleep. I wrote a title – 'Pictures of You' – then put my pen and notebook back on the table and turned out the light. It had been a hard day, but I had got through it. I'd marked two things off the list, but it felt like the hardest one of all was to come.

CHAPTER 13

EVERYTHING IS NEW

'Hi, Soph.' Mia smiled.

I tried to smile back, but the muscles in my face were frozen to ice. I glanced at the other kids from the village waiting at the bus stop. They must have all known what had happened to me. It only takes a conversation with one person at the village store or the chip shop for news to spread. It had been well over a week since it happened, so even kids who never listened to their parents' gossip were bound to know I was the girl who had gone deaf overnight.

My phone vibrated with a message from Mum.

Mum: Hope you're okay, love, and it goes well.

I thought of replying, but I couldn't lie. I wasn't okay. I was waiting for a bus with a friend who couldn't think of anything to say, apart from hi, and all the kids from the village, whose eyes were burning into the back of my head.

I looked back along the road towards my house. With Mum and

Dad at work, it was empty. I took a step, thought of going back, up to my room. And I would have gone back if it wasn't for noticing Liam's motorbike propped up against our fence. I wasn't in the mood for my stepbrother today.

My phone buzzed again.

Mia: Sorry, not very good at this.

I turned to Mia. She looked as scared and nervous as I felt. I wanted to tell her it was okay, that if a friend of mine went deaf, I probably wouldn't be able to think of anything to say either, but she just reached out and held my arm.

'What is it?' I asked.

I felt a rush of wind and spun around, just as the bus arrived.

Mia pulled me by her side, quickly. 'Just stay close to me,' she said.

'Okay.' I took a deep breath and leaned back against the glass of the bus shelter. Normally I'd have heard the bus's engine or the hiss of its brakes, but in the silence, it seemed to come out of nowhere. Mum hadn't been keeping on at me to go out for nothing. It was to save me from getting knocked over before I'd even left the village.

I was still in shock as the rest of the kids filed by. I watched as, one by one, they stepped on to the bus and showed their passes to the driver. I reached into my bag, fumbled though my pencil case and found mine. Mia edged forward, pulled me with her.

'It's all right,' I said. 'I'm okay now.'

Mia winced.

'Did I just shout?' I asked.

'Yeah.' She nodded. 'Just a bit.'

'*Sorry*,' I mouthed.

I showed my pass to the driver then looked down the bus for a seat. The kids from Rampton village sat at the front, and Powell Stevens and the rest of the kids from Bidstock village always sat at the back. I never really spoke to them, but sometimes they might burst out laughing whenever one of them had said a joke, or poke fun whenever anyone new got on. I didn't know if they did that to me this time, because I couldn't hear, and I never lifted my head. I just sat in our usual middle seats with Mia and faced the front.

Normally we'd talk about what we'd watched on Netflix the night before or share selfies on our phones, but as the bus pulled away my stomach twisted into a hundred knots.

I glanced at Mia. 'I can't stop shaking,' I said.

Mia smiled. 'I'm here, don't worry,' she said.

I felt a knock on the back of my seat. I wanted to look to see what it was, but I was too scared in case everyone was looking at me.

The chair knocked again.

Mia turned round and scowled at whoever it was, then picked up her phone.

Mine buzzed. I looked at the screen.

Mia: Just Josh Hyatt messing about with someone's bag.

I sighed.

Sophie: So no one's looking at me?

86

Mia: No. No one.

Sophie: Not even Powell Stevens?

Mia flashed a look towards the back of the bus.

Mia: No. She's just doing what we are.

Sophie: Really? She's not even dancing?

Mia giggled.

Mia: No, she's just looking at her phone.

I smiled with relief. But as we got closer to school, I felt another wave of panic coming. I remembered the things Miss Urbanski had said the school would put in place for me: sitting at the front of the class; having a hearing buddy and maybe a note-taker. People may not be looking at me now, but having those things would make me stand out, make me different. I didn't want to be different. I just wanted to walk into school and have lessons in exactly the same way as everyone else.

87

CHAPTER 14

AS SCARY AS HALLOWEEN

Mum had taken me for walks to get used to being out, and I'd been with Mia, but nothing had prepared me for walking with her through the corridors when I got to school. Boys and girls zig-zagged in front of me, mouths moving, arms waving, feet stepping as I clung on to Mia's arm. Normally I'd have been one of them, but now it felt like I had to negotiate a sea of silent random atoms, just to get to my classroom.

'You'll be okay, Soph,' Mia must have said ten times, but my heart stopped when I reached my form room.

Twenty-eight pairs of eyes staring at me as I walked into the room.

Twenty-eight mouths that had been open, suddenly closed.

Everyone had stopped what they were doing and were looking right at me.

Even Li and Harry had stopped playing Top Trumps.

Mia was by my side, but I felt alone. I stood there, right at the front of the class, in front of the whiteboard, with all those eyes wide open, gawking at me like I'd just walked in wearing a blood-eyed

Halloween mask. I felt like I was sinking into the ground until Miss Urbanski came and rescued me.

'Hi, Sophie.' She smiled. 'Good to have you back.'

I tried to say it was good to be back, but I'd been quiet for so long that my words were clogged in my throat. Miss Urbanski turned to the class. She must have said, 'Get on with some quiet reading,' because everyone reached into their bags and got their reading books, finally tearing their gaze from me.

Mia and I sat down in our seats at the front and I reached into my bag for my book, *The Shadow Creeper*, and started to read like we were supposed to during registration. Mia nudged me.

'You okay?' she asked.

I nodded that I was, but I could feel the stares burning into the back of my head as Miss Urbanski started the register.

Miss Urbanski was turned towards her computer, so I couldn't lip-read as she called out the names. And I couldn't see who replied because they were either beside or behind me. All I knew was that I was tenth in the register, and that Lois Grant's was the name before mine. I looked across the room to where she was sitting by the window. Form class and registration was usually quite fun. I'd say hi to a few friends, but now almost everyone had their heads down.

I glanced back at Miss Urbanski, head still turned to the computer, then back at Lois. All I had to say was two words, but for the twenty seconds leading up to it I said, *Yes, miss*, over and over in my head, like I was rehearsing for a school play.

I saw Lois reply to her name, then I looked back at Miss Urbanski, who said my name, and I blurted, 'Yes, miss!'

Amy and Ryan on the next table gave me a weird look, like I'd said it too quiet or too loud. I knew no one could see my deafness, but that didn't stop me feeling like I stood out.

Luckily for me, Mia knew I was stressing, and everywhere I went that morning, she went too, linked arm in arm with me like I was the new girl at school. We sat at the front in maths. I had worried about the teachers making a fuss of me, or that they'd walk around the classroom so much that I wouldn't be able to read their lips. But Mrs Doust hardly took any notice of me when I walked in, and she spent most of the lesson in front of the whiteboard, so it wasn't hard to keep track. The only time I got stuck was when she started calling out random multiplications for the class to answer, and I couldn't tell if she had said thirteen or thirty, so I decided it was best not to put my hand up at all.

When it got to break, Mia walked with me down the corridor. The only time she let go of me was when I went to the toilet, and even then she was waiting right outside the cubicle. She was still right by my side when we sat on the bench in the quad. Normally we'd have had to shout over the noise of the boys playing tag, but we just sat there, sometimes glancing at each other with nervous smiles as I watched the boys and girls running around, mouths open like they were shouting, but all the while I couldn't hear a sound. All I could think about was fast-forwarding to meeting the band at lunchtime, to get away from everyone. So I was glad when Mia tapped my arm and said the bell had rung for the end of break and we went back inside. Mia was amazing. Being with her was like having subtitles in real life.

It was a lot harder to follow Mr Bryant in geography because he liked walking around the room. I had to keep turning in my seat, trying to follow him, but I'd miss everything he said as he walked away from me. I'd pick up some words as he walked across the back row, then most of what he said as he walked towards me again, but even then I'd lose some of the words as the sun was behind him, making his head a silhouette, so I couldn't see his lips clearly.

By the end of the lesson, I knew there was a land bar somewhere in Devon, that it's six and a half kilometres long and there was a chance we might be going there on a field trip. But that's when he looked out of the window, and I've no idea if the trip is going to be at the end of the week, month or term, but luckily Mia had written it down for me. She'd also written, *Can't wait for band practice at lunchtime!* And I smiled, because even when I could hear, band practice was the best part of the day.

CHAPTER 15

BACK WITH
MY FRIENDS

It felt good just to be walking down the corridor with my guitar on my back at lunchtime, but the closer I got to the music room, the more I could feel my confidence draining away.

I stopped outside the door and peeked through the glass window. Inside, nothing seemed to have changed – Ty was fiddling with the amp, and Rocco was scratching his head trying to work out how to program the drum machine – the only difference was that me and Mia were on the outside looking in. *They don't really need me*, I thought. *They're only being kind, saying they want me to play. They could easily get someone else.*

Mia pushed the door open. I stood still.

'What's wrong, Soph?' she asked, turning back.

'This,' I said, pointing into the room. 'I think I've made a mistake.'

I backed away from the door. My guitar knocked against something, or someone.

I spun round. Mrs Hopkirk was standing behind me.

'Sophie.' She beamed. 'How lovely to see you!'

I smiled nervously. 'Thank you,' I said, taking another step backwards.

'I thought you were going in,' she said.

'I was,' I said, glancing back into the music room. 'But I changed my mind.'

Mrs Hopkirk put her hand on my arm and then looked at Mia. She must have said something, because Mia nodded and went inside.

Mrs Hopkirk turned back to me.

'I can see you're nervous, Sophie,' she said. 'And I'm not going to lie, I would be too. In fact, there's been many times that I've been to auditions, or getting ready to play, and I've stood at the edge of the stage wanting to turn back.'

'I know.' I sighed. 'But this feels different. I think the band are just being kind, that they don't really need me.'

'Oh.' Mrs Hopkirk grinned. 'That'll be why Rocco came to me first thing this morning, all excited that you were coming back.'

'Did he?' I smiled.

'Yes, he was going on about some computer thing I didn't quite understand . . . And here he is to tell you about it himself.'

I turned and saw Rocco in the doorway looking like the excited Labrador Dad said he was.

'What's up, Soph?' he said 'You are coming in, aren't you? I got something to show you.'

'See.' Mrs Hopkirk nodded. 'What did I tell you?'

'It's really cool,' said Rocco. 'But first, have you seen this?' He pointed at a poster on the wall.

Battle of the Bands
Semi-Final
Come and Support Your Bands
HiFi Dad, the Longshots, and the Band With No Name
Town Hall, Sunday 5th June

'That's us,' he said, pointing at the last band name. 'I was going to tell them we were called the Bees, but you hadn't agreed, so I left it. Cool, though. There's another poster in the reception area, and on the noticeboards in every corridor.'

I couldn't stop smiling. The band still didn't have a name, but we were in the semi-finals and, after all that had happened, I would actually get to be part of it.

'Anyway,' said Rocco, 'that's not what I wanted to show you. It's_____.' I lost Rocco's words as he walked away from me.

Mrs Hopkirk smiled. 'Think you'd better follow,' she said. 'You know what he's like.'

'Yes.' I grinned. 'I do.'

Mrs Hopkirk headed towards the instrument store cupboard as I followed Rocco to the back of the room, where Ty was helping Mia adjust her guitar strap.

'Here,' said Rocco, as he stood next to a laptop. 'I downloaded an app.' He turned the laptop to face me. 'Because we haven't got a drummer for you to watch, we just program the drum machine and you _____.' I lost Rocco's lips again as he looked at the screen.

'Rocco,' I said. 'You need to slow down. You're rushing me.'

94

'Oh, yeah,' he said. 'Sorry. Keep forgetting. Well, not forgetting, but, well, you know.'

'Yes,' I said, smiling slightly. 'I know.'

'So, Soph,' Rocco continued. 'Here it is.'

I looked at the screen. There wasn't much to see but a green line.

'Maybe it's best that I show you,' said Rocco. 'We can tweak it a bit so you can see it from a distance. You'll look like a techie in Kraftwerk.'

'Kraftwerk?'

'German computer band,' said Rocco. 'My dad went to loads of their gigs. They used computers all the time. Anyway, this is how it works. See that line?'

I stood beside him and looked at the straight green line, which cut across the screen.

'Now watch.' Rocco pressed a button on the drum machine. The line went jagged, peaking and troughing like a heartbeat on a monitor. I'd heard there were apps like this, but I'd never needed to use one before.

'It'll just be the drumbeat,' he said. 'It'll be easier with all the other stuff filtered out. Do you think it could work?'

I stared at the screen, mainly because I could feel the pressure of everyone in the band looking at me. Rocco might always be fooling around, appearing like he doesn't care, but he'd taken the time to find the app for me.

I nodded slowly. Everyone smiled with relief.

'Yes,' I said, grinning. 'I think it could work.'

'Great,' said Rocco. 'So, let's do it?'

I went to get my guitar out of its case, but Ty had already done it. I took it from him.

'And I got you this,' Ty said, holding out a black guitar pick.

I took the pick. It had the Elk logo on it from one of my favourite bands.

'Thanks.' I smiled as I showed it to Mia. 'Ty, that's really kind.'

'No worries. Just thought you'd like it.'

'I do.'

Ty smiled slightly awkwardly then bent down to his amplifier. Because he's the quietest out of all of us, it's hard to tell what Ty is thinking, and as I looked at the pick, it made me feel like I really was part of the band again.

Rocco stood behind the mic, then made sure I was watching as he pressed the button on the drum machine.

The green line dipped up and down as Rocco nodded his head in time. I imagined the beat – the bass, the snare. The bass, the snare. I saw Rocco grinning as I began to nod to a beat I couldn't hear.

Mia held her hands over the strings of her guitar. Ty tapped his foot in time as his fingers hovered over the keyboard. I put my left hand over the frets and held my pick over the strings.

Rocco grinned at me. *'Okay?'* he mouthed.

I smiled. This wasn't air guitar any more. This was for real.

I couldn't hear a thing, but I was back in the band. I was back in the band properly, and it wasn't just about the music; it was about doing something I loved and being with my friends.

Rocco held his hand above his head. 'Let's go,' he said. 'One, two, three!'

I looked at the screen. The green line blipped up and down. I checked my hands on the frets once more, then started to play, imagining each chord and note in my head. I glanced up as Rocco sang.

We have reasons
For being who we want to be
We have reasons
For not wanting to be alone.

I looked back at the green line on the screen, hoping I was still in time. I'd only taken my eye off it for a second, but I was already behind. I was struggling to keep up. The song must be sounding awful, like when we first started the band, and our bass didn't follow the drums, and Ty's keyboards clashed notes with my guitar.

I glanced at the rest of the band. Rocco was singing like everything was normal, and Mia and Ty were concentrating so hard that they didn't even look up. They could all hear the music, but all I heard was a hooting sound as my noise grew loud with the stress. I felt like stopping, but the rest of the band all seemed to be trying so hard to make it work. I watched Rocco's lips. Maybe following the green line *and* watching him might work.

We have reasons
We have reasons we want to be alone
Because we are all the same
Five feet tall, full of chromosomes.

I took a deep breath. *Keep going*, I said to myself as the green line blipped on. I moved the fingers of my left hand over the frets as I strummed with the fingers on my right –

Blip. Blip. Blip.

Yes! I smiled to myself as I hit the last *blip* smack on time, then again, and again. I looked at Rocco, who was grinning like he knew I had just worked it out. It wasn't perfect, but I had to keep going, because suddenly I realized that with a lot of practice, I might make it to Battle of the Bands after all.

Mum and Dad's faces seemed to be stuck on a permanent smile when I got home and told them how my day had gone. Mum kept asking questions like she wanted to know exactly what had happened in every minute of every lesson. I told her about how I think I made a mistake answering the register, and how I missed things in geography, and that the same happened in history during the afternoon. Mum said things like, 'It was only to be expected', and that 'things will get better', but I told her none of that really mattered because I'd had such a great practice with the band at lunchtime, it had made the rest of my day feel so much better. 'Should have known that was the main reason you're happy,' said Dad as he cleared the dinner plates from the table.

'It was brilliant,' I said. 'I mean, I've got to practise loads, which I did in my head all afternoon. It was probably the main reason I kept running while the rest of my class had stopped in the gym.'

They both laughed.

'I'm going up to practise again now,' I said. 'So I'll be even better when I meet the band again tomorrow.'

'Okay,' said Mum as I pushed back my chair. 'But, Soph, haven't you forgotten something?'

'I don't know.' I grinned. 'Have I?'

Mum glanced at Dad, then back at me.

'What's wrong?' I asked, suddenly worried.

'Soph . . .' Mum paused like she didn't want to spoil my mood. 'We've got to go to hospital for your scan results tomorrow at eleven.'

I felt my heart thud as it sank into my stomach. Mum had popped the fun balloon and brought me back to earth. She must've known because she stood up and gave me a hug, but after being so happy, all I wanted to do was go upstairs to my room.

'It's understandable that you're nervous,' Mum said, 'but isn't it better that we know what's going on, and what can be done to help?'

'Yes,' I said. 'I know you're right. I just need to be on my own for a bit.'

I left her in the hall as I went up to my room. I'd planned to spend the evening practising with the app Rocco had found, but now all I could think about was what would happen the next day.

I sat down on my bed and messaged the band, told them why I wouldn't be able to make practice. My phone seemed to vibrate with their replies seconds after I'd pressed send.

Mia: Good luck!

Ty: Good luck, Soph. We'll see you Thursday instead.

Rocco: 👍

Thumbs, I thought to myself. *I just told you I'm going for my scan results, Rocco!*

Rocco: Sorry, hit that by mistake 😊 Hope it goes okay, Soph.

I put my phone down next to me. I knew I had to get the scan results, but I was only just starting to get used to not being able to hear; now the thought of finding out what caused it, and if I would ever get my hearing back, was scaring me to death.

CHAPTER 16

SCAN RESULTS DAY

'So,' Dr Cowans said as I sat in his office with Mum and Dad. 'Let's run through what the scan revealed, and then we'll discuss our options from there.'

He turned and shared his computer screen with us. I'd been shaking with nerves in the car, and I couldn't stop myself still.

Dr Cowans smiled like he knew. 'It's okay,' he said. 'Even I get nervous with things like this. I imagine it's like getting exam results, only a hundred times worse.'

I laughed nervously.

'Now,' Dr Cowans continued as he picked up a pen and pointed it at the screen. It was full of areas of black, grey and white. 'I know all this looks extremely complicated, but this here is your brain, Sophie.' He circled an area of grey on the screen. 'But the areas we are going to focus on are here, and here.' His pen touched the screen left and right of what I assumed was a picture of the inside of my ears.

Mum and Dad were concentrating hard, judging by their

expressions, and I was trying my best to understand, but all the time Dr Cowans's lips moved, I was scared the next words he would say were going to be bad. I didn't want to know anything bad, not right here in his room. I glanced at Mum. She squeezed my hand, then we looked back at the screen with Dad.

'So –' I followed Dr Cowans's mouth – 'there appears to be some damage to the soft tissue, and to the nerves, which I'm afraid we won't be able to repair.'

My heart sank.

Dr Cowans kept talking, but my eyes had welled up with tears, so I couldn't make out the words.

No. I thought as I shook my head. *I don't want to know. I don't want to know that my hearing won't come back.* I looked at the ground as tears fell down my cheeks. My hearing had gone, but I didn't know that it would be like that for ever. I wanted to hear music again; I wanted to hear birds; I wanted to hear Mum and Dad's voices, not watch their mouths with no sound coming out.

Mum tapped me on the arm. I lifted my head and wiped the tears on my sleeve. Dad wrapped his arm around my shoulders.

'It's okay, Soph,' he said. 'We're all here to help. If there's something that can be done, I'm sure Dr Cowans will find it.'

Dr Cowans nodded, then gave me a caring smile.

'Sophie,' he said. 'It's easy for me to say, but I don't want you to worry. There are some positive signs here.'

Mum handed me a tissue as Dr Cowans continued.

'While we don't think we can get your hearing back,' he said, 'the good news is that your eardrum and your inner ear seem to be functioning correctly, which may well mean you could have a cochlear implant. Which, while not restoring hearing, can certainly offer an improvement on what you have.'

He handed Mum a leaflet and said something else, but I was wiping away more tears. I couldn't think about what help he could give me; all I could think about was what I had lost and that I was going to be stuck in a world of silence for ever.

It was like I was travelling with ghosts all the way home. Mum and Dad barely spoke, and I was so upset that when I got in, I went straight up to my room. It was like I'd secretly been expecting Dr Cowans to find a way to get my hearing back all along, and now he couldn't, it felt like I'd lost my hearing all over again. *This is what it's going to be like*, I thought to myself as I stared at the TV. Watching my favourite programmes in silence for the rest of my life with the subtitles on.

It was maybe half an hour later that Mum put her head round the side of my door.

'Is it okay to come in?' she asked with a cautious look on her face.

'Of course,' I said.

Mum came over and sat at the end of my bed.

'I would have left you longer,' she said. 'But I didn't want you to stay up here thinking you won't hear again.' She held up a leaflet. 'I know you can't have caught everything Dr Cowans said, and I've been upset too, but after reading this, I realized there might be more hope for things to improve than you might realize yourself.'

'But it won't come back, will it?' I said. 'It'll never be the same.'

'No.' Mum shook her head, then edged closer to me. 'But these people have had the same thing happen to them.'

Mum shared the leaflet with me, like when we used to read together when I was younger. On the front was a picture of a girl, smiling. She was about the same age as me. Above her was the headline – *Cochlear Implant: The Start of Something New.*

'It happens to all people of all ages,' Mum said as she opened the leaflet. Inside was a group photo of about eight people: some younger than me; some as old as my grandparents. 'And yes, you're right – they don't get their hearing back. But if you read through what some of them say, it seems to be a huge improvement on what they had before.'

I stared at the photos and the things people had said about the implants underneath, but I was still so shocked that none of the information went into my head.

'Can I read it later, Mum?' I said wearily. 'I'm just really tired.'

'Of course,' said Mum, putting it on my bedside table. 'There's no rush, and even if you did decide to have it done, it wouldn't be for a while as there's a waiting list. But, as Dr Cowans said, it's best to put your name down now, even if you decide not to go ahead.'

I nodded. I'd heard what Mum was saying, but suddenly it felt like too much was happening too soon. I wiped my eyes as the tears came again.

Mum wrapped her arms round me.

'Soph,' she said.

I felt her say something, but I didn't know what. All I knew was that I felt so scared that I didn't want her to let go.

CHAPTER 17

THE GIRL IN THE PHOTOGRAPH

The girl in the leaflet smiled up at me when I left the room to go down for tea. She was still there when I went back up to practise my guitar. And she was there all the while I answered the messages from the band, asking how I had got on at the hospital. At first I thought of waiting to tell them in person, but that would have meant telling Mia on the bus, and then Rocco and Ty again at school, and I wasn't sure how I would cope doing that with other people around.

Mia said she'd come around, but I said no because it was beginning to get dark. Ty said he was sorry, and Rocco said he was too, and then he asked if it was possible for me to have an implant like the person he knew. That's when I glanced at the girl on the front of the leaflet again. I reached over to my bedside table and picked it up. The girl on the front was still smiling, but there must have been a time when she was as upset as I was.

I opened the leaflet, saw the group picture as before, but this time I noticed another picture of the girl. She was side on, and I could see what must have been a hearing aid, only it wasn't fitted behind her ear; it was attached to the side of her head. I read the writing underneath, then on the next page. It explained that a cochlear implant is an operation where an implant about the size of a ten-pence piece is slid under the skin, and a processor is attached by a magnet on top, so you can take it off when you brush your hair or have a shower. Instead of transmitting the signal to the eardrum like a hearing aid, it transmits it to the bone around the ear.

I flicked to the back page, where it gave more details of the operation, how patients usually stay in hospital for one night, and explained how a cochlear implant was considered routine and safe. But, as with any surgery, there were risks. It could cause nerve damage, tinnitus, dizziness – and even though hearing could be restored in the majority of cases, it would not be of the same level or quality as the patient had before.

A wave of disappointment passed through my body. For a while all the smiling faces had given me hope, but as I re-read the last sentence, it felt like it had been taken away. I could go through the whole operation and still not be able to hear properly. What was the point in that?

I closed the leaflet and put it back down on the table. I was about to feel sorry for myself all over again when my phone buzzed with another message from Rocco on our group chat.

Rocco: Hey, Soph. I know you've had a hard day, and all that, but have you managed to practise at all? You know, with the app?

I shook my head as I imagined Rocco in his room, squirming while he wrote the message, wanting to check what I'd done, but also trying not to upset me.

I looked across at my guitar. Battle of the Bands was just a few days away. If I wanted to play properly, I couldn't sit in my bedroom feeling sorry for myself. I had to practise and get used to the app that Rocco had put on my phone.

Sophie: It's okay, Rocco. I'm going to practise now.

Rocco: Cool. See you tomorrow.

My phone buzzed again.

Mia: Rocco, you're terrible!

Rocco: What? ☺

Then Mia messaged me direct.

Mia: Soph, I'm sorry about Rocco. He's so insensitive!

Sophie: It's okay. He's right. I do need to practise.

I picked up my guitar and opened up the app on my phone. Rocco had recorded us yesterday lunchtime, so all I had to do was watch the green line and play along. I started to play. Music usually made me forget things that might stress me; it would take me into another world.

I played 'Reasons', but I couldn't stop there. I had to get it perfect by playing over and over again. But all the time I kept glancing at my bedside table, at the girl smiling up at me from the leaflet.

Of course she would be happy, I thought to myself. *They wouldn't put a picture of a sad girl on the front if they wanted to encourage people to have the operation.* But she looked genuinely happy, like she'd be like that even if the camera wasn't there.

I started to play again, but not 'Reasons' or any of our other songs, because as I strummed the strings, another tune and a lyric came into my head.

I nodded as I played.

Your smile lights up the page
Lights up my room
You made me happy
When I was feeling sad
Because everything looks fine
Everything looks great
When you're the smiling girl in the photograph.

CHAPTER 18

NO TIME FOR NERVES

The best thing about being in the band was that I was so focused on the Battle of the Bands that it stopped me constantly thinking about my hearing. Mia and Rocco did ask more about the implant when I arrived at band practice the next day, but once Ty arrived in the music room at lunchtime, all our attention was focused on Mrs Hopkirk as she explained what to expect at the semi-final at the weekend.

'It'll be similar to the school event,' she said as we gathered around her. 'Only this time there won't be any waiting around for people if they're late, like when the Pops from Year Nine were in the first round.'

We all nodded. For once even Rocco wasn't messing about.

'And remember, this is a much bigger event: far more acts from far more schools.'

'My dad asked if he could come,' said Rocco. 'But I don't think he can, can he?'

'No,' answered Mrs Hopkirk. 'There will be enough people with just the bands and supporters from schools, but parents will be invited to the final, which will make that all the more special.'

'Cool,' said Rocco. 'I'll tell Dad to book tickets for that.'

We all laughed at Rocco's confidence that we'd get through.

'Anyway,' said Mrs Hopkirk, looking all serious again. 'You're on sixth, after Weasel. So once you're called onstage, you've fifteen minutes to set up things exactly how you want. So, Ty, no fiddling around with the amp for ages. Mia, make sure your hair is tied back before you go on so it doesn't get tangled in the strings, and, Rocco, think about where you are going to stand. Sophie, you need to set the laptop screen so that you can see it clearly.'

We all looked at each other. We'd been practising and having fun, but suddenly what Mrs Hopkirk was saying made it sound serious.

'And when you're playing,' Mrs Hopkirk went on, 'concentrate on what *you* are doing, but also think about how you come across as a band. You could all be amazing musicians, but the audience and the judges aren't going to warm to you if you don't look like you enjoy playing and being together, not like the Calloway brothers in Big World.'

'What did they do?' asked Ty.

'Had a brawling fight in the middle of a field at Glastonbury,' said Mrs Hopkirk.

We all laughed. We'd all seen Glastonbury on TV and could picture ourselves fighting in the mud.

'Apart from that, we're good,' said Mrs Hopkirk, smiling. 'Aren't we? Oh, apart from your band name. Do you have one yet?'

We all looked at each other. We'd still not come up with anything since we'd talked about it in Rocco's garage.

'We're still undecided,' said Rocco. 'But we'll come up with something when we're practising at mine on Saturday.'

'Well, I hope you do,' said Mrs Hopkirk. 'The judges won't be too impressed if you turn up as the Band With No Name, should you make it to the finals.'

We all laughed. With the semi-finals only three days away, it felt like we were laughing with nerves rather than because it was funny. At least it definitely felt that way for me. Before I lost my hearing, everything felt natural – all I had to do was pick up my guitar and play. Now it felt like, because of me, everything and everyone had to be organized and in the right place, and at the right time.

Rocco and Ty walked towards the keyboard. Mia picked up her bass and fiddled with the tuning pegs. Mrs Hopkirk gave me a look like she knew what I was thinking. She put her hand on my shoulder.

'I'm not going to pretend it's not a big thing, Sophie,' she said. 'But I'd never have encouraged you to pick up the guitar again if I didn't think all this would be fine.'

'I know.' I looked at the others to check that they weren't listening.

Mrs Hopkirk stood closer. 'What is it?' she asked.

'I just don't want to let them down.'

'And you won't.' Mrs Hopkirk smiled as Ty, Mia and Rocco gathered round us. I thought I'd been whispering, but they must have all heard.

'We're in this together, Soph,' said Ty.

'Yeah, all of us,' said Mia.

'Yep,' said Rocco, holding out his arms. 'Group hug?'

I looked at them all.

'Okay.' I smiled. 'Go on, then.'

We wrapped our arms round each other. It was typical Rocco, acting like we were all in a rock movie, and for once I didn't care, because the semi-final was so close it was like the excitement and nerves were in everyone's hugs. *Now it feels like I'm part of it*, I thought to myself, and I never, ever wanted that feeling to go.

CHAPTER 19
THE SEMI-FINALS

Two men wearing denim jackets were on the town-hall stage, along with a woman wearing a long black dress, and another chewing gum, with eyeliner so thick it made her eyes look like deep holes. A presenter was standing between them, talking, until he walked up to the microphone.

I edged to the left of the stage so the microphone didn't hide his lips.

'Welcome, everyone,' he said. 'Welcome to the semi-final of Battle of the Bands. Twelve bands from six schools, but not all will make it through to the finals at Rock City. And, just to remind everyone who the judges are_____.'

I lost his words as he turned to the people beside him. They each nodded in turn as the presenter must have said their names.

'So –' he turned back to the audience – 'just to remind you what we're looking for. It's not about how you look; it's about the songs, the composition, how well you play live and how it all comes together.'

Rocco nudged me. 'We'll be fine, Soph,' he said. 'After all the practice at my place yesterday.'

'Hope so,' I said. 'My fingers are so sore from playing so long.'

'Yeah, my throat too.' He nodded across the hall, to where a band from Highcliffe Seniors were wearing leather jackets and leaning against the wall.

'They think they're so cool,' he said. 'But I heard them practise earlier and all their songs sound the same. The lead singer tries to dance and sing at the same time and ends up _____ like a _____!'

'Ends up what?'

'Oh, sorry.' Rocco opened his mouth into an *o*. 'Gulping like a goldfish!'

I put my hand up to my mouth and sniggered. I still found Rocco funny, even if it did take me a millisecond longer to get the punchline.

I looked around the hall. I'd seen some of the bands standing by their minibuses when we arrived – Derry Hill, Marshawn, Marine High, and others I couldn't remember. Some of them wore leather jackets like the group from Highcliffe Seniors; others wore long white shirts like bands in the eighties. Another group had safety pins attached to their clothes, like punks.

We'd arrived in our minibus with HiFi Dad, who sat in the front all the way, talking and laughing to each other, pretending we didn't exist. The Longshots, our sixth-form group, made their own way here because some of them had cars. There were also supporters from each school who were huddled in groups around the hall.

Twelve people had come from our school in a separate minibus, including Powell Stevens, who apparently had started singing 'Bohemian Rhapsody' by Queen on the way. She was now standing in the middle of the hall on her own.

My head buzzed with excitement when the presenter said the competition would start in ten minutes. I thought I'd be nervous, but I'd played to the app track so many times over the past few days that the tempo was ingrained in me.

Mrs Hopkirk walked over to us with a piece of paper in her hand.

'Remember,' she said. 'You're after Weasel, and you've got fifteen minutes to get ready.'

'Thanks, Mrs Hopkirk,' said Rocco, who was now jumping up and down with nerves like a boxer before a fight.

Mrs Hopkirk looked at him.

'Rocco.' Mrs Hopkirk chuckled. 'You might want to calm down, otherwise you'll have no energy left by the time you go onstage.'

'Yeah, you're right.' Rocco smiled nervously. Then he glanced in my direction and I could tell the competition meant as much to him as it did to me.

Mrs Hopkirk left us and walked over towards HiFi Dad.

'Okay,' said Rocco, blowing into his hands like he was cold. 'Let's just check which songs we're playing again.'

'It's only two, Rocco,' I said.

'I know, but just to be sure.' He pulled a piece of paper out of his back pocket. On it were the five songs we'd all voted on. Rocco pointed at the two with an asterisk: 'Nobodies' and 'Reasons'.

I nodded. Ty shrugged like it was a shopping list. Mia was

115

watching four boys from another school as they arranged their set onstage. Two were adjusting the position of the competition's drums and microphones, while the other two unfurled a homemade banner that read THE GERBILS in giant red painted letters. Some members of the other bands were smirking, as was Rocco. But I didn't know why he found it funny, because not only did we not have a banner, but we'd also not been able to come up with a name.

I looked around the room: everyone was sat down or leaning against the wall, trying to look cool, especially HiFi Dad, who were made up of boys and girls from Year Nine. They'd been in the semi-finals of Battle of the Bands last year, and everyone had thought it was unfair when they didn't make it through to the finals.

Mia came and stood beside me.

'I'm suddenly feeling nervous,' she said, holding out her shaking hand.

'It'll be okay,' I said. 'We've practised loads. But if it makes you feel any better, I think most of the bands feel the same.'

'You think?'

'Yeah.' I nodded across the hall at a band dressed like pirates. 'That girl in black just told the boy next to her that she's so nervous she needs to pee, and that Rocco's an idiot.'

Mia laughed. 'What? You can read that?'

'No.' I laughed. 'I made that last bit up.'

'He can be, though.' Mia grinned.

We both watched Rocco as he sat laughing with Ty. He looked like he was on a day out with his friends, not about to perform in the most important competition of our lives. He seemed so carefree and confident, but deep down I knew he was anxious, too, and only pretending to be relaxed in front of the other bands.

Back on the stage the drummer of the first group adjusted the stool behind the kit. The two guitarists stood either side of the stage, and in between them, the lead singer edged slowly to the front. He looked out at the judges, who were sitting at the judges' table in the middle of the hall. He said something I couldn't make out, then he looked at his fellow band members.

The drummer lifted his arms.

I put earplugs in my ears, then pulled up my headphones stuffed with foam. Mia had already tested them during the rehearsals. She said it was like I was wearing three coats in the middle of summer, but I'd promised Mum and Dad.

The lead singer walked up to the microphone. I waited for him to take it off the stand and jump around like Rocco, but he just stood there like he was trying to hide behind it.

Mia and I looked at each other, wondering how they had got through. Part of me wanted to laugh, but I'd have hated it if anyone did that to me. I didn't know if he had a good voice or not, but at least the drums and bass were in time.

Mia nudged me. I thought she was going to say something, but she just nodded at my feet. I looked down. My right foot was tapping in time with the bass and drums.

'Can you feel it, Soph?'

'Yeah.' I grinned. 'I wasn't even thinking about it, but I can feel the beat through the walls and the floor.'

Mia smiled.

I grinned as I kept tapping. It felt so good being able to listen to music again, even if it wasn't the same way as before. I kept tapping my foot, then my hands against the wall behind me. If I could feel this and have Rocco's app when we played, I was sure nothing could go wrong.

Even though the bass was great, I had no idea if the band were any good. I couldn't tell from the audience alone, and the judges were busy making notes, and the other bands looked like they were too cool to dance. Some teachers and parents were standing at the back nodding their heads. The only one who was dancing was Powell Stevens; she kept flicking her hair and flailing her body and arms around like she didn't have any bones. She did that all the way through the first song, and the second. It was like she thought she was back on TV.

'What did you think?' Rocco asked when they had finished playing.

'Okay,' said Mia.

'Okay?' Rocco laughed. 'The lead singer was like a robot.'

Mia opened her eyes wide as the lead singer went past.

'Oops – oh well.' Rocco shrugged. 'Not my fault. What did you think, Soph?'

'I couldn't really tell,' I said. 'But they seemed a bit nervous.'

'But she could feel the bass,' said Mia.

'Ah, cool.' Rocco beamed. 'Well done, Soph. Bet that felt great.'

I nodded, because it had. I was about to tell Rocco how I'd felt it through the walls, but while he had been pleased for me, he was already focusing on the next band.

'Let's see what they're like,' he said as they went by. 'Bet they won't be as good as us.'

'Rocco!' I said. 'I think you should calm down. No one likes a bighead, especially not the judges.'

'Yeah, true.' He glanced at the judges, then back at me. 'I'll behave, miss,' he said, putting his hands behind his back as a grin spread across his face. 'Oh, by the way,' he added as Ty joined us, 'James from HiFi Dad reckons you're going to be listening to a backing track through your headphones and he thinks that's cheating.'

'Even if I was, it's not cheating,' I said defensively. 'Loads of bands do it. But tell him he can try them on if he wants.'

'It's okay,' said Rocco.

'Ty told them you were deaf.'

'*Temporarily* deaf,' said Ty, looking sheepish. 'I told them *temporarily*.'

He stopped talking and looked awkwardly towards the stage. The next band had unfurled a banner behind the drums. The Pins.

I looked back at Ty and the rest of the group. Had they all been going round telling people I was deaf? I wasn't sure I liked the idea; it was up to me if I told people or not, even if most of the people in my school already knew.

The Pins began to play, and I felt the vibrations again, only this time they were lighter and quicker. It was the band with the safety pins, and they all jumped up and down on the stage. I loved how they didn't seem to care what they were doing or what anyone thought of them. I wished I felt the same way about my deafness.

The Pins' songs were so short that they played four, one after the other. Their energy seemed to be infectious; a group of teenagers had moved forward and had started to jump around behind the judges.

Rocco was standing still with his hand up to his chin, like he was thinking. He nodded to himself like he'd decided they were good. I just couldn't tell if he thought they were better than us.

But I do know he thought the third band were rubbish because they didn't write their own songs and they just stood in the middle of the stage reading the lyrics off their phones.

We watched another band, then Weasel, the band that was before us. Now that I'd seen the other competitors, I realized how much I wanted to win, and when I caught Rocco out of the corner of my eye, clenching his fist and saying, 'Come on!' to Ty, I knew how much it meant to them too.

I was so nervous I couldn't feel my feet as we all walked on the stage. Mia looked even more anxious than me as I passed her and plugged my guitar into the amp. Rocco fiddled with the switches and pads on the drum machine that he'd set up on a table between me and the microphone.

I looked out into the hall. The other bands were talking, huddled in their groups, while the judges leaned back in their chairs and chatted among themselves. Powell Stevens was behind them. It wasn't a huge stadium packed with people, but I didn't care. I was onstage and suddenly it didn't matter if everyone knew I was deaf. I was with my friends in a band, holding my guitar, and it was the best feeling I could have.

We all looked at each other and nodded that we were ready.

Rocco took the microphone off the stand and stood back so I could see him.

'We haven't thought of a name for the band yet,' he said. 'But these are our songs.' He turned to me. 'This first track is called "Nobodies".'

I placed my fingers over the strings and frets.

'One. Two. Three.' Rocco switched on the drum machine.

The green line peaked up and down on my screen. I played the first chord. Then the bass drum thudded through my feet as Rocco started to sing.

'I was on the rooftops. You were below on the street. I wanted to shout. You wanted to scream.'

Bands aren't supposed to look happy when they are playing; they're supposed to look moody and cool. But as Rocco went into the chorus I couldn't stop myself from smiling.

'We are young. We are free. We are Nobodies. And we don't care if it's just you and me.'

I glanced up and saw Powell Stevens dancing, two of the judges nodding, and along the sides of the halls the other bands just stood and stared, except for a girl from the Pins, who was smiling like she thought we were good. All the bands must have practised as hard as we had, but that didn't stop me from hoping that we would be the best.

I checked my tempo with the peaks on the laptop screen. I was still on time as Rocco took the microphone off the stand as we went into the second verse. My screen suddenly blipped. I wondered if Rocco had blocked the Bluetooth signal with his body, like it sometimes did with my phone. A wave of panic went through my body, but the bass was still thudding through my feet. I kept playing. Rocco stepped back straight away, like he realized what he'd done. But I was going to be okay, anyway. It was just repeat chorus, then bridge, then final chorus.

One of the judges made a final note on her pad as the song finished, and Rocco put the microphone back on the stand. '*Sorry*,' he mouthed in my direction.

We all took a deep breath. We'd just played the hardest song; now we could relax and enjoy performing the next one.

Rocco put his hand over the drum machine once more and counted me in.

The green line peaked. I played the intro of 'Reasons'. Rocco wouldn't have to start singing until the end of the second bar. I kept my head down, glancing at the screen as my hands moved up and down the neck of the guitar, pinching the strings against the frets. I nodded in time.

End of the first bar, into the next.

I glanced up, the bands were still staring as before, but all the judges had looked up from their notepads like something had gone wrong. Even Powell Stevens was stood still with an expression on her face like, *What on earth?*

I didn't know what was going on, so I kept playing until out of the corner of my eye I caught Rocco walking towards me waving his left hand.

What's he doing? Why isn't he singing?

'Soph,' he said, shaking his head.

122

'*What?*' I mouthed.

'You're playing the wrong song!'

'I'm not.' I stopped playing. 'It's "Reasons".'

'No, Soph.' Rocco came closer to me like he didn't want the audience to hear. 'We swapped it out.'

'When?' I asked.

He glanced at the audience, then back to me. 'When the Pins were on. We agreed to change.'

'But no one told me.'

'We did, Soph.' Rocco looked at me like I was being deliberately stupid. 'You nodded when we told you.'

I stared at him and tried to gather my thoughts, but the stress suddenly made my noise ring in my head. I had no memory of the conversation at all, and as I looked out to the audience, I saw everyone was still staring, and I was so embarrassed that if there had been a trapdoor in the stage, I would have lifted it up and dived down it.

Rocco stood in front of me.

'So, we're playing "Pictures of You",' he said slowly, like he was making sure I got it this time.

'No,' I snapped. 'We haven't practised that one enough. And stop talking so slowly. It wasn't that I missed what you said. It's because I wasn't there!' I stopped talking. A slight movement offstage caught my eye, and I could see some of HiFi Dad laughing behind their hands. I wanted to scream and shout, but I knew that arguing with Rocco onstage would only make things worse.

Mia walked over to us, shaking her head like she knew what I was thinking.

123

'It's okay, Soph,' she said. 'Just play the song and we'll talk about it afterwards.'

I looked down at my screen and got ready to play, but my hands were shaking so much that there was no way I would keep tempo. At that moment, I wished Mum and Dad had been in the audience. They would have understood how I was feeling, and maybe a smile from Mum would have calmed me down. But instead all I felt like doing was walking off, or better still, picking up Rocco's microphone and whacking him over the head with it. But then I saw the pick between my fingers, the one Ty had given me, and I remembered how amazing I'd felt that day.

You have to do this, I told myself. I was furious with Rocco – there was no way we were going to win after messing up so badly – but I couldn't just give up.

The green line blipped on the screen.

I held my pick over the strings and began to play.

CHAPTER 20

ALL CRIED OUT

I sat on the steps outside the town hall while the next band played, waiting for Mum to come and pick me up. Mia had followed me out, but I told her I wanted to be on my own. She went back inside and sent messages instead, like, *It wasn't your fault, Soph* and *I'm not sure anyone even noticed.* But, of course, everyone had noticed. I'd been playing the wrong song for thirty seconds, swimming away in a world of my own. It was more embarrassing than when I'd worn my Winnie the Pooh onesie to school when I'd thought it was Pyjama Day. I just wanted to go home to my room, but Mum seemed to be taking ages.

I looked at my guitar beside me. I was stupid to even think I could play it again.

My phone buzzed in my hand.

Mia: Soph, come back in. The next group are really good.

Ty: Yeah, they are.

I muted my message alerts and stared out at the road as the traffic passed by. Mia was only trying to help, but reminding me the competition was still going on when I couldn't hear a thing just made me feel worse. All I could think of were the judges and the other bands staring at me like I was an alien who'd lost its spaceship. I hated Rocco for changing the song, and I hated the stupid look on his face, like, *Duh*. He had no idea what it felt like, and he hadn't even bothered to check if I was okay afterwards. My heart sank into my stomach as the scene played over and over in my head. It was my worst nightmare and I just wanted someone to shake me awake.

I felt a tap on my shoulder.

'Mia,' I said. 'I told you I'm okay. I just want to be left alone.'

A shadow crept across the steps as she sat down beside me.

'Please, Mia. I'm so angry and embarrassed that all I want to do is cry. And I'll just end up shouting at you.' I turned. 'And I don't want to do—'

I stopped mid-sentence. Powell Stevens was sat next to me, smiling. She'd probably come to gloat about how she'd danced in front of millions of people while I'd messed up in front of a hundred.

'Eating is the worst,' she said slowly.

'Sorry?'

'Eating.' She pointed at her ears. 'It's the worst. Especially crisps – sounds like bones are crunching inside your head.'

How did she know about my eating? I'd only told Mum. I looked at her ears to see if there were any wires from hearing aids sticking out.

'Not me.' She smiled. 'My brother. He says eating is the worst.

He actually says it's like his skull is caving in, but I didn't want to worry you.'

'It's okay.' I nodded. 'He's right. That's exactly what it feels like.'

'That's all I wanted to say really. That, and that you'll be okay. He is.'

'I didn't know you had a deaf brother,' I said.

'Not many do. He doesn't like people treating him differently; that's why we never told the people from *Banned-It*! You know how they have background stories about the families . . . We didn't want to get to the next round just because people felt sorry for my brother. It wasn't even about him. As it turned out I would have needed more than a sibling-related sob story anyway.' Powell laughed. 'Anyway,' she said, 'I better get back in. His band are on next.'

'Which band is he in?'

'The Ultratones.'

'From Marine?'

'Yes. He went there because most of his friends did. He didn't want me to come in case I embarrassed him. But how could I embarrass him?' Powell grinned as she stood up. 'Are you coming?'

'No,' I said. 'I don't want to see the rest of my band. Especially—'

'Your lead singer?'

'Yes.'

'Oh, don't worry about him. He's like the rest of us lead singers – precious and full of themselves. But, honestly, I thought your band were good.'

'Thanks.' I smiled.

'No, really,' said Powell.

I reached for my guitar as I stood up.

'That's it!' said Powell, like she thought I was going back in. 'Come on.'

'No,' I said, nodding at a red car that had pulled up. 'My mum's here.'

I'd managed to control myself in front of Powell, but I started crying as soon as I got in the car.

'Love, what's wrong? What happened?'

'I can't tell you here,' I sobbed. 'I just want to go home.'

'But if someone has upset you, I need to know. That girl you were talking to, wasn't she on *Banned-It*? Was it something she said?'

I shook my head.

'No,' I said. 'Please, can we just go?'

All I could see was Rocco's stupid face staring at me, like everything was my fault, and then the audience watching me, laughing. I just wanted to go home and forget the whole thing had ever happened.

CHAPTER 21

THE WORST THING EVER

'I thought the Incredible Hulk was in the house, the way you stormed past me earlier,' Dad said when he and Mum sat on my bed with me that evening. 'Thought your door was going to come off its hinges when you slammed it closed!'

'I'm sorry.'

Dad smiled, doing his best to cheer me up. 'It's okay, Soph,' he continued. 'Like the Hulk, I think we all know it's best to wait for you to calm down.'

I smiled.

'So, do you want to tell us now?' asked Mum.

I told them how the first song had gone really well and how I'd managed to keep in time using the app Rocco had given me.

'Well, that's great,' said Mum. 'What's to get upset about there?'

'Because Rocco changed the next song without telling me. He said he had, but I didn't hear, and I ended up playing the wrong song for thirty seconds.'

'But that's his fault,' said Dad.

'I know,' I said. 'But if I wasn't deaf, it wouldn't have happened. I wouldn't have played the wrong song and looked like a dummy.'

'It's fine, Soph,' said Mum, like she knew I was getting upset all over again. 'Are you sure anyone even noticed? You know how self-critical you can be, like when you were sure you'd failed your grade seven guitar, but you ended up with a distinction.'

'Oh,' I said. 'They definitely noticed. Everyone was looking at me. I was so embarrassed I could feel my face burning.'

'Well,' said Dad. 'I'm sure it wasn't as embarrassing as when I drove over the instructor's foot before my driving test.'

Mum and I laughed.

'But seriously, Soph,' said Dad. 'These things are always worse than they seem. Try not to think about it for too long and things will go better next time.'

'There won't be a next time,' I said. 'I'm not playing any more. Not after that.'

'Give it some time,' said Mum. 'But you should know we're both proud of you. Remember you thought you'd never play guitar again; now here you are back onstage playing in front of people.'

'Yes,' I said. 'And making a complete idiot of myself.'

'Soph,' she said, stroking my hair. 'You really are being too hard on yourself.'

'Definitely,' said Dad. 'Just give it some time. Maybe I'll dust off my guitar and we'll play a bit.'

'It's okay,' I said. 'I want music that will cheer me up, not the depressing stuff you play.'

They both laughed.

I was feeling down, but was quite pleased with my joke.

'That's right,' said Dad, standing up. 'Make fun of your dad.'

'Didn't mean it, Dad,' I said, smiling. 'Well, not much.'

'It's okay.' He smiled. 'Anything to cheer you up. On that note, we're getting pizza – what do you fancy?'

I lay back on my bed as they went to order the pepperoni pizza I'd asked for. Mum and Dad were only trying to be kind, but they didn't understand. They'd never messed up as bad as I had. If Dad posted a letter through the wrong letterbox by mistake, he only had to knock on the door and get it back, or the person might leave it on their mat for him to pick up the next day. The only people who would know would be him and that person. When you mess up like I did, you know it's going to get around the whole school.

Why couldn't I have looked up, just for one second? I could have pretended my guitar was out of tune and stopped. But no, I had to keep my head down. I was stupid to think I could play in a band in the first place. The people Mrs Hopkirk had shown me were blind or had lost fingers, which was bad enough, but actually *not* being able to hear music seemed to be the hardest thing to overcome. Beethoven must have found that, but then he was a genius. I wasn't a genius and the semi-final had highlighted that I was so cut off from everything that I could never be part of the band again.

I picked up my phone. I'd muted it ever since I'd left the town hall to stop Mia's messages, but I knew she'd be worried about me. Even though I didn't want to talk about what had happened, I should at least let her know that I was okay.

I unmuted my phone. It vibrated straight away, then again, and again. Message alerts, one after another, scrolled up my screen. The first was from Mum saying she was stuck in traffic; the next was from Mia, asking if I was okay; but the next six were from our group chat:

Mia: Soph, where are you? We got through!

Rocco: Yessss! Get in!!!!!!!!!!!!!!

Ty: We did it! WE DID IT!

Rocco: Yes!!!!!!!!!!!!!!! Rock City, here we come! We need to practise. Every lunchtime and one last practice at mine, the day before.

I stared at my phone. The result could only just have been announced because the messages were still coming through. I didn't know whether to celebrate or not when we'd messed up so badly, but no one else seemed to care.

Mia: I'll be there! Anywhere 😊

Ty: Any place, any time.

I couldn't help smiling.

Rocco: Great. Soph! We did it! We did it!

I shook my head as I read Rocco's message. Earlier he'd made me feel as small as an ant, but now I wished I was in the same room as him, celebrating.

My phone buzzed again. Another message from Rocco that only me and him could see.

Rocco: Soph, I'm really sorry about what happened. I was just nervous. And lost it a bit.

Sophie: A bit?

Rocco: Okay, a lot 😊 But I am sorry. Maybe chat at school tomorrow? I've got an idea.

Sophie: What idea?

Rocco: I'll tell you tomorrow. But we're through, Soph! We're through!

Sophie: 😊

Rocco: I'm 😊 😊 😊 but also really 😣 😣 😣

I smiled.

Sophie: Okay, okay. I get it. You're happy and you're sorry.

Rocco: Tomorrow?

Sophie: Yep. Tomorrow. But you're still an idiot 😊

I put my phone down on my bed. Ten minutes ago I was crying because I was sad and angry at Rocco, but now I was crying because I felt great. Rocco was an idiot, and he had hurt me, but maybe I had overreacted. Feeling emotional was one of the side effects of the steroids I'd been taking – maybe it was that? I knew I should tell Mum and Dad we'd got through, but suddenly my head was buzzing – but this was a good buzz. The buzz that would come when I got ideas for songs in my head.

I leaned over the side of my bed and picked up my lyric book. I might not have been able to hear my guitar for real, but that didn't mean I couldn't write lyrics to a tune in my head. I flicked through it – 'Reasons', 'Nobodies', 'Fade Away', 'Big Town' and lots of other songs I'd written before I'd gone deaf. Songs about how I was feeling, and places I'd lived.

I'd written 'Pictures of You' and 'Girl in the Photograph' since then. Just because I couldn't hear, it didn't mean I had to stop writing. It just meant I might write about different things, and different feelings.

And right now the feeling I had most was, *This is Amazing!*

CHAPTER 22

WALKING ON AIR

Me and Mia couldn't stop smiling as we sat on the bus to school the next morning. For a while we just kept saying, 'We did it!' Like we had to convince ourselves it was true.

Then Mia told me about the bands that I'd missed. One of them was the Motson Twins from Somerfield. Mia could hardly stop herself laughing because being identical meant the Motson Twins were identically singing out of tune, and identically singing out of time.

And after them there had been a group of boys from Marine, who'd turned up with no instruments but had danced and sung to a backing track, but Ty had said the other band from Marine, the Ultratones, were great, and that he hated to admit it, but HiFi Dad were also brilliant.

Mia was telling me about a band called Grit when I felt a tap on my shoulder.

I spun round. Powell Stevens was sat sideways on the seat behind me.

'Just wanted to say congratulations!' She beamed. 'Told you your band were good.'

'Thank you,' I said. 'I really didn't think we'd get through. Did you honestly think we were that good?'

'Yeah,' said Powell. 'Wouldn't say if I didn't.'

The bus began to slow. I didn't know what to say next.

Powell smiled. 'Anyway, congrats again.' She stood up. 'See you around, Sophie.'

'Ooh.' Mia knocked shoulders with me as Powell walked towards the back of the bus. 'New Friend. New Friend.'

I laughed. 'I don't think so.'

'But nice she said something though.'

'Yes,' I said. 'But she caught me by surprise. I should have told her Ty said the Ultratones were good.'

'Why?'

'It's her brother's band.'

'Oh,' said Mia. 'Didn't know. Maybe tell her later when you meet her for lunch.' Mia winked.

I pushed her on the arm and we both laughed because we knew that would never happen.

When we got to school, kids I'd never spoken to were coming up to me in the corridors and saying well done. And teachers who'd never taught me were saying things like, 'I bet you're on cloud nine,' and, 'You must be feeling ten feet tall.' And even the head said she was very proud of all of us, and that maybe we might get our photo in the local paper.

During geography I daydreamed what the headlines would be, *if* we won: 'THE BAND WITH NO NAME WINS BATTLE OF THE BANDS'. In fact, I didn't mind what the headline was, as long as it wasn't, 'DEAF GIRL WINS AT ROCK CITY'. Like Powell, I didn't want to win anything by playing the sympathy card.

But all the excitement made me want to write more. In maths I added some lines to finish 'Pictures of You' and then wrote another song called 'Dreams'. The first verse was about how we can all have them, and the second was about how we can make them come true. All I had to do was come up with the chorus, which was usually the bit Rocco was good at. It was like I could write the serious bits, and he could come up with the catchy bit that everyone could sing along to.

I was so excited about us all meeting at lunch that my guitar was bouncing on my back as I ran down the corridor towards the music room. The band had seemed so happy on the group chat that I couldn't wait to see them. I was glad I'd spoken to Rocco too and cleared the air. They were all in the corner of the music room when I got there. Ty had his head down, pressing keys on his synthesizer. Rocco seemed to be listening, and Mia was getting her bass out of her case, like she'd only just arrived.

They all looked up as I walked in.

'Soph!' Mia beamed when she saw me. 'You're here.'

'Of course!' I said.

Ty walked towards me with a huge smile on his face. 'We did it,' he said, giving me a high-five.

I waited for Rocco to come bouncing over, but he smiled

awkwardly. I thought maybe he was still feeling bad about what had happened onstage.

'I wrote us a new song,' I said. 'For the finals. And I worked on "Pictures of You" so we can play it in the final.' I showed them my lyric book.

'Oh ... yeah ... yeah,' Rocco said, barely looking at me.

I gave Mia a quizzical look. I thought Rocco would be excited, but he was acting like he did when his hamster died. He was always the most confident out of all of us, but it was like he was too embarrassed to even look at me. It was as if something had happened since we'd chatted.

'So,' I said, trying to carry on as normal. 'Did you want to work on this song today?'

Rocco turned to Ty and said something. Ty nodded.

'Rocco,' I said. 'I can't hear.'

'Oh, yeah.' He looked back at me. 'Sorry. We will work on it, but ...' Rocco flashed a look up at the clock.

'Do you have to go somewhere?' asked Mia.

'Yeah,' said Rocco, seeming on edge. 'I do. I need to get to the canteen.'

I didn't know what was going on. I had thought I'd be the awkward one today, but Rocco was taking it to a whole new level.

'Rocco,' I said. 'Is something wrong? I thought we sorted everything out.'

'We did,' he said, picking up his bag. 'I just can't write when I'm hungry.'

'But we always meet at lunch,' said Mia. 'Besides, maybe we need to clear the air after Sunday.'

Rocco wiped his hands on his trousers. 'Nothing to talk about. I sorted it with Soph.'

'Yes,' I said. 'We did. But, Rocco, we chatted, but we have to make sure it doesn't happen again.'

'It won't,' he said, looking at the clock once more. 'Come on, Ty. I need the toilet on the way.'

Ty looked as confused as me and Mia.

'Rocco,' he said, 'why are you acting so weird?'

'Nothing, it's just, I think I've made a mistake—'

The music-room door opened.

Kai Bridges walked in with his guitar on his back.

'We've booked the room,' said Ty.

'Yeah, I know,' said Kai, looking around the room. 'That's why I'm here, for the guitar audition.'

'Guitar audition?' asked Ty.

'Yeah.' Kai turned to Rocco. 'You did mean today, didn't you?'

'Yeah . . .' Rocco stammered. 'I mean, didn't you get my message this morning?'

'No,' said Kai. 'My phone died.'

We all exchanged glances. Mia was open-mouthed; Ty was blinking like he'd just got up. I might not have been able to hear everything, but I'd caught enough to work out what was going on.

'Rocco.' I glared at him. 'Have you got Kai to come and play guitar?'

'Yeah.' Rocco's face was red. 'But, Soph, it's not what you think.'

'Not what I think?' I must have shouted really loud, because Rocco stepped back. 'What is it, then? An audition for any other guitarists to come join our band?'

'It was ...' stammered Rocco. 'I mean, it is. I thought it would help.'

'Help!' I said. 'How does this help?' My blood felt like it was thudding in every part of my body. I looked for Mia and Ty to back me up, but they still looked like they were in shock.

'So that's it, then,' I said. 'I make one mistake and you kick me out?'

All the band's mouths moved, but it was too hard to read all their lips at the same time. Kai Bridges must have said something, because he was edging back towards the door.

'No,' I said, picking up my bag and songbook. 'You stay. You can have them, but just remember they won't let you make one single mistake!'

My guitar knocked against his and my leg caught the corner of the table as I made my way to the door. It hurt, but not as much as what the band had just done to me. I don't know if anyone shouted after me, or tried to follow, as seconds later I was in the corridor. I had only just got over what happened at the semi-finals, yesterday, and now *this*. I could barely hold back my tears as I rushed past kids and classrooms to get outside as quickly as I could.

The afternoon lessons passed in an angry blur. Mia was with me in history. She was my friend and my hearing buddy, but I was too upset to look at her notes or talk. I couldn't believe what Rocco had done, or that she and Ty had just stood by and let him do it. I wanted her to explain, but I knew whatever she said would just make me angrier and I didn't want to fall out with her, especially not in front of everybody at school.

Rain was pouring down as I walked on my own to the bus stop. I thought about what I was going to say to Mia on the bus back home, but every time I decided on something, it felt like no matter what words came out, they would just make me cry. For months we'd all been together in the band, meeting every lunchtime, sometimes after school, and nearly every weekend at Rocco's house. In fact, my dad was always complaining that Rocco's dad saw me more than he did. All those times, all that practice, and now it was all over.

Cars passed by as I kept walking, waiting for Mia to catch up and tap me on the shoulder, because the more I walked and thought, the more I just wanted a hug. But she never tapped my shoulder, and she wasn't at the bus stop, and even though the bus waited for five minutes, she never got on. I wondered if I'd upset her by not looking at her in history, but she knew me so well, I'm sure she would have said.

I stood my guitar in front of Mia's usual seat as the rain poured down the glass. A lady in a blue coat stopped beside me and smiled.

Really? You want to sit here?

I looked around me, saw all the other seats were full.

I slid my guitar and put it on my lap. The old lady sat down beside me.

Please don't talk to me, I thought. *Please, I don't want to explain that I can't hear you or read your lips if you look away.*

141

The old lady started to talk. I pulled my headphones up over my ears and looked out of the window. I felt bad for blocking her out, but all I wanted was to get home.

He'd got Kai from Year Eight. From a band that didn't even make the semi-finals. How could Rocco do that? How could he let me down after all the time we'd spent together writing songs? They weren't just songs; they were moments we'd shared because we wanted the same thing. I took a deep breath, then another, but that was the worst thing I could have done because all it did was replace my anger with tears.

A noise started in my head, first like a hiss, then a *whoosh*, like the sound of heavy rain falling. And it kept falling, so hard and so long that it felt like there was no escape.

CHAPTER 23

MISSED STOPS

I had my eyes closed, trying to calm my noise for so long that I didn't notice the bus passing through Montsfield.

And I didn't notice it passing through Rampton, or any of the journey after.

And my noise was still raging when the bus driver tapped me on my shoulder and said, 'Hey, this is the last stop.'

I looked around the bus – all the seats were empty. Outside, the rain was pouring down, but instead of the rows of cottages in my village, there was a church and a stone wall around a graveyard. I was in Bidstock; I'd over-stopped by two villages. And I felt so confused, like I'd woken up with a start from a crazy dream.

The bus driver bent down.

'Hey, my love,' he said. 'Are you okay?'

I nodded. I had stopped crying, but it felt like they had made tear tracks on my face. I picked up my bag and guitar.

The bus driver gave me a concerned look.

'Are you sure?' he asked. 'Only, I can't turn back, but can you call somebody?'

'Yes,' I said. 'I've got a phone.'

The bus driver said something else, but all I wanted to do was get past without bumping into him with my guitar.

I stepped off on to the pavement. The bus pulled away and left me standing in the rain that was coming down so hard that in seconds I could feel the drops soaking through my jumper to my skin. I'd told the driver I could call someone, but I didn't want to get Mum out of work, and I remembered Dad saying he was helping a friend from the post office move some stuff. But, most of all, I didn't want them to think I couldn't cope.

I peered across the road to the bus stop on the other side. The yellow letters on the screen were lit up bright in the rain, telling me the next bus wasn't due for fifty-five minutes.

I sat down on a bench. The rain dripped off my hair as I looked at my phone.

A message from Mia:

Mia: Hey, Soph. Sorry, Mrs Donnesh stopped me and asked if there was something wrong, then I couldn't find you. Hope you get home okay.

Another from Rocco:

Rocco: Soph, I'm really sorry, but I think you must have misunderstood. Can we talk?

144

No, I didn't misunderstand, Rocco, I thought. *You got another guitarist in and you kicked me out.*

I put my phone in my bag. My house was only six kilometres away, but I felt so lonely that it could have been on the other side of the world. I thought that losing my hearing had been bad, but I didn't think that would mean I would end up losing my friends. It was like all I was left with were my thoughts, and my noise, which was now piercing through my head.

My clothes were so wet they were sticking to my skin when I sensed someone standing next to me. I didn't want to talk to anyone, so I pretended something was amazingly interesting on my phone, even though my fingers were too wet to make it work.

I felt a tap on my shoulder and looked up. Powell Stevens was standing above me holding a bright yellow umbrella.

'Seems like we're making a habit of this,' she said, clearly, but not obvious like some people.

'What's that?' I asked, pulling my headphones off, even though that wouldn't help me hear.

'Me, finding you alone in places.'

'Yeah.' I forced a smile. 'But I'm okay. The bus will be here in a minute.'

Powell looked up at the sign, then back at me.

'Make that fifty-three.'

'Yeah,' I sighed. 'Got me.'

Powell laughed.

'Anyway,' she said. 'My mum says you should come in. She

doesn't know you, but she's still worried you'll catch pneumonia. You know what mums are like.'

She looked across the street towards a big house set back from the road. A woman was standing in a first-floor window, waving. I didn't feel like talking to anyone, not Powell or her well-meaning mum.

I looked down the road, hoping by some miracle the bus would be coming towards me, but there was only a car parked at the side of the road.

'Please yourself,' said Powell, like I had upset her. 'Like I said, it's my mum asking, not me.'

I shivered as rain trickled down my neck.

'Okay,' I said, standing up.

'Well, don't force yourself,' Powell said with a scowl.

'Sorry,' I said. 'Thanks for the invite, but I'll just message my mum and dad first and tell them what's happened.'

'Do it inside – it's chucking it down now.'

I slung my guitar across my back and followed Powell to the other side of the road.

'Mum's busy working,' she said as we walked up the garden path. 'So we'll go in the kitchen.'

'Okay.' I smiled nervously as Powell's house towered above me as we got closer – three floors and a window in the attic. It must have been three times the size of mine, with a proper garden path, not one that took two strides to get from the front door to the street. After climbing four steps, she pushed the front door open. Inside, the hall floor was covered in coloured tiles, and there were huge pictures of lakes and mountains on the walls.

'Yeah.' Powell grinned when she saw the look of surprise on my face. 'My mum likes lakes and mountains. Bit much, I know.'

'No,' I said, not wanting her to think I didn't like them. 'All we've got on ours is one picture of me with my first guitar when I was six, and another of Liam go-karting. Speaking of . . . I better quickly message them.' I fired off a text to Mum to let her know I was safe.

Powell laughed. 'Still better than mountain goats. Oh,' she said, pointing at a hook above a radiator. 'You can leave your coat there.'

I could tell she was used to talking to her brother because she always seemed to find a way of signalling to get my attention, like moving her arm, or standing right in front of me.

I left my guitar and bag in the hall and followed her into the kitchen where there was a huge wooden table and an American-style fridge that was covered in picture magnets.

'Don't look at those,' Powell said, waving her hand like she wanted to take the pictures down. 'Mum takes her camera everywhere. I especially hate that one of me with the presenter at *Banned-It*! She told us to smile, but his cheesy grin gave me the creeps . . .'

I laughed, although I did think it quite cool to have a picture taken with someone I'd only seen on TV.

Powell opened the fridge. 'Juice?' she said, turning to me.

I nodded. She was being so kind. At school everyone – including me – thought she was a show-off, but she didn't seem like that at all in her own house.

Powell poured orange juice into two glasses then got a packet of Oreos out of a cupboard.

'You can sit down,' she said, nodding at a chair by a radiator. 'Might even dry off.'

She handed me a towel and I sat down. As I dried my face, I glanced at the clock. Powell was being so friendly, but she was five years older than me, and I wondered what we would have in common to fill the next forty-five minutes.

'So how did it happen?' Powell put the drinks and Oreos on the table and sat down opposite me.

'Oh,' I said, putting the towel on my lap. 'I just didn't get off.'

Powell laughed. 'No,' she said. 'Not the bus. This.' She pointed at her ears.

'Oh,' I said. I was surprised by her question – everyone else seemed to tip-toe around the subject.

'It's okay,' she said, picking up a biscuit. 'You don't have to say.'

'No, it's all right,' I said. 'I'm just not used to someone being so . . .'

'Direct?'

'Yes,' I said. 'But it's okay. I prefer it.'

'Best way,' said Powell, munching. 'Tom hates it, says he can sense it whenever he meets new people. I got him a T-shirt with *I'm Deaf* on it.'

'What?' I didn't know whether to laugh or be shocked.

'Yeah, it's okay. He loved it. Here, help yourself.' She slid the plate towards me.

I took a biscuit. Powell was right, I much preferred people to talk normally rather than walk on eggshells around me.

'My hearing started to go about a year ago,' I said. 'Not really bad, but I noticed I couldn't hear my primary school teacher when she had her back turned, writing on the whiteboard, and then it gradually got worse until I noticed it was so bad I'd started to watch TV with subtitles.'

Powell munched on another biscuit.

'Go on,' she said. 'I'm listening.'

'Well,' I said, 'that was it really. I just thought it would stay like that, but then, *bam!* I woke up with nothing.'

'Nothing?'

'Yeah.' I sighed. 'Nothing, except . . .'

'Except what?'

'The noise,' I said. 'In the middle of my head.'

Powell nodded like she knew what I meant.

'Does Tom get it?' I asked.

'Why don't you ask him yourself?' she said, gesturing at the window.

I looked out as a boy with blond hair, wearing a blue school uniform, ran up the steps with a pair of headphones on. Powell had told me he was a member of the Ultratones, but I didn't know which one.

'That's your brother?' I asked.

'Yeah,' said Powell. 'Not many people guess he's deaf because he doesn't sign. Some used to give him strange looks because he spoke a bit different at first, but you can hardly tell now.'

I looked up. The lights flashed on and off like the power was cutting in and out.

'You obviously haven't got that in your house, then?' Powell laughed. 'The lights are linked to the doorbell, so Tom knows when it rings, but he does it when he comes home just to annoy us even though he's got a key.'

I smiled. 'We haven't got those,' I said, 'but it's quite cool.'

Powell smiled like she could tell I found it exciting. 'You can do it through an app on your phone. Tom's got a lot of stuff like that. You should look it up.'

'I will,' I said. 'But I'm hoping this is only temporary.' I pointed at my ears. 'I'm still having tests and stuff.'

'O-kay,' Powell said slowly. 'I mean, I hope so.'

She seemed uncertain. Powell hadn't said how Tom had lost his hearing, but I wondered if he had been told to hope for the same and that it had never happened.

'I'm sorry,' I said. 'Did the doctors say Tom's was temporary too?'

'No.' Powell shook her head. 'His was meningitis when he was ten. It destroyed all the nerves. He doesn't really like talking about when it actually happened, because it was horrible.'

'Yes,' I nodded slowly, understanding that I shouldn't ask Tom about that. I didn't like talking about it either because when mine went it felt like the worst day of my life.

'But he'll tell you everything about how he copes now,' said Powell, looking brighter. 'Especially about drums. So ask away, because here he is now.'

CHAPTER 24

TOM

I'd never met anyone who was deaf. Some of the people in the waiting room at the hospital may have been, but I'd not actually spoken to them. So, when Tom walked into the kitchen with rain dripping from his head, I didn't know what to expect.

'Hi!' he said, pulling his headphones down round his neck.

'This is Sophie,' said Powell.

'Yeah, I know.' Tom smiled at me. 'Saw you at Battle of the Bands – thought your band was good. Or at least everyone said you were.'

'Thanks,' I said slowly, unsure of how quickly to speak. 'I'm sorry I missed yours, but you must have been good to get through.'

Tom laughed. 'It's okay, you can talk normally. But, yeah, we're okay.'

I felt my face burn with embarrassment. I'd done the same to Tom as people had done to me and I knew how irritating that was. But Tom didn't seem to mind because he just opened the fridge and picked up the carton of orange juice.

'But we need to be better to win,' he said, before taking a swig from the carton.

'That's disgusting,' snapped Powell. 'We all have to drink from that.'

Tom grinned and wiped his mouth on his sleeve. I tried to think of something to say, but suddenly my words had dried up.

Powell glanced at me. It was almost like she knew I was stuck.

'Sophie's got a question for you, Tom,' she said. 'She wants to know if you get a noise in your head.'

Tom must have seen the shocked look on my face, but he seemed used to how blunt Powell was.

'That's Powell for you.' He shrugged. 'Says it as it is. What else has she said? *Let's go to my house and meet my deaf brother?*'

'No,' I said, awkwardly. 'I just missed . . .'

'I'm joking.' Tom's face cracked into a grin. 'But, yeah. I get it. People think we can't hear anything, and some don't, but I do. Sometimes it's like a rumbling bus; other times it's like the wind or waves.'

'Yes.' I nodded. 'That's it. Just like that. And then the screeching sound?'

'The worst,' said Tom.

'Like aliens,' I said.

'Yeah, exactly that. I think I had it a bit before my hearing went, but I noticed the noise more when it was the only thing I could hear. But you get so used to it that you kind of forget it until the noise changes pitch, then you notice it again. And Powell already told you about the crisps thing?'

I looked at Powell.

'Sorry,' she said. 'Just told him stuff.'

'It's okay,' I said. 'I don't mind.'

Tom took another swig of juice. He seemed so happy and carefree, and if I hadn't known he was deaf, I would never have been able to tell. And best of all, he acted like it was no big thing.

'I'm off down to the basement,' he said. 'Maybe catch you later, you know, if you want to ask me anything else.'

'Thanks,' I said, as he walked out of the door.

'That's him gone for a bit,' said Powell. 'Now tell me about your stepbrother.'

'Who, Liam?' I said, surprised.

'Yeah. Sorry. Bit random. Mum said I get it from my dad. Wherever he is. But your stepbrother. What's he like? He was in my class, but he left when I went into sixth form. He was always messing around, ate a goldfish in science once.'

'So that was true!' I said. 'He came home saying he wished he hadn't because he could feel it swimming in his stomach.'

'It was already dead before he ate it!' Powell laughed so much her eyes filled up with tears. 'No way!' she said, taking a breath. 'What's it like living with him?'

'A pain,' I said. 'He always comes into my room stinking of burgers.'

'And Lynx deodorant,' said Powell.

'Yes,' I said. 'All boys stink of that.' I stopped talking as the table began to vibrate through my elbows.

I lifted them up like I'd had an electric shock.

153

Powell laughed. 'He doesn't take long.'

The surface of my orange juice vibrated in concentric circles, like when you throw a stone in a pond.

'What is it?' I asked.

'Tom,' Powell replied. 'He's downstairs playing his drums.'

'I thought it was an earthquake.'

'Yep, should have warned you; we get a lot of earthquakes around here. It's like that because he's below us in the basement, but it's okay. It's only when both me and Mum are in here that we ask him to not play so loud.'

'Yeah,' I said as I felt the thud through the floor. 'Mum and Dad used to complain if I played my guitar along to loud music, but they won't have to worry about that any more.'

'Why not?'

I'd been so wrapped up being with Powell that I'd forgotten the reason I'd overshot my bus stop in the first place.

'Rocco, our lead singer, got another guitarist to join the band today.'

'What?'

'It's because I messed up.'

'But he can't do that? Wasn't it partly his fault too?'

'Well, yes.' I shrugged. 'But he still did it anyway.' I thought of saying more, but it was hard to concentrate with the vibrations of the drums.

'I know what it's like to be pushed aside,' said Powell. 'One minute you're great and everyone is dancing and singing with you; the next it's all gone, and you're left with nothing . . . Well, nothing

154

except people laughing.' Powell turned and rinsed her cup under the tap. I felt bad for her. She seemed so confident when she was at school and when she'd been on TV, but all the while she'd cared about what people thought of her, and it seemed to hurt her.

As she dried her hands, the drums beat so hard I could feel them vibrating though my shoes up into my legs. I giggled to myself.

Powell turned round.

'What's so funny?' she asked.

'Nothing,' I said, not wanting her to think I was giggling because of her. 'It's not funny; it's just amazing.' I put my hands flat on the table. 'I can feel the beats through my whole body.'

Powell grinned, then glanced up at the clock. My heart sank. The bus would be here in twenty-five minutes, but after being worried about what we were going to talk about, I now didn't want to leave.

'Come on.' Powell stood up.

I picked up my bag.

'No,' she said. 'You don't need that. I'm taking you down to the basement. It's the happiest I've seen you look.'

I smiled with relief.

Powell pointed at my headphones. 'Don't forget to put those on ... Actually, stay there a second.'

I waited at the top of the stairs while Powell ran down to the basement. I wondered if she'd changed her mind, or if she was going to check Tom was okay with it. But I didn't have long to think about it, because a minute later Powell was running back up the stairs, holding out her hand.

'Put these in first,' she said.

I looked at two pink earplugs in the palm of her hand.

'It's okay.' She smiled. 'He's not worn them. This is a spare pair. It's kind of double protection for the eardrums. In fact, triple.' Powell held out two pieces of foam the size of my palm. 'It seems weird when the doctors say he won't get his hearing back, but he still protects his eardrums, just in case they discover something new that might get his hearing back in the future. But then, you already know that.'

As I put the triple protection on, I couldn't help feeling sad that Tom was fifteen and five years on he still hadn't given up hope that he might hear one day. But I didn't have long to think that because Powell had given me the thumbs-up, then turned down the stairs. I felt myself grinning with excitement because on every stair, I could feel the drums vibrating through my teeth.

CHAPTER 25

FINDING MYSELF AGAIN

It was like I was walking into the darkness of a nightclub that I'd seen on TV – beat thudding, and lights flashing as I made my way down the stairs. When I reached the bottom, I saw Tom sitting on a stool in the middle of the room, smashing the drums with his headphones on.

He grinned when he saw us, and kept playing. Every time the pedal beat against the bass drum, a red light flashed on and lit the room.

Powell picked up another pair of headphones and slid them over her ears.

'Come on –' she beckoned me – 'sit here.'

I sat down next to her on a sofa opposite Tom and his drum kit as he kicked the bass and hit the snare and toms then cymbals. It was so much more exciting than watching Rocco crouched over a table pressing buttons on the drum machine. Tom smiled at me and kept playing with the red light lighting up his hair. He was totally lost in what he was doing, like nothing else mattered except smashing the drums.

I smiled back but felt a bit embarrassed, even though I'd already spoken to Tom. It felt like whenever Liam had his friends around and I didn't know what to say to them.

I looked around the room. The curtains were drawn, but I could make out posters of rock bands on the wall – Big World, PopArts and the Demon Days – and there was a set of bongo drums on the floor in a corner. It was a perfect place to play drums, just like Powell had said, but this felt like Tom's space, and even though I loved feeling the beat, I wasn't sure I should be there. And how could I ask him questions while he was playing drums?

Powell raised her hand like she was in class.

Tom stopped playing.

'What?' he said.

'Oh, great,' said Powell. 'Sophie gets a smile and I get "What?"!'

'So?' Tom grinned. 'You're my sister.'

I thought how much they were like me and Liam.

Powell nudged me. 'Go on,' she said. 'I know you want to ask him loads of questions.'

I hesitated. I had questions in my head, but they wouldn't come out.

'Okay,' said Powell. 'I'll ask for you. She needs your help, Tom. She's a really good guitarist and songwriter, but she just let the lead singer of her band walk all over her.'

I flashed a look at her. I had questions, but that wasn't one of them.

'What?' She shrugged. 'It's true.'

'Well, yes,' I said. 'I suppose it is.'

'See,' said Powell. 'So, tell her, Tom. Tell her to ignore him and get back in the band.'

Tom shrugged. 'It's up to you,' he said, looking at me. 'You got to do what you want to do.'

'What?' Powell snapped. 'You're supposed to back me up and tell her to go back and kick him out.'

'I know.' Tom knocked his sticks together like he was thinking. 'That's what you would do, but you're not the one who's deaf. Sophie might not feel ready. Look at me when I first joined the band. I felt like everyone was looking at me, like everyone knew I was deaf.'

'Yes.' I nodded. 'Exactly like that.'

'Besides,' said Tom. 'You can't kick him out; he might have been a bit of an idiot, but he did have stage presence.'

'Oh,' said Powell, standing up. 'You mean like me?' She started to spin in a circle with her arms flailing.

Tom smiled and shook his head.

Powell stopped spinning. 'Don't know what you're smiling at. At least I'm better than that boy from the Pins; he flailed like a fly swimming in custard.'

Me and Tom laughed, then he looked at me, straight-faced, and said, 'But, seriously, only go back to the band if you're ready.'

'But how will I know?' I asked.

Tom shrugged. 'Not sure,' he said. 'I think it just sneaks up on you. One minute you feel like you're on the outside looking in; the next you feel like you're in the middle of it.'

I nodded. 'Yes,' I said. 'I know what you mean. I definitely feel like I'm on the outside at the moment.' I went to ask how long it had taken him, but I saw Powell looking at her watch.

'Nearly time for your bus,' she said. 'Don't want to miss the next one.'

I sighed inside. I'd only spoken to Tom for a few minutes, but for the first time I'd met someone who knew exactly how I felt.

I stood up.

Tom picked up his drumsticks, hit them together three times, then hit the snare, then the cymbals, and the lights flashed again. Powell headed towards the stairs. Tom checked she wasn't looking at us.

'*Don't let her boss you,*' he mouthed. '*Do what you want.*'

I smiled.

'*I will,*' I mouthed back.

The thud of the bass drum followed me up the stairs and it felt like it was still throbbing through my body as I stepped out of Powell's front door. The sun was shining between the storm clouds, making the puddles glitter on the path.

'Cool, wasn't it?' asked Powell.

'Yes,' I said.

Powell reached out and lifted my headphones off my ears, before sliding them down on to my shoulders.

'Just looks weird when I'm talking to you,' she said. 'People will think you're blocking me out because I'm boring you.'

'I don't need to be wearing headphones for my mum to think that!' I laughed.

'Me neither.' Powell grinned. 'But I've not got the same excuse . . . Here.' She leaned back inside the door. 'Take this,' she said, handing me a small, folded umbrella. 'Just in case it starts raining again.'

'Thanks,' I said.

'That's okay,' Powell said. 'Just Mum would get annoyed with me if she thought I'd let you get wet again.'

'No,' I said. 'I meant thanks for letting me come in. It was great, and I really liked the drums.'

'But not Tom?'

'Yeah,' I said. 'Him too.'

'You need to go,' she said as the bus pulled in.

I ran across the road, climbed on and found a seat by a window. Powell was standing watching and she waved as the bus pulled away. I took out my phone to tell Mum I was on my way. There were three messages from Mia, and two on the band chat, but I didn't want to read them because for the first time in weeks, I'd had an hour where I almost didn't notice I was deaf. No one asked me questions; no one asked how I was feeling because they knew how it felt. No one treated me differently. No one opened their mouths extra wide or mimed like they were playing charades. It was great watching Tom play the drums and seeing him have fun, but most of all I liked being treated like me. I wasn't Sophie-the-deaf-girl, or Sophie-the-girl-who-went-deaf-overnight. I was just Sophie.

And I liked being just Sophie again.

CHAPTER 26

AN UNLIKELY ALLY

'POWELL STEVENS,' Liam said with a sarcastic expression on his face when he came into my room after he got in from work. Which became even more annoying when he used air quotes, when he said, 'Not "The" Powell Stevens?'

'Yes, *The* Powell Stevens,' I snapped. 'And stop saying her name so much, you'll wear it out.'

'It's my *Banned-It* presenter's impression.' He grinned. 'THE FAMOUS POWELL STEVENS!' He peeled a banana that he'd been using as a mock microphone, and took a bite.

'I know,' I said. 'I could tell. I just don't find it funny any more.'

Liam pretended to choke. 'What do you mean? You were doing it last year. You even did her dance in the living room. What was it?'

'The Octopussy.' I sighed.

'That's it!' Liam grinned. 'The Octopussy. One of the judges said she danced like an octopus and sang like a cat.' Liam waved his arms wildly in the air.

I tried to keep a straight face, but I couldn't stop a smile from leaking out.

'See,' said Liam. 'She might be your new buddy, but even you are laughing now.'

'I know,' I said. 'But she's different to how I thought she was.'

'Anyway, do you want me to beat him up?' said Liam, suddenly changing the subject.

'What?' I asked, confused.

'Sorry.' He took another bite of his banana. 'I said . . .'

'Not with your mouth full, Liam,' I said. 'Can't make out the words.'

'Oh, yeah. Sorry.' He swallowed and started again. 'I said, do you want me to beat him up? This Rocco.'

'How did you know I was upset about him?'

Liam shrugged. 'Dunno, lucky guess. Anyway, do you want me to?'

'What? No.' I shook my head at the same time. Rocco had upset me, but I wanted to make sure Liam got the message. 'No. I don't want you to beat him up.'

'But he sounds like a real idiot.'

'He is,' I said. 'But I don't want anything bad to happen to him.'

'Suit yourself. But you shouldn't let him get away with it. He might think it's his band because he's the lead singer, but you write the songs.'

'I know,' I said. 'But I messed up badly.'

'So?' Liam shrugged.

'So, I looked stupid onstage. I was really embarrassed. Everyone was looking at me.'

'That's your problem.'

'What do you mean, that's my problem?' I snapped. I wasn't in the mood to get a lecture from anyone, especially not Liam.

'No.' Liam shook his head. 'You got that wrong. I'm not saying, that's your problem, *finito*. I'm saying that's your problem, in that you worry about what people are thinking about you too much.'

'What?' I said. 'You think I should be more like you and care about no one but myself?'

'Ooh –' Liam put his hand over his heart – 'that hurt.' He grinned. 'But for once I'm being serious. You should be feeling good about what you did, not be sat up here, sulking.'

'I'm not sulking,' I said. 'I'm just mad with Rocco.'

'So you *do* want me to beat him up?'

'No!'

Liam smiled. 'I'm kidding,' he said. 'But just forget about him and do what you want to do.'

I smiled. I couldn't believe I was listening to my stepbrother, and for once he wasn't messing around. It was like he cared.

'Thanks,' I said.

'No worries.' He threw his banana skin, punched the air and said 'Yes!' as it flew into my bin. 'That'll be a tenner,' he said, holding out his hand.

'For what?'

'For sorting out your life.'

'No way.' I laughed.

Liam turned to leave, then stopped.

'Oh, one more thing,' he said, pointing his bum towards me.

'No, Liam!' I shouted as I picked up a cushion. 'You dare fart!'

He grinned.

I threw the cushion at him as he disappeared out of the door.

He was normally a bigger idiot than Rocco, but as I lay back against the wall I realized that he had made me smile. And maybe he was right – I was worried about what other people were thinking too much.

My phone buzzed beside me on my bed. I glanced at the screen as three messages popped up from Rocco.

Rocco: Soph, can we talk? I made a mistake. Was only trying to help. Come to the music room again tomorrow?

Sophie: No! You can't do that to me!

I stared at the message, but I never pressed send. Instead, I reached into my bag for my maths books and opened the homework Mrs Doust had set us.

Simultaneous equations.

$$2x + y = 9$$
$$3x - y = 1$$

I tapped my pen on the page and looked at the question again.

$$2x + y = 9$$
$$3x - y = 1$$

I felt the pen tapping through my book on to my thigh.

I knew the answer, but all I could do was stare at my bed.

I could feel it. It didn't have to be Tom whacking the bass drum; I could feel *this* ... the pen tapping through my body on to my leg.

I moved the pen to the edge of the page, tapped it quickly three times, then moved it back to the centre of the page and tapped again. Vibrations, light at the edges, heavier in the middle.

I kept tapping. Two full beats. Two half beats.

Two full beats. Two half beats.

I picked up *Of Mice And Men*, put it on my knee.

Two full beats. Two half beats. Two full beats, two half beats.

I picked up another exercise book, put it on my left thigh. Started tapping. A beat, a rhythm. A smile crept across my face. I'd played on the drums when I first started music. Mrs Hopkirk said it was a good way to feel the rhythm. She said I was a natural at it, but all I ever wanted was to play guitar. But now, as I tapped, *Of Mice And Men* was my bass drum, my exercise books were snares. I looked at the books spilt on my bed, ripped two pieces of paper out of my geography book and put them on my knees for cymbals.

I kept tapping, repeating the rhythm, finding the metre, just like I'd felt when Tom was playing. I imagined him there now, smashing the drums down in the basement, making the whole house shake. Tapping the books didn't do that, but at least I could feel it through my legs.

$$2x + y = 9$$
$$3x - y = 1$$

I knew the answer, but instead of writing it down, I ended up writing a song called 'Simultaneous Equation'.

The rhythm stayed in my head all evening and when I put my head on my pillow to go to sleep, the beats were still there, only heavier, like Tom was in the house next door playing the drums. I imagined him sitting behind the kit with his headphones on, nodding his head and smiling like he didn't have a care in the world. I loved my guitar, but maybe Rocco was right to replace me. The judges and the competition would be much harder in the final. There would be no second chances if I messed up again.

I closed my eyes.

The bass drum was still there . . .

Let Rocco replace me, I thought. *I don't need him or the band. I just need this – the* boom, boom, boom. Boom, boom, boom, *beating as regular as my heart.*

CHAPTER 27

I FEEL LIKE A YO-YO

Mia was quiet on the bus the next morning, but once I'd told her about my visit to Powell and the buzz I got from meeting Tom, she understood why I'd not replied to her messages until late last evening.

'I'm just pleased you feel happier,' she said. 'I remember seeing him onstage. I didn't know he was deaf though. I thought he was wearing headphones so he could hear the click track.'

'Don't think he was,' I said. 'But, Mia, it was amazing feeling the bass. I'd love to go back.'

Mia gave me a suspicious look. 'Soph,' she said. 'You're not thinking of joining their band to get back at Rocco, are you?'

'No,' I said. 'Course not. I told you, I'm not going to be in any band. It was just nice being at Powell's house. Her and Tom just made me forget I was deaf for once. Besides, maybe Rocco is right, trying to replace me on guitar.'

'But he's not though, is he?' Mia linked her arm into mine as we crossed the road. 'I know you, Soph. You're just putting on a brave face so people don't think you're hurt by it.'

'Might be, might not be, but I do know it feels weird walking to school without my guitar on my back.'

'Yeah.' Mia grinned. 'Like a snail without its shell.'

'You saying I'm a slug?' I said.

We both laughed as we walked through the school gates.

'But seriously, Soph.' Mia hugged my arm. 'Please don't leave; just let Rocco explain himself.'

'What, and then listen to him asking me to teach Kai Bridges the songs?'

'I give up,' said Mia. 'You two are as stubborn as each other.'

'Well.' I smiled as we walked through the main doors. 'That's one thing you've got right.'

I told myself all morning that I didn't care about being in the band, and it wasn't just because of falling out with Rocco; it was that I wasn't sure any of them understood how it felt to be deaf. Ty and Rocco kept forgetting I was, and would turn away when they were talking. Mia had been great, though. She understood, and I could see how much she cared, but she couldn't make me feel like I had at Powell's house, like being deaf didn't matter; it was considered normal. All I wanted to do was work out a way of going back there without looking like I was desperate.

I saw her coming towards me on my way to the canteen at the beginning of lunch break. She was with a group of her friends. I tried to catch her eye by half raising my hand, but she was busy talking and laughing. I thought maybe she didn't want to be seen talking to a Year Seven, but I needed to give her umbrella back at some point, and it might as well be now. I reached into my bag as she got closer. For a moment I thought she was going to walk by like I wasn't there, until she glanced at me.

I held out the umbrella. She stopped. All her friends stopped behind her like cars braking in traffic.

'I thought I'd better give you this back,' I said nervously.

Powell looked at the umbrella.

'Oh, that.' She waved her hand like the umbrella didn't matter. 'Can you keep it for a bit? I don't want to carry it around all afternoon.'

'Okay,' I said, feeling embarrassed that I'd even said anything, especially as all her friends were looking at me. One of them must have said something, because the rest started to giggle. A wave of heat passed through my body, thinking I was being talked about.

Powell smiled. 'Give it to me on the bus,' she said. 'Actually . . .' One of her friends tugged her arm, turning Powell away. If she was still talking, I couldn't see what she was saying. Powell walked on, then glanced over her shoulder and said something, but now she was too far away for me to read her lips.

No, I thought to myself. *I have no idea what you just said. You should know that.*

I thought of running after her as she disappeared into a sea of blue uniforms, but I didn't want to look stupid in front of her friends.

I went to the canteen and sat on a table on my own. A couple of kids from my year came over and congratulated me for getting through to the final of Battle of the Bands. I didn't tell them I wouldn't be playing. But sitting on my own did make me realize that

I'd spent nearly all my lunch hours in the music room and that there was a massive hole in my life where the band used to be.

It was when I saw Ty walking across the quad that I realized how big that hole was. I sat and watched him as he pushed open the doors and turned right down the corridor towards the music room. My heart ached. There would be no more butterflies in my stomach through morning lessons as I looked forward to the practice. No strumming of guitars or playing of the keyboards, waiting for a tune to come. No watching Rocco mess around, dancing and swinging the microphone above his head. No sitting down with him, sharing my lyrics with him, telling him what they meant. No laughing when he suggested funny lines. No, *WOW*, when he came up with brilliant ones. No Ty recording our voices and turning them into funny noises on his synthesizer, even though I wouldn't be able to hear them now.

I looked down at my food, but I couldn't think of eating a thing. No matter how much I'd tried to convince myself that I wouldn't, I missed the band. I missed everyone, even Rocco. Part of me wanted to run into the music room and tell them that I'd met Tom, and he was the drummer in a band. Maybe I could do the same? But maybe I was being stupid just thinking that. He'd practised for years before he'd got into a band; all I had done was sit in my room hitting a few books and pieces of paper with a pen. I'd felt a few vibrations in my legs, that was all, and tapped out a rhythm and got a tune by accident.

I looked up as three more kids came over and said well done, then two girls from Year Eleven who know Liam did the same. They seemed happy for me, but also apparently couldn't believe someone who was remotely related to Liam had done something successful. I was beginning to feel like a yo-yo. One minute I felt like I should be signing autographs; the next minute as if I wanted to go into hiding.

Yay! I can play guitar.

Argh, I made a mistake.

Yay! I love the feel of drums.

Argh! I'm not in the band.

Ever since the day I woke up deaf, I'd been battling, battling, battling . . .

My phone buzzed on the table.

A message on the band chat.

Rocco: Hey, Soph, are you coming or not?

I looked at the screen. Rocco was acting like nothing had happened. He'd said he was sorry, but if he was sorry, if he really wanted me in the band, he wouldn't be messaging me from the music room; he would be here trying to get me out of the canteen. Another message pinged.

Rocco: Soph, we're starting. I haven't got the lyrics for 'Pictures of You'. I can remember the chorus, but if you don't come, I'll try to make the rest up.

No. I felt so angry, it was like Rocco was in front of me. *Those are my lyrics. It's my song. You weren't even there for the scan.*

My blood thudded through my body – *thud, thud, thud* – just like it had when I was in the scanner. I remembered the bright lights, the buzzer in my hand, and the headphones clamped tight round my head as I slid towards the hole.

You don't know what the song is about, Rocco. You really don't know.

My eyes started to sting with tears as I looked around the canteen. Hundreds of mouths opening and closing in silence. I wanted to head for the corridor, but it felt like the walls were closing in.

Don't cry, I told myself. *Don't cry – not here in the middle of the canteen.*

My phone buzzed again.

Leave me alone, Rocco, I thought. *Leave me alone.*

I was doing well – that's what everyone was saying. But I didn't feel like I was doing well. I felt like I was drowning in the middle of the ocean and there was no lifeboat to rescue me.

CHAPTER 28

I'M NOT ALONE

'It's only natural to get emotional . . . It's only natural that you will have these ups and downs . . . In fact, it wouldn't be natural if you didn't.'

I was in the Student Support room with Mrs Hopkirk. I was too upset to say anything, so I just sat in the chair with a box of tissues on my lap while she spoke.

'It's good that you have a strong character. It's good that you are tough, but you need to let things out, talk to someone. Some people can explode if they keep it all in. I know I do. You just ask my husband; I'm forever losing my temper with him.'

I wiped my eyes, then smiled at Mrs Hopkirk.

'I know,' I said. 'I think I just did. I just wish I hadn't started crying in the middle of the canteen.'

Mrs Hopkirk smiled kindly. 'Oh,' she said. 'Don't worry about that. I once burst out blubbing when a boyfriend dumped me in the middle of an Indian restaurant.'

I laughed as I wiped away my tears. I hated crying, but if I was going to do it, I was glad I was with Mrs Hopkirk.

I told her how things had felt up and down, and that Rocco's message had been the tipping point.

'Well, isn't that Rocco,' she said, when I showed her the text. 'I honestly think he's so wrapped up with this Battle of the Bands thing that he doesn't think he's doing anything wrong.'

'Maybe,' I said. 'But I think it's more than that. We used to sit side by side for ages and write songs, but it's like since I went deaf, he hardly even looks at me.'

'People do react in different ways,' said Mrs Hopkirk. 'Of course, it's nowhere near what you've had to cope with, but he's had to see his friend go through this. Mia obviously copes by being with you. Maybe Rocco just doesn't know how to act, so he's either cracking jokes or acting like he doesn't care.'

'Well, I don't care about him,' I said stubbornly. 'Nor the band.'

'I'm not so sure about that.' Mrs Hopkirk smiled. 'You seem very upset for someone who doesn't care.'

'I don't know what I think,' I said, even though deep down I knew I did care about the band. 'I just feel so confused. One minute I'm thinking about playing guitar, then drums, then not being in a band at all.'

'Drums?' asked Mrs Hopkirk.

'Yes,' I said. 'I went to Powell Stevens's house and saw her brother, Tom, playing them. He was amazing.'

'Well.' Mrs Hopkirk grinned. 'He must have been, because that's the first time you've smiled since you've been in here.'

'He was. And the best thing was I could feel the beat through my whole body.'

'That's wonderful,' said Mrs Hopkirk.

'It was,' I said. 'I mean, it is. Tom is deaf too, but you can't tell.'

Mrs Hopkirk shook her head as if she'd forgotten something. 'I don't know why I didn't include her name on the list of musicians I gave you.'

'Whose?'

Mrs Hopkirk spun round to her computer and started to type.

'Eve_____.' She pointed.

On the screen was a picture of a woman: Evelyn Glennie, a deaf percussionist.

'She plays in orchestras all over the world,' said Mrs Hopkirk. 'I saw her a few years ago at the Royal Albert Hall. She was incredible. Feels the music through her hands and feet.'

'That's what Tom, does,' I said, excitedly.

'Sounds like you had a great time.'

'I did,' I said. 'I'm hoping I might get to go back.'

Mrs Hopkirk clicked the print icon on her screen, then got up and walked over to the printer. 'I'm not saying give up on the guitar,' she said, handing me the piece of paper. 'But I did always say you had a natural rhythm for drums.'

'I know,' I said. 'I remember that.'

I looked at the picture of Evelyn Glennie hitting a huge concert bass drum with a mallet. Underneath it said she had gone deaf when she was just a year older than I was.

'Thank you,' I said, looking up.

'No worries,' said Mrs Hopkirk. 'I'm just happy to see you smiling again. How about you let me know how it goes with Powell's brother?'

'Okay,' I said. 'I will.'

'And don't worry about Rocco,' she said. 'Let's leave it a day and let me talk to him. You are good friends, after all.'

'Were,' I said.

'Sophie.' Mrs Hopkirk gave me a sideways look.

I laughed as I went out of the door. As I walked back to my lesson, I thought even though she wasn't deaf, Mrs Hopkirk understood how I was feeling, but she hadn't just given me sympathy; she'd got how much I missed music and was trying to find a way for me to get my love for it back.

CHAPTER 29

CAN YOU FEEL THE NOISE?

'I knew I should have gone to the canteen with you,' said Mia, as we took the bus home.

'You can't be with me all the time,' I replied. 'Besides, it's me that's fallen out with Rocco, not you. And I'm beginning to think he was right to get Kai in anyway. Ever since I've been back it's not felt the same. I've been playing, but it's felt out of control, like a runaway train. Oh.'

Mia laughed as I reached into my bag and wrote *out of control like a runaway train* in my notebook.

'See?' she said. 'How can you say you've given up music when you're still writing songs?'

'I haven't given up,' I said. 'It's just that I'm going to try the drums.'

Mia glanced over her shoulder, even though we both knew Powell hadn't got on the bus. 'So, you're still going there, then?' she said. 'To her house.'

'Yes.' I held up the umbrella. 'How else am I going to give this back?'

'At school tomorrow, obviously,' Mia said with a sarcastic look on her face.

'Well, I could, but then I wouldn't get to play the drums.'

'Is it just the drums?'

'Yes,' I said. 'But I liked meeting Tom.'

'Ooh,' Mia nudged me with her elbow.

'He's fifteen!' I said. 'And that's not the way I like him. It's because he understands everything. He knows what this is like.'

'Okay, I believe you.' Mia gave me a sideways look as she picked up her guitar. 'Message me later, then?'

'Yes,' I said. 'I will.'

Mia walked down the aisle as the bus stopped outside the chip shop in our village.

I felt a bit bad that I hadn't messaged her to come when I was having a meltdown in the canteen, but she'd already been with me in nearly every lesson, writing notes, listening to me going on about not being able to hear and helping calm me down when my noise got too much. She had been great, but she couldn't help me in the way I felt Tom could. Mia could say things like, 'It must be horrible' or 'I can't imagine what it feels like.' Whereas in the short time I had spoken to him, Tom had known exactly how it was.

But as I waved to Mia as the bus pulled away, I began to doubt if I should be going to his house at all. Like Mia had said, taking an umbrella back was pretty strange. But the thought of feeling the drums again and talking to Tom kept me going. I'd loved being in a place where I'd almost forgotten about my deafness.

When I got off the bus, I stayed by the church for a while looking at the house. Powell had been friendly the day before in the kitchen and when she'd taken me down to see Tom in the basement, but she'd barely spoken to me when she was with her friends earlier today. It was like she was two people: a friendly one at home, and a too-cool-to-talk-to-a-Year-Seven one when we were at school.

I began to feel so nervous that I looked for places I could leave the umbrella, by the front gate, or resting against the front door. I could ring the bell so they'd come out and find it, but with Tom's app, all the lights in the house would flash and the whole village would know I was there. Mia was right. It was desperate. I started to turn away. Then stopped as Tom came walking towards me.

'There's nothing worth stealing.' He grinned. 'My Xbox is broken, and Powell's only got *High School Musical* DVDs.'

I laughed nervously. 'No,' I said. 'That's not what . . .' I reached into my bag for the umbrella.

'Just kidding,' said Tom. 'I'm amazed that for once Powell didn't forget.'

'Her umbrella?'

'No.' Tom shook his head. 'To give you the message. That is why you're here isn't it? For the drums?'

I shook my head in confusion.

'Powell was supposed to tell you. We talked after you left yesterday. Basically, I know what it's like to lose your hearing, and we just thought you might like to know more about the drums as you seemed to enjoy them so much. But obviously she didn't say.'

'Well, she might have,' I said. 'I saw her in the corridor, but she was too far away for me to read her lips.'

'Yeah.' Tom nodded as he looked up and down the road. 'I think she must be at a friend's, so we'll go on in and get started. I got some stuff ready to show you.'

'Okay,' I said. 'Thanks.'

Tom took a step towards the house and we walked side by side up the garden path. I tried to think of something to say, but I was still surprised that after thinking about how to meet him again, he'd been expecting me all along.

'Did you sort your thing out with your lead singer?' he asked, looking across at me.

'No,' I said. 'Not really. I've avoided him all day.'

'It might work out,' said Tom, reaching for his keys. 'Our band fall out all the time, but we're excited about the final; the whole school is. Our head even said we can have time to practise during PSHE.'

I was used to having to tell people to turn their heads so I could read their lips, but Tom had put the key in the lock and pushed the door open all while still looking at me. Being with him was so much less stressy than having to lean forward to read other people's lips.

'Put the umbrella there,' he said, pointing at a stand by the door. 'I'll just let Mum know I'm home.' He tilted his head back. 'Hi, Mum!'

The lights in the hallway flashed twice.

Tom laughed. 'That's Mum replying. It's cool isn't it?' he said. 'She could come down, but I like to scare my friends into thinking we've got a poltergeist.'

I laughed.

Tom put his bag down in the hallway.

'I'll get us a drink,' he said.

I stayed in the hall as he walked into the kitchen. I'd been worried that I had imagined how I'd felt the last time I was here, but I'd only been in the house a few seconds and I was already as normal and relaxed as I had been the day before.

'Here you go.' Tom handed me a can of drink. 'Come on,' he said. 'We'll go on down.'

I followed him across the hall, then down the stairs into the basement.

'So where would you like to start?' Tom held out his arm.

I looked around the basement. Tom had moved the drum kit and sofa towards the walls, and on a rug in the middle of the room, he'd laid out every percussion instrument I'd ever seen, and some I hadn't known existed: a tambourine, a xylophone, a triangle and drums (so many drums!), some small bongos, some big enough to stand on their own, and colourful painted mosaics made of pottery and wood. It was like I'd walked into an antique store.

'They're amazing,' I said.

Tom grinned. 'Most of them come from Morocco,' he said, 'apart from the congas.' He nodded at two drums shining like they were painted with red nail varnish in the corner. 'I got them from Cuba. And those –' he pointed at two smaller drums joined together like bongos – 'the Batá drums, I got them from Nigeria.'

'And you can play them all?' I said.

'Pretty much! Well, some better than others.' He picked up the triangle off the rug. 'But this is what I started with. Mum got it for me after I went deaf because it's one of the easiest things to feel notes on. Here, try to listen.' He struck the triangle with a metal bar.

I titled my head on one side thinking that by some miracle I might actually be able to hear it.

Tom smiled, like he'd seen the look of disappointment on my face. 'Yeah,' he said. 'Nothing. But you don't listen with your ears; you feel it, like this.' He struck the triangle again, then held his finger as close to it as he could without touching it. 'You can feel the vibrations.'

I held up my hand. It felt a bit weird. What if I couldn't feel the things he did?

'It's sound waves,' he said, striking the triangle again. 'Can you feel the noise?' His eyes flashed excitedly, like he was willing me to be able to.

I nodded. 'Yes,' I said. 'Just a bit.' I wished I could have said it was amazing, but really it was just a tingle, like an ant crawling over the top of my finger.

Tom put the triangle down.

'Okay, then.' He scanned the room. It was like we were in a shop and he was trying to find some sweets I liked. He picked up a set of bongos. 'Let's try these,' he said.

'Okay,' I said. 'I played them a bit at school, before, you know.'

'Yeah, they're great fun. I use them with the band to save moving my kit every time.' He sat down on the rug and placed the bongos between his legs. He started to hit the skins of the drums with the tips of his fingers and his palms. All the time he was staring ahead, concentrating on the rhythm.

'It takes you to another place,' he said. 'Like, I remember Mum with the triangle; I remember a school trip and playing these around the campfire. Do you get that?'

'Yes,' I said. 'Well, I did. I remember Dad getting me my first guitar one Christmas. I didn't think I had anything. He put it behind the tree because from the shape it was obvious what it was.'

Tom smiled and kept playing.

For a moment I remembered opening my guitar and feeling the excitement I had when I ran my fingers over the strings for the first time. Tom was right, instruments do bring back memories, but suddenly I felt sad because as Tom hit the bongos, I couldn't hear or feel a thing. There was no tapping, and no thud – just his hands moving so fast they were a blur in a speeded-up film. It was useless. How could he feel it when I couldn't? For a moment I felt jealous of him, like his hearing couldn't be as bad as mine. But I realized that was stupid. He couldn't hear a thing either.

Tom suddenly stopped playing and looked at me.

'You okay?' he asked.

'No,' I said, shaking my head. 'Not really. I can't feel a thing.'

'Sorry,' he said. 'My mistake. I was getting carried away. I'll roll the rug up, then you sit next to me.'

I felt bad for showing my disappointment. I thought about saying I would come back another time, but Tom was already rolling up the rug.

'Sound vibrates better through wood,' he said, looking up at me. 'I discovered it on the school stage, but it works just as well here. Come on.'

184

I still wasn't sure I would feel anything, but he seemed determined that I shouldn't give up.

I sat down beside him and crossed my legs like he had. He passed another set of bongos to me. I waited for him to give me instructions, but he just held up his left hand. 'Just play,' he said. 'Whack it, have fun. I know it sounds corny, but don't search for the sound; let it find you.'

I looked down at the bongos. I tapped the middle of the biggest drum, then the middle of the smaller one. I could feel Tom watching.

I hit the drums, left hand, then right, first slowly, then quicker. Could I feel the drums or was it my wrist knocking against my knees? I raised my arms, set my elbows at right angles, then hit the drums again. My ears were silent, but I could feel the vibrations through the floor and through my knees: heavy when I hit the drums in the middle; lighter when I tapped my fingers on the edge. I kept playing, fast, then slow, fast then slow. I repeated it over and over again, until a rhythm started to form, in my hands, in my body, until I had imagined sound. Suddenly it felt like I had music in my head again and I couldn't help smiling.

I sensed shadows cross the floor. I glanced up.

Powell had walked into the basement and sat down on the arm of the sofa.

'Bet he made it sound like he'd been to all the countries to get them,' she said.

I nodded but kept to the rhythm.

'Truth is, he got them all off eBay.'

I glanced at Tom, who was smiling. 'True,' he said.

I laughed. The one advantage of us both being deaf was that

Powell could talk, but we didn't have to stop playing to understand what she was saying.

Powell reached on to the sofa and picked up a tambourine, then nodded in time with the beat Tom and I were playing. It was like we were holding a skipping rope and she was waiting to jump in. Tom hit his drum on my offbeat, then again on my on. Off beat, on. Off beat, on. And all the time Powell tapped her tambourine against her thigh.

A grin cut across Tom's face. I felt a smile crack mine. This is what it was like jamming with my band, except there were no guitars or keyboards. It was just Powell on tambourine, me on bongos, and Tom, who had now reached across for a mallet and was banging it against his huge bass drum. Every hit vibrated through the air and the floorboards and into me.

Powell stood up, and for a moment I thought she was going to stop, but instead she started flailing her arms, left one above her head, right out by her side, then on the next offbeat, she switched arms.

Tom smirked, then shook his head like he knew he shouldn't.

'*Keep going*,' he mouthed to me.

I kept hitting the bongos and watching Powell. She was doing the Octopussy in the middle of the room. Part of me wanted to laugh, but the other part loved it that she didn't care what anyone thought of her; she was just doing what she wanted. She spun around in a circle, arms flailing.

'You dare tell anyone,' she said.

'I wouldn't,' I replied.

'What?' Powell leaned forward, held her hand to her ear.

'I said, I wouldn't,' I shouted.

'Just checking,' she said. 'And you've got to remember these.' She bent down and lifted my headphones on to my ears. 'You should have told her,' she said to Tom.

'Sorry,' Tom said. 'Forgot.' He kept beating the drum, turned his face so only I could see. *'She's so bossy,'* he mouthed.

'I know what you said,' said Powell.

We all smiled, and kept playing as Powell threw her head back and did the Octopussy again. I could hear nothing, but I never wanted it to end. For what seemed like ages I'd hidden myself in my room thinking I would never be able to play music again. And when I did play, it had all gone wrong. Being here was different; it was like there was no wrong, like I was free. You just hit drums and danced. It was like being in a band for the very first time, but we were sharing music through vibrations, not sound.

Powell circled in front of me.

'Isn't it amazing!' she said.

'Yes.' I grinned. 'Amazing.'

I was only playing bongos, but it didn't matter. I just wanted us all to keep dancing and playing, and never stop.

The beat of the drums seemed to stay with me on the bus on the way home. It was like my tinnitus, only it was a good feeling that wasn't in my head – it was in my bones. As the drums eventually faded, my noise started again. It was like it had come back to spoil my fun. But this time I wouldn't let it ruin a brilliant day.

CHAPTER 30

SORRY, DAD

'Drums?' Dad almost choked on his coffee when I first got back from Powell's.

'Yes, Dad,' I said. 'Drums. I can't hear them, but I can feel them through my hands.'

'Soph,' he said. 'It's great to see you so enthusiastic . . . but where did you get those?' He nodded at the bongo drums that Tom had let me borrow.

'A friend,' I said. 'But these are just the start,' I added excitedly. 'I need a full kit.'

Dad shook his head, said something I couldn't lip-read.

'Dad,' I said. 'You're doing that thing when your mug is hiding your lips.'

'Oh, sorry.' He put his mug on the counter. 'I said, I love to see you so happy, but really it can't happen. Dr Cowans told you to avoid loud music.'

'It's fine, Dad,' I said. 'I've got triple protection.'

'Triple protection? Sounds like a deodorant.'

I laughed. 'No, it's not. Look,' I said, reaching my hand in my pocket. 'I put these in my ears, and I've got extra pieces of foam stuffed in my headphones.'

Dad shook his head slowly. 'I'm not sure, Soph,' he said. 'Where did you get that idea from?'

'Powell Stevens's brother,' I said.

'The girl off the TV?'

'Yes,' I said. 'Her brother, Tom, is totally deaf, and he has a whole drum kit that he plays in his basement.'

'Let me think about it,' he said. 'Next-door are going to be chuffed. They already knock on the wall when Liam plays his music too loud.'

'But Mrs Hopkirk thinks it's good,' I said, even though that wasn't true. 'She told me to watch this person –' I took my phone out of my pocket – 'Evelyn Glennie. She went deaf at roughly the same age as me, and now she plays in orchestras all over the world.'

'Okay, okay. You don't have to show me.' A smile crept across Dad's face, which usually meant *I* was winning.

'Please, Dad,' I said.

Dad rubbed his face, suddenly red-eyed and tired-looking. But he'd given me a glimmer of light; now I just had to bust the door open.

'Okay.' He sighed. 'But we can't go too expensive. And you've got to help me take the stuff out of the shed.'

'Yes!' I said. 'Of course.' I wrapped my arms round him. 'Love you, Dad.'

Before, I would have heard him make an *hmm* sound like I'd got my way, but now all I could feel was the rumble through his chest.

I went upstairs to my room and started to play the bongos again. I'd been gently tapping them on the bus all the way home. After our jam with Powell, he'd shown me how to listen with my hands: if I hit the bongos on the edge, the vibrations were sharp and light; if I hit them in the middle, they were longer and heavier; and there were a whole lot of other vibrations in between. He said I had a natural rhythm, and that was key, but using my fingertips and palms to 'listen' was like learning music all over again.

My hands were beginning to ache when I noticed Mum and Dad standing in the doorway smiling at me.

'The happiest you've been in ages,' said Mum.

'Yeah, it is,' I said.

'Just as long as you look that happy when you're helping me clear out the shed,' said Dad. 'Because it'll be too noisy in here.'

'The shed's fine,' I said brightly, then I laughed because Mum was standing behind him giving me the thumbs-up, probably because she'd been on at him to clear out the rubbish for ages.

They stood and watched me for another five minutes. They always looked so proud of me when I played guitar, and it made me feel great to see the same warm look on their faces as they watched me play the bongos.

'It's brilliant, Soph,' they seemed to say at the same time.

'It is,' I said. 'Just imagine what it'll be like when I have a whole kit.'

'Yeah.' Dad rolled his eyes. 'Just imagine.'

We all laughed, then Mum and Dad left me and went downstairs to watch TV.

As soon as they left I picked up my laptop and started my search for the whole kit. Tom said I could borrow other small things like the triangle, tambourine and xylophone, so I wouldn't need those for a while. He also said I could go over and use his drum kit whenever I wanted to, but I couldn't go there every day, even though I'd have liked to. I had to find my own.

There was a six-piece Mapex set in Dumbarton in Scotland. And a five-piece Premier kit with Sabian hat (whatever that was) in Gloucestershire, but both were hundreds of kilometres away. I'd never get Dad to drive that far, let alone pay over three hundred pounds for a kit.

I kept searching for something cheaper and closer. I found a complete CB set for one hundred and twenty pounds (including local delivery) in Tolworth, which Google Maps said was only ten miles from our house. I sent a message, saying I thought I might be able to afford seventy pounds and I could save them delivering it because maybe my dad could get a friend to pick it up in a post-office van.

While I waited for the reply, I was already planning how to carry the bass drum through the hallway, out of the kitchen door and down the garden path to the shed. It might be cold and dusty in there, but I thought maybe I could take one of my beanbags from my room, and I was sure there was already an old rug in there that Dad was supposed to have taken to the dump. It might not be as cosy as Tom's basement, but at least it would be somewhere I could create music and write lyrics, some place where I could just be myself and try to forget about my deafness for a while, just like I did whenever I was at Tom's ... And right then, I found myself smiling because I'd realized that's what I wanted more than anything else.

CHAPTER 31

A TRICKY CONVERSATION

I was excited about the drums, but that didn't stop me from feeling empty when I knew the band were in the music room at lunchtime the next day. I ate my lunch on my own, watching YouTube videos of Evelyn Glennie on my phone. She could play every percussion instrument; some I'd never even heard of or seen. There was a video of her giving a lecture at a university. Someone in the audience asked her how she first started, how she first felt music. She kicked off her shoes and stood in the middle of the stage. *'When this happened,'* she said, striking a huge bass drum. *'When I realized I could feel vibrations through the soles of my feet.'*

I smiled as I remembered feeling the same thing in Tom's basement.

I looked around the canteen as everyone filled their plates with food, walked over to their tables and ate. The videos were great, but as I sat on my own, it still felt like the world was moving around me. Then I spotted Mrs Hopkirk walking towards me.

'How's today going, Sophie?' she asked.

'Okay,' I said. 'Just watching YouTube videos.' I turned my phone towards her.

'Brilliant, you've found her!' Mrs Hopkirk's face lit up as she sat down opposite me. 'Isn't she amazing? Apparently there's over a thousand instruments she can make music from ... I can't even think of that many.'

'Me neither,' I said. I tried to think of something to say, but after being sat on my own for so long, nothing came into my head.

Mrs Hopkirk looked at me like she knew what was bothering me.

'Have you and Rocco spoken yet?' she asked.

'No,' I said. 'But it's okay.'

'I'm not sure that's true,' said Mrs Hopkirk.

I shrugged.

'Look,' she said. 'I know you're moving on with your drums, and that is great, but does that really mean you have to leave the band behind? I chatted to Rocco in the music room, like I said I would. He's putting on a brave face just like you, but I can tell he wants you there at the finals. Why don't you go and meet him?'

'He's practising.'

'He is,' said Mrs Hopkirk. 'But I've told him to finish ten minutes early so you can chat before the bell goes.'

'Really?' I asked.

'Well, someone has to sort you two out.' Mrs Hopkirk smiled. 'Even if you don't get back in the band, it'd be good for you to see your friends again.'

I nodded.

'So, you'll go, then?'

194

'Yes,' I said. 'I'll go.'

'Good.' Mrs Hopkirk pointed at my phone. 'Then how about you show me some more videos of Evelyn Glennie?'

Normally I would have been full of excitement when I walked to the music room, planning out songs and sorting lyrics in my head. But as I headed to meet Rocco, I was shaking like I was caught in a snowstorm without a coat. I had no idea what I was going to say. I'd made up my mind to leave the band, but that didn't stop me from being mad with him. Me and Rocco were always having little arguments about lyrics or the melodies, but that was to make them better. We'd never fallen out about something as serious as this.

I stopped outside the music room and peered through the glass in the door. Rocco was at the back of the room, looking at the wall. *Well, at least he stayed behind*, I thought. I gathered myself, tried to think what I would say. Should I just be cool and pretend that I wasn't bothered by what happened, or should I just tell him how upset I was straight away? I still hadn't made my mind up. *Don't laugh at his jokes*, I told myself, *even if they are funny. He needs to feel bad for what he's done.*

I pushed the door open.

Rocco spun round.

'Hi!' he said, lifting his hand sheepishly.

'Hi,' I said.

He smiled shyly. For a moment we just looked at each other like Mum did when she didn't know how to finish talking to strangers on a dog walk. Eventually Rocco pointed at the wall.

'Have you seen this?'

I walked towards him. He stood back and showed me the poster on the wall.

'There's one in reception too,' he said. 'And I heard they put one up in the sixth-form block, which is weird when the Longshots didn't get through.'

I looked at the poster.

Battle of the Bands
THE FINAL!
Come and Support HiFi Dad
and
The Band With No Name
Rock City, Sunday 19th June

'Looks great, doesn't it?' Rocco said, still looking nervous. 'Maddy from HiFi Dad did it. Probably explains why their name is first.'

'Yeah.' I nodded as I turned back to study the poster. Around the writing, Maddy had drawn a set of drums, a keyboard and two guitars and eight caricatures of each band's members. 'It's good,' I said, looking back at Rocco.

'Not sure which one is supposed to be me, though,' he said.

'Easy,' I said. 'The one with the biggest head.'

'Yeah.' Rocco chuckled. 'I probably deserved that.'

We both returned to looking at the board like neither of us knew what to say next. I couldn't make up my mind if I wanted to tell Rocco what I thought of him or if I should give him a chance to apologize first.

He nudged me. 'You look cool in your headphones though.'

He was trying to be nice, but seeing him made me realize how much I was hurting inside. I'd not known what I was going to say, or how I was going to say it, but suddenly the words blurted out.

'How could you do it, Rocco?' I asked. 'How could you even think about replacing me?'

'No, Kai wasn't there to replace you.'

'What was he there for then?'

'To help you out. I thought you could play together so no one would know if . . .'

'If I messed up!'

'Well, yeah,' Rocco said, sheepishly.

My anger blew up inside me. He was still blaming me for what happened at the semi-final.

'But *I* didn't mess up, Rocco.' I pointed at myself.

Rocco glanced around the room, even though no one was there.

'Soph,' he said. 'You're shouting a bit.'

'I don't care if I am. You still don't get it, Rocco. It was YOU who changed the song!'

'Okay, okay!' Rocco held up his hands. 'I changed the song, but I thought you'd got that.'

'Well, I hadn't, obviously.' I stared ahead at the poster, so angry I felt like ripping it down.

I hated falling out with Rocco. I just wanted things to go back to how they were. I took deep breaths, trying to calm myself down.

Out of the corner of my eye I saw Rocco's lips moving.

'Rocco,' I said, turning to him. 'Can't hear.' I pointed at my ears. Even I was doing that now.

'Sorry, Soph,' he said. 'I always forget. I was just saying I didn't mean to upset you. Maybe it was a stupid idea.'

'It was,' I said. 'I get that you were trying to help, but imagine what it did to my confidence. What if we got another lead singer? You'd be so destroyed you wouldn't be able to open your mouth.'

Rocco nodded.

'I know, I AM sorry. I just want you back, Soph. It's not the same without you. All I want _____.'

He held his hand up to his throat and swallowed hard. I hadn't been able to make out what he said, but from the pained expression on his face, I could tell that he'd meant it. But I couldn't get back with the band; I'd made up my mind.

'Rocco,' I said. 'I can't come back. What happened just proved that I can't. I don't feel part of it any more; it's like I'm stood outside a window watching you all play.'

'But we can fix that,' he said. 'We'll find some way, like we did with the app. And you can't pull out.' He pointed at the wall. 'Your picture is on the poster.'

'I know,' I said. 'But it's not just the band; it's all my hearing appointments and stuff. It's so stressy.'

'Oh, yeah,' said Rocco. 'I forget how often you have to go to hospital ... I mean, I don't forget; it's just—'

'It's okay, Rocco,' I said. 'I understand.'

'So does that mean you're going to stop playing drums as well?'

'How do you know about the drums?' I asked, surprised.

'Mia. She said you'd started playing them.'

'Well, I have,' I said. 'But it's different. It's just for fun at Powell Stevens's house.'

'Not POWELL STEVENS?' He opened his eyes wide and clutched his heart in mock awe. '*THE* POWELL STEVENS?!'

'Not you too,' I said. 'You're as bad as Liam.'

'But everyone finds her so irritating.'

'I know,' I said. 'But she's not like that when you get to know her. Bit like you, really.'

'What?' Rocco looked hurt. 'I don't do that weird dance or nod my head.'

'You don't?'

Rocco laughed. And I couldn't help myself either. Rocco had upset me, but it was nice to be joking with him again. He looked at the poster then back at me.

'Are you sure you won't come back, Soph? Like I said, it wasn't to replace you. Loads of bands have bass and two guitars.'

'I know,' I said. 'But that's not what I want. I don't want to stand up onstage and feel that bad again. But it's okay – you can still use my songs, and I'll teach Kai the chords if you like.'

'Thank you, Soph,' he said, looking awkward. 'I didn't know whether to ask or not. But I'm glad – that way you're still part of it. Maybe you could be our guru or something. You know, like that guy who worked with the Beatles.'

'Rocco.' I laughed. 'I really don't think you should compare the band with the Beatles.'

'Maybe not.' Rocco grinned. 'But we can dream.'

'Yeah, Rocco.' I smiled. 'We can dream.'

'So, we're friends again?' he said.

I nodded.

'Cool.' Rocco opened his arms.

'What? You want a hug?' I said. 'Really?'

'No.' Rocco grinned. 'I want to give you one.'

'Oh.' I smiled. 'Well, that's different.'

We both laughed as we hugged each other. *We're friends again*, I thought to myself. And I was so glad we were.

CHAPTER 32

A BIG SURPRISE!

I should have known something was up a week later when there was no one in the house when I got back from school.

And I definitely should have got suspicious when I saw the shed door open at the bottom of the garden with compost bags and parts of the old lawnmower strewn over the grass. Dad really had meant it when he said he'd clear out the shed for my drums, but I hadn't even bought them yet.

I walked down the path and saw Mum's hand on the top of the shed door, holding it open.

'What's going on?' I asked as I got nearer.

Mum peered round the door.

'Oh, Soph,' she said, looking at her watch. 'I didn't know it was that time already.' She stepped away from the door, smiling.

I kept walking.

'What are you do—?' I stopped dead.

'I was trying to get it done before you got here.' Dad grinned as he looked up at me from the shed floor. 'But I don't know which bits go where.'

'It doesn't matter, Dad!' I said, putting my hands up to my face in disbelief as I looked at all the pieces of drum kit scattered on the floor – the snare drum, the bass, the toms and the cymbals. 'I can't believe it,' I said, taking my hands down. 'How did you get it?'

'The guy messaged back when you were at school,' said Dad. 'Saw it on the laptop when I got in, so I borrowed the work van and picked it up. But that was the easy bit.' He stood up. 'So many different pieces,' he said. 'I can't even figure out the stool.'

He sat down on the stool and put his hand underneath, searching for a lever.

'See, one minute it's not working then—' The stool bumped down. Dad fell back against the wall. 'See!' he said. 'The things got a blimmin' mind of its own.'

Mum and I burst out laughing.

Dad rubbed his head, then looked up at me. I had tears in my eyes, but I couldn't stop smiling. A whole drum kit. My own drum kit, right in the middle of our shed.

Dad stood up.

'You happy, Soph?' he asked.

I nodded, and tried to speak, but no words came out.

'Just remember, I know it's a pain, but . . .'

'I know, Dad,' I said. 'I'll wear them, the earplugs, the foam, and the headphones.'

Mum still looked a little concerned.

'I will, Mum,' I said, trying to reassure her. 'I'll even wear Liam's motorbike helmet if I have to.'

Mum laughed, but it seemed to end too soon. She glanced at Dad.

202

'What's wrong?' I asked.

'Nothing's wrong,' said Mum. 'It's just we've had an email from the hospital.'

I sighed. 'Have I got to go for another test?'

'No.' Mum took a deep breath like she was about to tell me some bad news. 'Soph, I know you might have put this out of your mind as we've not spoken about it for ages.'

'Mum,' I said impatiently. 'What is it? You're scaring me.'

'The cochlear implant,' said Dad. 'There's been a cancellation and there's a chance you could have the operation, a week this Friday. '

'A week this Friday?' My head hooted with the shock. 'But that's only nine days away!' I said. 'I thought it would be ages, and I've not even decided yet.'

'I know,' said Mum. 'But please don't worry. If you're not ready to decide, then we'll just tell them to wait.'

'I don't know what I want,' I said, panicking. 'I've not really thought about it.'

I'd been so happy about the drums, but now it was like a rubber band was tight round my chest. I sat down on the stool as I felt tears build up behind my eyes.

Dad knelt down by my side.

I felt the warmth of his breath on my cheek as he pulled my hair out of my eyes. I looked at him.

'Hey,' he said. 'Just tell me what scares you?'

I wiped my tears on my sleeve.

'Everything,' I sobbed. 'Having my hair shaved, the magnets, the wires, and then wondering if it will work or not.'

'Well, I'm not sure it'll hurt,' he said. 'Maybe it'll be a bit sore. I read the leaflet too. It's a small cut, here.' I felt his finger gently touch the skin above my ear. 'Then they stitch it up and your hair will grow back, unless you're going bald like me, in which case it won't.' He was trying to be funny and considerate at the same time.

'But *I'll* know it's there,' I said.

Mum knelt down on the other side of me.

'We're talking the size of a pound coin, Soph,' she said, holding up an imaginary coin between her thumb and index finger. 'Okay, maybe slightly bigger.'

'But people will be looking, and I'll be able to feel it when I brush my hair back with my hand.'

'But isn't the hope that you might get some hearing back worth more than worrying about what you look like?' said Mum.

I shrugged.

'Maybe we can talk about it later,' said Dad. 'After all, we didn't go to all the trouble of setting up your drums for you to be upset.'

I glanced up at the drums. A minute ago I couldn't wait to play them; now all I could think about was the operation. I hadn't forgotten about it at all. I'd written a song about the girl, and the leaflet was still in my room; it was just every once in a while, the girl's smiling face would get hidden under tea plates or my schoolbooks. If it was any other leaflet, Mum would have thrown it out when she tidied my room, but this was too important to put in a bin. So I hadn't forgotten about it; I'd just decided I didn't want to think about it.

Dad ruffled my hair as he stood up. I felt like saying he wouldn't be able to do that if I had the operation, but from the kind look on his face, I knew he was only doing his best to help.

'We'll leave you, Soph,' he said, handing me the drumsticks. 'I can finish setting this up, after work tomorrow.'

I smiled.

'Thanks, Dad,' I said.

Mum hovered, like she wasn't sure she should leave me.

'It's all right, Mum,' I said. 'I'm okay.'

She nodded and followed Dad back down the path. I looked at the drum kit. I'd had such a great time at Tom's that I hadn't been able to wait to play it, but the thought of having the operation had triggered a high-pitched whine in my head. I closed my eyes, took a deep breath to try to calm the noise down, but that just made it screech louder. I knew I had to think about the cochlear implant, but every time I'd been to Tom's I'd been so relaxed that being deaf hadn't mattered. I didn't know if it was because of Tom or because we played drums, or maybe it was both. All I knew was that I wanted to feel like that all the time.

I rested the tips of my drumsticks on the rim of the snare. Mum and Dad said they'd talk to me later about the operation; I'd think more about it then. I held up the drumsticks and beat a rhythm on the snare then searched for the bass pedal with my foot, but Dad had set it up too far away from me. I bent down and slid it across the floor. I remembered what Tom had said about every drum kit feeling different, that you have to position the kit so everything feels natural to hit. I pulled the snare a little closer and lowered the top hat a few centimetres. I hit the snare again. The drum kit was perfect.

I just wished everything else in my life was as easy to fix as that.

I'd thought Mum and Dad would want to talk to me about the operation during tea, but all they did was ask how the drums were. It was like they knew I was too stressed to talk about it. I told them that it was still weird hitting something but only being able to feel it, but after the first hour I had got used to it, and had even had a go at playing some of the band's songs by playing along to the app that Rocco had put on my phone. Mum and Dad thought that was great, but the truth was I'd only followed a basic beat because that was all Rocco could do on the drum machine.

It used to be my guitar that I was drawn to like a magnet in my room, but when I went up after tea, it was the girl smiling up from the cochlear implant poster that was impossible for me to ignore. I lay back on my bed and read through the leaflet again. The bits about having to have my hair shaved so they could fit the implant and how I would only have to stay in hospital for one day still scared me. And the waiting for three weeks for activation day scared me even more. I imagined those weeks would feel like months and how horrible it would be to go through all that and then find out the implant hadn't worked.

But for the people in the leaflet it had worked, because underneath their photos were quotes from some of them, saying things like, 'The implant is amazing' and 'I've discovered hearing again'. And then a quote from the girl on the front, which read, 'At first I was worried, but having the implant has changed my life.'

206

It changed her life, I thought to myself, *but how do I know for certain that it will change mine?*

I looked up as my bedroom door opened.

Liam put his head round the side.

'Liam,' I said, annoyed. 'Can't you—?'

'Knock?' Liam smiled, and I realized that wouldn't work anyway. 'Maybe we should set up a system instead.' He grinned like he'd had a great idea. 'Like I could text, *Hi, I'm outside. Can I come in?*'

'That'd just be weird, Liam,' I said, putting the leaflet down. 'But Tom has an app that flashes the lights.'

'Cool,' said Liam. 'Or I could just use my hand.' He reached back to the light switch by my door and flicked it off and on, off and on . . .

'Liam,' I said. 'That's just irritating. What do you want anyway?'

'Nothing.' He grinned. 'Just checking how you are.'

'Really?' I shook my head. 'You can't do better than that? You must want something.'

'No, really. I want to know how you are. Dad said you've had some news.'

'Yeah,' I said, lifting up the leaflet. 'I could have the implant in nine days, but I'm not sure whether to have it.'

'Nine days! Woah!'

'I know,' I said. 'That's why I'm freaking out.'

'Maybe it's best you don't get long to think about it, though, like when your mum springs the dentist on us.'

'True,' I said. 'But I'm still undecided.'

Liam walked over to my window and sat on the sill.

'Well, if you can't make a decision, maybe you should talk to someone.' Liam touched the strings on the top of my guitar. 'Maybe Powell Stevens's brother.'

'Liam,' I said, suspiciously. 'Are you sure Mum and Dad didn't send you in?'

'No, they didn't. I just thought you'd been hanging out with him.'

'I have,' I said. 'And he said I could, but I'm worried I might upset him by talking about it, because he's never had the chance to get any hearing back.'

'Then maybe that really does make him the best one.'

I looked at Liam. We were always messing around, or irritating each other, but ever since I'd lost my hearing he'd been so much more sensible and caring. He was right. Tom would be the best one to ask, but that still didn't stop me thinking Liam was up to something.

'Liam,' I said, cautiously, just in case I was wrong. 'I don't want to be horrible, but this isn't like you. You must want something.'

'Okay.' He smirked.

'There.' I pointed at him. 'I knew it! What is it?'

Liam ran his thumb over the strings on the neck of my guitar again, then suddenly looked embarrassed.

'Okay,' he said again. 'Me and my mates are setting up a band, and, well, I was wondering if I could borrow your guitar.'

'You're starting a band?'

'Yeah. Why not?'

'But you can't play anything,' I said.

'I know,' Liam said. 'But Luke has been having lessons and he said he'd teach me.'

'Luke,' I said, trying not to laugh. 'Your friend Luke is going to teach you?'

'Why not?' Liam stood up and looked at me with a hurt expression on his face. 'I knew I shouldn't have asked you. It's okay for you. You can play guitar, and I heard you on the drums that Dad got you. You can play anything, and I want to try too. I don't want to be stuck cooking chips and burgers all of my life.'

Liam walked towards the door. He was being serious, and I felt bad for laughing.

'Liam, wait,' I said. 'You can. You can borrow my guitar.'

Liam stopped and turned round. 'Really?' he said.

'Yes,' I said. 'Just be careful with it.'

'Course.' He smiled. 'Unless I get famous and smash it onstage, but then I'd have enough money to buy you a hundred.'

'You wish!' I laughed as I stood up. 'Make sure you always carry it in this.' I slid the guitar case out of the gap between the wardrobe and the wall.

'Will do ... and thanks.'

'No problem,' I said. 'But you owe me, Liam.'

I'd never have thought in a million years that I would ever let anyone borrow my guitar; it felt like it was a part of me and it hurt so much to let it go. But it was the right thing to do. At least this way someone else would get to enjoy playing it, instead of it sitting unused in my bedroom, forever out of tune. Now it was going to be Liam's. It was horrible watching it go, but seeing the smile on his face as he left made me feel happy too. I'd always thought he was satisfied just hanging out with his friends, and grilling burgers, but all along it seemed like he had dreams, just like I did. And I thought it was cool to have another musician in our house, even if I wasn't in a band.

My phone vibrated on my bed.

A message from Tom.

Tom: Hey, come over again tomorrow. No need to bring an umbrella 😊

I went to reply, but Tom sent another message as I typed.

Tom: Got something to show you – might have something else here too 🥁 😊

I smiled. Just reading Tom's messages made me realize Liam was right – he was the right person to ask. And now I didn't even need an excuse to get to see him again. But I still didn't want to spring it on him. I typed my reply.

Sophie: Thank you. I'll come. But do you mind if I talk to you about something too?

Tom: Course. What's up?

I thought about explaining, but typing the words seemed more complicated than saying them.

My messages scrolled up as Tom sent another.

Tom: Is it about hearing?

I nodded as I typed.

Sophie: Yes.

Tom: Thought so 😊

My heart lifted. I'd felt awkward about asking, but just seeing the smiley face made me think it would be okay.

CHAPTER 33

DOING THE RIGHT THING

It felt weird as I sat in the drama room teaching Kai the songs the next day. He'd been playing along to recordings that Rocco had given him, so he knew almost all the chords and key changes, but it was like he still wanted to check with me.

'They're your songs, Sophie,' he said when we met. 'I want to play them the way you wrote them.'

'You better,' I joked, which made him and everyone else in the band laugh. It was like they felt as weird as I did, but at least what I said had broken the ice.

We sat side by side as the only bit he was stuck on was the bridge on 'Pictures of You'. I showed him the chords and he moved his fingers over the frets and nodded. I think he may have said something, but unlike the rest of the band, he hadn't learned to look at me. But from the way he nodded and repeated the sequence, I knew he had got it right.

Then it was time for him to join the rest of the band onstage, with Rocco prowling around. And as Kai started playing, I thought how kind he'd been to say he wanted to play the songs like I'd written them. He didn't have to do that, but it made me feel better that he had.

'I think maybe you could drop the mean look,' Mrs Hopkirk said, looking over at Rocco. 'You look like Lewis Grainger.'

'Lewis who?' Rocco asked.

Some of the kids from HiFi Dad sniggered. Apparently, Lewis Grainger was in Uploaded, one of the biggest bands ever.

'It doesn't matter,' said Mrs Hopkirk. 'All I'm saying is people might warm to you a bit more if you smiled. And do you really think the hat is a good idea?'

'I thought we could all wear them,' said Rocco, taking off his police officer's hat. 'You know, like Ty could wear a fire-fighter's hat?'

'What?' said Ty. 'No way.'

'Rocco.' Mrs Hopkirk smiled. 'You don't want to distract the audience from your music.'

'Okay.' Rocco walked towards me, bent down and took a drink from his bag. 'Any good?' he asked, looking up at me.

'Yeah,' I said. 'I think so. But I think maybe you could be a little less hyper.'

'Can't help it.' He grinned. 'It's because of the new songs. I was worried when they said we couldn't play the same ones as the semi-final, but I think these two are better.'

I nodded because even though I couldn't hear the tune, I loved the new songs I'd written.

Mrs Hopkirk walked towards us. 'Okay,' she said. 'Maybe now is a good time to remind you about the judging. In fact –' she clapped her hands – 'everyone should hear this. Yes, including you, HiFi Dad.'

The members of HiFi Dad walked towards us, trying to be cool, like they'd done Battle of the Bands before, which I suddenly remembered they had.

'So,' Mrs Hopkirk said. 'Here's how the marking works. Four judges give marks out of ten, like in ice skating, or gymnastics, but we won't know what those marks add up to until we get to the end.'

'What if it's a draw?' asked Rocco, tipping his hat.

'It'll be a play-off,' said Mrs Hopkirk. 'Just the bands that have tied.'

The lead singer of HiFi Dad said something I couldn't see. The rest of his band laughed.

'We'll see,' said Rocco.

'Yes, we will see,' said Mrs Hopkirk, looking at her watch. 'Although neither of you are going to stand a chance if we don't get on with this practice. Rocco, are you going to get your band ready for the next song.'

The group split. Rocco put his drink bottle back by his bag.

'So, we'll play "Girl in the Photograph" next?' he said to me. 'Soph?'

'It's okay, Rocco,' I said, 'You don't have to check in with me every time.'

'Oh, sorry. Just don't want to make same mistake, twice.'

We both smiled.

'Rocco,' said Mrs Hopkirk. 'Can we have you back here? We want to hear both bands' songs, not just yours.'

'Yep, coming.' Rocco walked away from me, then spun round. 'Just in case . . .' He pointed at Mrs Hopkirk. 'She said I had to go.'

'I know, Rocco,' I rolled my eyes. 'I got that.'

'Cool.'

'But, Rocco?'

'Yeah?'

'I think Mrs Hopkirk is right. You should lose the hat.'

'Oh, right.' He took off his hat and threw it like a Frisbee towards his bag. I waited for him to run back to the stage, but he just stood looking at me. 'Soph,' he said. 'Are you sure you don't want to be in the band? I know you only just started drums, but maybe you could play a tambourine.'

'Rocco!' I laughed. 'There's no way I'm just going to stand onstage and tap a tambourine.'

'Sure?'

'Yes,' I said. 'But thanks.'

I smiled as Rocco ran away from me, then jumped up on to the stage. I was glad he'd invited me along. He'd seemed nervous at first, but now it was like he understood what was going on with me. I felt bad that we'd fallen out and made each other so unhappy, so it was nice to see him back onstage having fun.

I put my earplugs in and pulled my headphones up over my ears. Ty turned a knob on his amplifier, Mia had her head down, and Rocco set the drum machine for the second song, 'Reasons'. My song. Kai stared ahead. Mrs Hopkirk had always said that when onstage it was best to try to focus on one point. For Kai that point seemed to be the doors at the back of the drama room. He was getting ready to play my song.

For a moment I wished I was back up there, feeling the buzz of getting ready to play, the excitement that came with the sound, but I knew that playing my guitar in silence was no longer fun, not like the drums.

Rocco counted them in. I watched Kai set his hands on the guitar and track his fingers over the frets as the band started to play 'Reasons'. After the first verse, Kai looked at me. I nodded. He was doing everything right; the band were going to be fine.

Mrs Hopkirk came and stood beside me as Rocco swung the microphone above his head. We exchanged smiles, then she leaned forward a little and said, 'I don't know if it's because you've turned up, Sophie, or because he's been drinking too many fizzy drinks, but this is the happiest I've seen Rocco this past week.'

'I know,' I said. 'I'm glad.'

On the stage Rocco was singing at the same time as trying to play air guitar. I smiled. He was totally lost in the music, forgetting where he was, probably imagining he was playing in front of hundreds and thousands of people at T in the Park.

Rocco took a breath, got ready for the chorus, and I felt myself singing the lyrics with him, word for word.

Your smile lights up the page
Lights up my room
You made me happy
When I was feeling sad
Because everything looks fine
Everything looks great
When you're the smiling girl in the photograph.

I was proud of the lyrics, even though I couldn't hear the tune Rocco had helped me put them to, but most of all, it suddenly reminded me of the girl in the leaflet on my bedroom table, and it made my heart race ... but I felt sad at the same time.

Mrs Hopkirk put her hand on my shoulder. 'Everything okay, Sophie?' she asked, like she could tell how I was feeling.

I nodded. 'Yes,' I said. 'I'm fine.'

I looked down, saw my foot tapping to a beat I couldn't hear. I might have missed being in the band, but I had made the right decision. Tom was right: once a musician, always a musician. And I could feel that with every tap of my foot, and every beat of my heart. But all the time I was watching the band, I was thinking about the girl in the photograph; how I couldn't stop myself thinking about how I would 'hear' music for the rest of my life.

CHAPTER 34

WHY WAS I
SO WORRIED?

Tom had said I could ask him anything, but that didn't stop my stomach turning over with nerves as I followed Powell off the bus after school that day. I wanted to ask her if she thought it would be okay, but she just told me to go on down to the basement because she was bursting for the loo. Which meant I just got even more nervous as I stepped down every stair on my own.

When I reached the bottom, Tom was sitting on the sofa. His drum kit had been moved towards the wall and there was what looked like a large circular table covered by a cloth in the middle of the room. For a moment I stood and watched him. Sometimes I wondered how I came across to others, now I couldn't hear, but watching Tom made realize that we look the same as any 'ordinary' person watching videos on our laptop screens. The only difference is that we can't hear what's being said, or what music is being played.

I walked slowly, so as not to make him jump.

He looked up. 'I knew you were there.' He smiled.

'How?'

'I'm psychic.'

'Really?'

'No.' He grinned. 'Powell sent me a text from the loo.'

I laughed.

'I was just watching this,' he said, turning his laptop towards me.

I grinned. 'Evelyn Glennie? I know. Isn't she amazing?'

Tom nodded. 'I've watched it before, but each time it gets better. I'd love to go and see her, even meet her. This is her talking about how deafness shouldn't be a barrier in music.'

I sat down on the sofa next to Tom and read the subtitles as Evelyn Glennie told a story about a deaf man in Germany whose parents were going to send him to a special deaf school when he was a kid, and how he didn't want to go. Now the man is twenty years old and is a percussionist after discovering rhythm by hitting his mum's pots and pans with spoons. He now performs all over Germany and Europe.

'My mum would kill me if I used her pots and pans,' I said.

'Yeah.' Tom laughed. 'Mine too.'

The video finished. Tom flipped the screen down on his laptop.

'So,' he said, turning to me. 'What did you want to ask me?'

I smiled. I'd known him and Powell for a while, but I still couldn't get used to how direct they were.

'Well.' I paused. 'It's just . . . I heard from the hospital yesterday. I've been on the waiting list for a—'

'Cochlear implant,' Tom jumped in.

'Yeah.' I nodded. 'How did you know?'

'I looked it up, obviously. I think it's great, but you don't look so sure.'

'I'm not,' I said.

'What? You're mad.' Tom beamed. 'You've got to go for it. I would if I could. My ears are just things stuck on the side of my head; yours are still connected to your brain. So yeah, why wouldn't you?'

'Really?' After being so nervous about asking him, I was surprised by his reply.

'Of course. I mean, there are risks and things. I read all about it years ago. I know they're not nice, the loss of balance and stuff, and we already got the tinnitus, but if I had the chance of getting my hearing back I would.' I sat back and blew my cheeks out in relief.

'What?' said Tom. 'Don't tell me you were going to say no?'

'I don't know,' I said. 'I just wanted to talk to someone like you, but then I was worried because you never really got the choice.'

'Nope,' said Tom. 'But hey, I still got the drums.'

For a moment, he stared at the floor. I'd not wanted to upset him, but it looked like I had.

'I'm sorry,' I said. 'It feels like I was just thinking about myself and not you.'

Tom waved his hand in the air.

'Don't worry about me,' he said, suddenly smiling. 'I do okay. Besides, it's more important what's ahead of us, not what we've left behind. So when is it?'

'When is it?'

'Your operation!'

220

'Oh, eight days' time,' I said.

'Blimey!'

'I know!'

'That's quick,' he said. 'But maybe it's best to have less time to worry.'

'I still will though.'

'Of course.' Tom put his laptop on the floor, then turned to me. 'So come on,' he said, looking enthusiastic. 'Tell me about it.'

I sat back and told Tom all the things Dr Cowans had discussed with me and Mum. Every time I told him a new detail, like the preparation for the operation, or how long it would take, he nodded like he already knew, and any doubts that I'd had started to fall away. He'd told me he was fine, and he looked fine, but for a few moments, after we'd stopped talking, I couldn't help wishing that somehow, sometime, someone might discover how to help repair the nerves that connected his ears to his brain.

'I'm excited for you,' he said when I'd finished talking.

'Thanks,' I said.

Then he suddenly stood up and said, 'Anyway, how are you getting on with your drums?'

'Good,' I said, thinking how suddenly he was able to change a conversation, like Powell did. 'Or at least I think so. It was hard to concentrate last night, but I played for two hours, and even had a go at a couple of the band's new songs. I love them.'

'Cool,' said Tom. 'I'm not sure our new ones are so good, but maybe I just have to get used to them. Anyway –' he nodded at the table covered in a cloth – 'haven't you been wondering what that is?'

'A table?' I shrugged.

He laughed then held on to the corner of the cloth like a magician about to reveal the end of a trick. 'Not quite,' he said, pulling the cloth.

In the middle of the cramped basement, Tom had managed to squeeze in a huge concert timpani drum.

'Amazing, isn't it?' He beamed. 'Hired it from the Drum Bank, in town. I've got it for a week; might even use it for Battle of the Bands.'

I walked over to the drum; it was as high as my waist and its skin stretched almost to the width of my arms.

'It's incredible,' I said in awe.

Tom reached down and picked up two mallets with blue fabric tips.

'It came yesterday,' he said. 'Played it for ages. So loud Mum and Powell said it shook the whole house. Thought you'd like a go, too. Evelyn Glennie says—'

'Start with the loudest instruments and work backwards.' I grinned. 'That way you can develop your senses rather than go searching for them.'

Tom laughed. 'Yeah,' he said. 'You watched that part of her video too. But get this –' he stood over the drum – 'put your fingers on the sides of the drum skin. It's amazing.' He smiled. 'I hardly have to hit it. It's like I only need to tap it gently to feel it, like a small pebble disturbing the surface of the water. That was Evelyn Glennie too – she said that's the best way to picture it. That the mallet is the pebble, and once you hit the middle, imagine the ripples of water

222

moving from the centre to the edge ... Actually, I'm talking too much. We'll just do it. Close your eyes. Oh, headphones first.'

'Oh yeah.'

We both pulled our headphones up over our ears. I loved how enthusiastic he was, and I just hoped that I would feel the same sensations he had.

I put the tips of my fingers on the side of the drum and closed my eyes. My head was totally silent, my eyes so tightly closed I couldn't see the drum or any light. I waited, but I didn't know what to expect; I thought I'd feel the whack of the mallet, but I didn't know what else.

I felt a vibration across my fingertips, then another, like waves of sound rolling across the drum and then fading away. Then another wave, and another. Still gentle, but arriving faster.

I opened my eyes, expecting to see Tom's hair flying round as he smacked down on the drums. Instead, I saw him leaning over, listening, lifting the mallet high, then dropping it down on the drumskin softly.

'How do you do that?' I asked. 'You make the mallet look like it weighs stacks, then let if fall gently like a feather.'

'I know.' Tom beamed. 'It's not all about whacking drums; it's also about doing it gently. And the weird thing is that it makes your arms ache more, trying to control it. And it's not just through the drum skin you feel it; it's through the stick too. Here, have a go.'

I took the mallet and held it in my hand, gently across my palm, just as Tom had done, then put the fingers of my left hand back on the edge of the drum. I lifted the mallet as high as my shoulder, then brought it down gently. The vibrations passed through my palms and my fingertips. It was like when I discovered rhythm hitting my books in the bedroom, only a thousand times better.

I lifted the mallet high and brought it down again.

'You learn to control it,' said Tom. 'I'm getting better. Only trouble is, I love it so much I don't want it to go back to the shop.'

I laughed, then saw Powell standing at the bottom of the stairs.

'Let me know when you start playing properly,' she said.

'This is properly,' said Tom. 'This is the pitter-patter of raindrops before the storm.'

'Blurgh!' said Powell. 'Where did you get that line from?'

Tom and I looked at each other, like we both knew it was a good line for a lyric.

'Go on,' he said to me. 'You can have that one. I know you want to write it down.'

'No,' I said. 'I'll remember.' I made a note of the line in my head.

'Okay,' said Tom. 'So, try the mallet again, but this time, just lay it across your fingers.'

I did as he said.

'Can you feel it?'

'Yes,' I said.

Powell shrugged like it was no big deal.

But it was. It was the biggest deal since I'd stopped playing guitar, even better than the first time I heard the drums in the basement. For the first time in a long time I felt like I was part of the music, not just sat on the outside watching. It was such a big deal that I wished there were two timpani so me and Tom could stand and hit them, side by side, and feel the noise.

'You two should dump your bands and play together. You'd go down a blast at Rock City.'

I smiled. It was as if Powell had read my mind. 'I don't think I'm ready for that just yet,' I said.

'But you are going to Rock City?'

'Of course,' I said. 'I'm going to support the band.'

'Oh, thanks.' Tom pulled a face, pretending to be offended.

'And your band, of course,' I added.

'Get a room.' Powell laughed as she slumped down on the sofa.

'Ignore her,' said Tom, picking up another mallet. 'But let's try playing together.'

We both put our left hands on the edge of the drum, then held up the mallets. Tom brought his down.

I loved playing the drums with him, but most of all I loved being with him because he didn't make me feel deaf, which was weird when we both were. I just hoped that if I got any of my hearing back, it wouldn't change any of that. Especially when the afternoon was going so great. At first we played together, matching rhythm, then he'd play sequences that gradually got more and more complicated, and I'd play them back to him. It wasn't that we were trying to beat each other; it was just us trying to play better.

'Why don't you play one of your own songs,' he said, after we'd had a break.

'I'm not sure,' I said. 'Because we've only used simple beats on Rocco's drum machine, I kept them quite simple in my head.'

'Even better, then,' he said. 'It's like a blank canvas, where you can start all over again.'

I didn't have time to think about it, because Tom had already handed me the drumsticks and was adjusting the stool to my height. I looked at Powell to see what she thought, but Tom and I had been playing so long that she had her head buried in a magazine.

I sat down on the stool. It felt a little high, so Tom gave it another turn.

'Go on,' he said. 'Just imagine one of your songs, and then play along. You know, like we do when we cover a famous song. Only it's not famous; it's yours.'

We'd been playing for three hours, but suddenly my hands were tense. It should have been natural to play one of my own songs, but I felt nervous, like I imagined Rocco must have felt whenever we wrote a new song and he'd be scared he'd forget the words in front of everyone.

I closed my eyes for a second, imagined I had a vinyl copy of 'Nobody' in my hands and was placing it on Dad's record deck. The record started to turn ... One ... Two ... Three. I opened my eyes and started to play.

For a moment there was no one around me with a spotlight shining down on me – just my hands, the sticks and the drums – and as the record kept turning, I kept playing, a simple beat of snare and bass drum, then adding more beats, more complicated than anything Rocco had put on the drum machine, but Tom could keep the beat, because as I played he stood next to me, moving his hands like he was hitting every beat with me.

'Keep going,' he said. 'It's great.'

We both smiled as I kept playing, and I thought about how he'd helped me make my decision. And I hoped if the implant was successful that I wouldn't lose moments like this.

CHAPTER 35

ROLLER-COASTER RIDE

I messaged Mia about the operation appointment on the way home. I thought she would be upset that I'd wanted to talk to Tom about it, but she said it had been the right thing to do; she could only imagine what it felt like, whereas he knew exactly how it was. I smiled at my phone with relief, but I should have known how she would react. We were such good friends that we often knew what the other was thinking.

I'd told my best friend I'd decided to have the operation, now it was time to tell Mum and Dad. But the house looked empty as I walked up the path. There was no flicker of the TV in the lounge window, and when I opened the door there was no smell of anything cooking for tea. I thought maybe they were still at work, until I looked out of the back door and saw Mum by the shed, holding a piece of chipboard, the same stuff Dad had used to floor the loft. I'd only had my drums a day, but now it was like they were turning the shed into a summer house.

I walked out into the garden. Mum looked up and smiled when she saw me.

'Hi, Soph,' she said. 'How was it at Tom's?'

'Good,' I said, walking towards her. 'But what's going on?'

'Oh, your dad,' she said, nodding into the shed. 'He's soundproofing it so you don't disturb the neighbours. At least he would be if he hadn't hit his thumb more times than the nails.'

'It's the hammer,' Dad said, looking up at me, red-faced, from the floor. 'It keeps slipping.'

'A bad workman blames his tools,' said Mum.

'No.' Dad wiped sweat from his forehead. 'A bad workman blames his wife.'

Mum laughed. 'Well, if you're going to be like that, I'll go inside.'

'No,' I said, holding out my hand to stop her. 'Don't go.'

Mum looked surprised, like I might have just shouted.

'Sorry,' I said. 'But I've got something to tell you – both of you.'

Dad put the hammer down and stood up. 'What is it, Soph?' he said. 'Anything wrong?'

'No.' I smiled as they both looked at me anxiously. 'Nothing's wrong.'

'Then what is it?' asked Mum.

'I've decided to have the operation.'

'What?' they both said, their expressions utterly confused.

'The cochlear implant,' I said.

Mum's face cracked into a smile. 'That's wonderful, Soph,' she said.

'Yes,' said Dad as he took a step towards me. 'It is. What happened to make you decide?'

'My friend Tom,' I said. 'I told you he was deaf too, and he said if he had the chance, he would go for it.'

229

'Aww, he sounds lovely.' Mum teared up and I don't know if it was because she was happy for me, or sad for a boy she didn't know, but from the way she wrapped her arms round me, it might have been both.

'It's great,' said Dad. 'I'm sure you're still a little scared, and uncertain about what will happen – this has been a real roller coaster.'

I smiled as Dad walked towards me and hugged us both. *It is a roller-coaster ride*, I thought to myself, and it was like Mum and Dad were on it with me, and no matter how high or twisty the ride, none of us were going to get off.

That's a great line for a song, I thought. It was like making the decision had relaxed me, because it was the second line I'd got that afternoon.

I gently pulled away from the hug.

'What is it?' said Dad, sniffing his armpits. 'Do I stink?'

'No.' I smiled. 'I just got an idea for a song. I need to write it down. But you do smell a bit too.'

Mum and Dad laughed at the same time.

'Laters,' I said as I ran back into the house and went up to my room.

I made a note of the line about the storm that I'd got from Tom earlier, but the roller-coaster line was fresh in my mind.

I started to write, not thinking too much, just letting the words go straight from my brain to my pen.

Round and round
Up and down

230

In and out
No place to run
No place to hide
But it's okay to be scared
It's okay to be fine
Because I am not alone
On the roller-coaster ride.

I closed my eyes and waited for the next line to come, but all that came was my noise. The noise that I never seemed to escape from, even though the stress of making the decision had gone. Dr Cowans had said he couldn't be sure that it would go and that he couldn't guarantee the operation would be successful, but I hoped it would, because that night my noise pierced, then droned, and by the time I felt like I could sleep, it was rumbling, rumbling, rumbling, on and on and on, like an electricity generator at a fair.

CHAPTER 36

OTHER PEOPLE'S DREAMS

'"Roller-Coaster Ride"! I love it!' Mia said as we sat on the wall outside my house. 'It's too late for the finals, but have you sent it to Rocco?'

'No,' I said, putting my notebook down next to me. 'It's not finished yet. I'm not even sure whether that's the verse or the chorus.'

'But you will show it to him?'

'Of course. But you know what he's like. He'll go all hyper and want to play it at Rock City tomorrow.'

Mia laughed. 'Yeah,' she said. 'That's him, all right.' Then she looked at me, and I knew what was coming next, because she'd asked me what it felt like a hundred times at school the day before. 'Soph,' she said. 'Are you sure you won't come to the final practice at Rocco's?'

'Yes, I'm sure,' I said. 'You've got all the songs, and Kai has had plenty of time, so he'll know them off by heart.'

'But it's not the same without you, Soph. I mean, what else are you going to do?'

'I'm okay,' I said. 'I've got some schoolwork to catch up on, then, with a bit of luck, I'll go out to the shed and play drums.'

'Okay.' Mia smiled. 'But you ARE coming to Rock City tomorrow?'

'Yep,' I said. 'Wouldn't miss it. Might not be in the band, but they are my songs, and I promised Tom I'd be there too.'

'Oh, well, then you'll definitely be there!'

'He's just a friend,' I said. 'But he is great. I even played some of our songs yesterday.'

'Brilliant,' said Mia.

'It was only simple beats,' I said.

'Yeah, I bet!' Mia grinned. 'I know you, Soph. I bet it was more than that. Anyway –' she nodded at her mum's red car as it came towards us – 'last chance. You coming to practice or not?'

'No, I'm fine,' I said.

'Yeah,' said Mia. 'And it's okay to be fine . . . See, your song's in my head already.'

She walked towards the kerb. Her mum waved as Mia opened the door and got in. I stood and watched the car pull off.

I'd woken up thinking I would go to Rocco's house, but the more I'd thought about it, the more I'd realized I'd just be in the way.

I turned and walked back into the house. Mum looked up from her phone, surprised, as I passed her in the kitchen.

'Didn't feel like going?' she asked.

'No,' I said. 'I thought they'd be better without me. I know if I was Kai, I would feel weird having the person I'd replaced there.'

She nodded, like she understood, and went back to her phone.

I walked back out to the shed and sat on the stool behind the drums. I started tapping them. Normally an idea would come in a few minutes, but all I could think about was the band playing at Rocco's. They'd be running through the songs, Ty playing keyboards at the back of the garage, next to Mia with her bass, and Kai might sit on the old washing machine like I used to, while Rocco jumped around with the mic, making sure he didn't jump so high that he knocked his head on the garage door. And when they finished, I imagined Rocco telling them all about what the band would do after they'd won the final – go on TV, play Glastonbury, go on a mega tour of the world, eating doughnuts and hot dogs in the back of a huge tour bus. That's what me and Rocco used to tell each other. We knew it wasn't realistic, but like Rocco always said, it didn't hurt to dream. The only problem was we weren't dreaming together any more.

I kicked the bass pedal, hit the snare, and imagined the band playing 'Pictures of You' with Rocco's voice in the middle of my head.

Bright lights
Black hole
Bright lights
Black hole
Sliding
Sliding
Press the button if you panic
Press the button if you panic
Thud. Thud

Boom. Boom
We're taking pictures
We're taking pictures
We're taking pictures of you.

I kept playing. It didn't matter if I was too slow or too fast because no one else was there to listen. I began to wish I was going onstage with them. It was great that they were going to play my songs, but no one would know that. Everyone remembers the performers, not the people who write the songs. The performers get mobbed in the streets while the song writers can go shopping without even getting noticed.

Tomorrow the band and Tom would play in front of two hundred people at Rock City, and here I was playing on my own, in the garden shed.

CHAPTER 37

ROCK CITY

Rock City smelt of sweat and boys' deodorant as the lights shone on the drum kit and the amplifiers that all the bands would use. As I stood with the Band With No Name, I looked around the room. Most of the groups were huddled in dark corners like they were cold. The only ones I recognized were HiFi Dad and Tom's band, the Ultratones, but that was only because he'd waved at me when he came in. I thought about going over and talking to him, but I thought he'd want to be focused on being with his band, making sure they were ready. Which is what Rocco was supposed to be doing, only he was so nervous he couldn't stop talking.

'Soph, do I look okay?'

'You look fine, Rocco,' I said for the tenth time. 'But I told you, you don't need the dark glasses and I'd definitely lose the grandad hat.'

'But I like it,' he said. 'And it looks better than what that lot are wearing.' He pointed across the hall at a band from another village dressed in black and wearing loads of make-up. 'Looks like they dressed for Halloween.'

I laughed, but it was a nervous laugh, almost as nervous as Rocco, who had bounced away towards Mia, presumably to ask her the same questions he had just asked me. I smiled. It was like he was full of nerves and excitement at the same time, even more than he was at the semi-finals, which usually meant he'd give a great performance.

I looked up at the stage. There were six amplifiers, twice the size of ours, on each side, and in between was a drum kit and three microphones set on stands. And behind the drums, hanging down from the ceiling, was a huge banner saying WELCOME TO THE FINAL OF THE BATTLE OF THE BANDS. Just reading it made me feel excited and nervous, and I wasn't even playing.

All around the hall it felt like band members were getting more and more animated as the competition start time got closer. One band's drummer was hitting his sticks against a radiator. Another band's member was tuning his guitar while chewing gum as the lead singer was opening her mouth wide like she was doing vocal exercises. Next to them were two students from Mittlesham High. I'd seen them at the semi-finals – a boy about my age, and a girl with long brown hair, whose face was skewed like she was in pain. They both looked even more anxious than Rocco, who was now bouncing up and down in front of Ty.

The hall suddenly seemed to fill as people swelled around me. Hundreds of mouths moving up and down like piranhas chasing after food.

I felt a hand on my shoulder and turned round.

'Hey! You all right?'

Tom was standing in front of me with his headphones on.

'Yes.' I nodded. 'I think so. Just feeling a bit stressed.'

'Me too,' he said, 'but I'm trying to block it out. Otherwise, you know what happens.'

I nodded. I knew he meant the noise.

'How's your band?' he asked.

'Fine, I think. Rocco's his usual self – all over the place.'

'Yeah, looks it.' Tom's eyes flitted to Rocco.

We both laughed. I was about to tell him that Mia was on edge too, but stopped as the lights flashed on the stage.

'No, that wasn't me.' Tom grinned as the lights had flashed just like they did when someone rang the bell at his house. 'Just means they're ready. I'll catch you later,' he said, looking back at his band. 'Think we're going to run through the songs one more time before we go on.'

'Okay,' I said. 'Good luck.'

'Thanks,' he said, tapping his drumsticks against his palms. 'We won't need it.'

As he turned away, I noticed his spare drumsticks tucked into his jeans. He seemed as prepared and confident about playing in front of two hundred people as he was on his own in his basement.

I went to join my band, but Rocco had them huddled like he was a coach giving a team talk. For a moment I wished I was there with them, feeling the buzz of excitement, but being on the outside just brought it home – I still thought of it as *my* band, but I wasn't part of it any more. For a moment that made me sad, but I didn't have time to think about it for long because Powell was walking towards me with a huge grin on her face.

'So exciting,' she said, flicking her hair back. 'Poor Tom is as nervous as anything.'

'Really?' I said. 'He seemed quite calm.'

'Yeah, he's good at hiding stuff, but he must have peed ten times before we left the house.'

I laughed.

'Ooh!' Powell clapped her hands together, then nodded towards the front as the judges walked on to the stage. 'I think it's about to start,' she said.

I could feel the rumble of the crowd cheering. Some even put their fingers in their mouths to whistle, as one of the judges stepped forward towards the microphone.

Powell looked at me like she knew I couldn't see his lips.

'Just boring stuff,' she said. 'About the rules and band order. Basically, while one band is playing, the next one has to get ready in the dressing room behind the stage so there's no time wasted between performances. Oh, hi!' Powell waved across the room at someone she must have known.

'He's so cute,' she said, doing a little jig of excitement.

I smiled, then looked around the room at all the bands waiting. Although I couldn't hear a thing, from the way they shuffled about, I could feel the tension and excitement in the room.

The judges moved to the side of the stage and the band from Mittlesham High walked on. They started to plug their instruments in while the drummer sat on a stool and adjusted the kit.

This is it, I thought. *This is Rock City, where loads of famous groups like Big Jam and Petrolhaze have played.*

I wouldn't be able to hear a thing, but at least I was here, and in two hours' time, people would get to hear my songs.

Rocco said the first band's singer sang out of tune, and Powell said that the girl on the keyboard could only play two notes, which made me laugh because Powell had danced manically all the way through while the rest of the audience's feet seemed to be stuck in cement.

At the end of the set, the band left the stage, and the next band came up from the direction of a waiting room at the back. I went to ask Rocco how he was feeling, but he was now standing with Mia, Kai and Ty, and seemed to be talking to them seriously. I knew how much it meant to him, but I'd never seen him looking so determined. Back on the stage the band were getting ready, and two of the stage group unfurled a banner that read FOREVER YOUNG, and I thought it was a great name for a band, and an even better name for a song.

The crowd swelled in excitement as the lead singer took the microphone off the stand. She smiled and shook her bright pink hair. I had no clue what she said, but I gathered the band must have brought lots of fans, because as soon they started playing, a group of students began jumping up and down in the mosh pit at the front.

Powell tapped me on the shoulder. 'Oh, these are good.' She grinned. 'I'm going over there. Coming?'

I shook my head. It was weird enough watching a band that I couldn't hear; it would be even weirder jumping up and down pretending I could. Plus, I couldn't risk someone knocking my headphones off my head.

Powell stepped forward. 'You sure?'

'Yes.'

She pushed her way into the crowd, and I lost her for a while, but then caught her blonde hair bobbing up and down every time the flashing lights caught her head. I looked around the room – people were nodding and tapping their feet. I caught sight of Rocco's mum and dad standing with Mia's mum. I didn't know what Kai and Ty's parents looked like, but I guessed they were here somewhere.

For a moment I thought how much Mum and Dad would have loved to have been here too, but I hadn't seen the point in them coming as I wasn't playing. I still missed them just the same though. I loved how they weren't pushing me to do anything, simply leaving me alone to make up my own mind. My thoughts were quickly interrupted by Rocco stepping in front of me.

'Soph,' he said, still looking jumpy. 'Can I talk to you?'

'It's all right, Rocco,' I said with a little frustration, thinking he was going to ask me if I was okay for the hundredth time. 'I told you, I'm fine.'

'No, it's not that. Can we go outside into the foyer?' He pointed at his ears. 'Can't hear you because of the band.'

I turned to follow him, then noticed that Kai, Ty and Mia were leaving too.

'What's wrong?' I asked Mia as she passed me.

She shrugged and kept walking. I wondered if Rocco was thinking of pulling out because of nerves, or if Kai had suddenly forgotten the chords. But nerves usually made Rocco more wired and the chords were simple.

I followed the band through the door out into the foyer. They all turned round with serious looks on their faces.

'What's wrong?' I asked. 'You should be watching the competition or getting ready to play.'

'We are,' said Rocco, glancing at the band, then back at me. 'We're getting ready here, with you.'

'But you don't need me,' I said. 'I've taught Kai the chords.'

'No.' Rocco stepped forward. 'We all decided we want you to play with us.'

'No, Rocco.' I laughed. 'You can't. I'm not getting it wrong again. And besides, you can't just dump me in there with my guitar when there's less than an hour to go.'

'Not guitar,' said Mia with her eyes open wide. 'Drums.'

'Drums?'

'Yeah,' said Rocco. 'We know you've been playing, and you can't say you haven't played our songs because you must have.'

I couldn't lie, I had. But how did they know for sure? Had they been camped outside the shed listening the day before? The thing is, I had been practising, but not in a hall full of other bands and their fans.

'No, Rocco,' I said, looking around. 'I'm not ready. Not for this. Not for anything.'

'You've got to be.'

'Why?'

'Because I left the drum machine at home.'

'What?' I panicked. 'Then go back and get it.'

'No time,' Ty said.

'Too much traffic,' said Mia.

242

'But you have to,' I said. 'You can't play without ...'

One by one, the band's expressions turned to grins.

'Have you planned this all along?' I said.

'Pretty much,' said Rocco. 'But only once Mia said you'd been playing our songs.'

I turned to Mia. 'I told you it was simple beats!'

'I know.' Mia shrugged. 'And I told you I knew what that meant.'

Everyone laughed, but it was like they were building pressure on me.

'But, I'm not ready ...' My voice cracked. 'I could seriously mess up.'

'Doesn't matter, Soph,' Rocco said. 'It wouldn't be the same winning without you. We'd just be like a cover band, playing songs that we didn't write.'

'But why didn't you say before? Why now?' I glanced at my phone. 'With only fifty-five minutes to go?'

'Because we didn't want you to stress,' said Mia. 'We know what that does to your noise.'

'What's going on?' Powell seemed to appear out of nowhere.

'He's left the drum machine behind,' I said, nodding irritably at Rocco.

'What a muppet,' Powell said.

'I know,' I said. 'But he did it deliberately so I'd have to play.'

'Oh.' Powell laughed. 'Good one.'

'No, not a good one,' I said, shocked. 'You saw what happened last time, and it'll be even more obvious if I lose track and the drums stop!'

'Nah.' Powell waved my excuse away. 'You'll be fine,' she said. 'I've heard you with Tom. I think you can do it, Sophie.' She looked across the room to where Tom was standing with his band. 'Come here.' She beckoned to him.

I took a deep breath as Tom made his way towards us. More than anyone, he would know how I was feeling.

'What's up?' he said.

'They want me to play,' I said.

'Cool,' said Tom.

'No,' I said. 'Not really.'

'But it is.' Tom tapped his drumsticks against his palms. 'You know you can do it.'

'But I can't,' I snapped.

Tom glanced at Powell and the band, then pulled me to one side.

'Look,' he said. 'I know you're a bit shocked, but you know you can do it. I know you can do it. Just remember the stuff we did, imagine the click track in your head, and get them to follow you – not the other way round like it was with the guitar. If my band can do it with me, I'm sure yours can. And you've been practising since we played at mine, right?'

I took a deep breath and looked around at the band. Part of me had hoped Tom would give me a good reason to get out of it, but instead he was pushing me into it like the others. It felt like I had no choice, especially now Rocco had left the drum machine behind.

Tom glanced across the foyer towards his band. 'Look,' he said, 'I've got to go, but you'll be fine, Sophie.' He started to walk away, then turned back. 'Oh,' he said, reaching round his back. 'If you use the kit on the stage, you might be needing these.' He held out his spare drumsticks.

I still hadn't said yes, but I couldn't stop my hand from reaching out to take them.

Tom smiled.

'Wait,' I said. 'Were you part of this too?'

'Might have been.' He smiled. 'Just don't smash the drums so hard you break them.'

'I won't.' I smiled nervously, but suddenly as I held the sticks in my hand a wave of excitement took over me. I couldn't believe what was happening. Was I going to play at Rock City after all? Ever since I'd lost my hearing it had seemed impossible, but then I remembered how bad I'd felt the day in the rain when Powell invited me into her house. If I hadn't gone down into the basement and met Tom, I would have given up music altogether.

'Well?' asked Tom. 'You're not thinking of changing your mind, are you?'

'No.' I shook my head. 'I just wanted to say thanks.'

'What for?'

'You know,' I said. 'Everything.'

'No worries,' Tom said with a grin. 'Just don't beat us.'

Tom walked back to his band, who were now waiting to go back into the main hall. I turned. Powell, Rocco and the others were looking right at me, waiting for my answer. After all they had done to make this happen, it felt like if I said no, I would be letting them down. But most of all, I realized that I'd been blocking out the idea of playing with the band, when deep down I knew I still desperately wanted to.

'Okay,' I said, blowing my cheeks out. 'I'll do it!'

'Well that's a blimmin' relief,' said Powell.

'We've got just under an hour,' said Rocco. 'Let's set up over here.' He led us all to the stairs where Tom's band had been gathered.

Everything seemed to be happening so quickly. One minute I'd been watching the bands with Powell; the next I had to get my head around playing. The very next thing I knew I had to do was message Mum and Dad and get them to come down to Rock City. They'd dropped me off and were spending the afternoon in town. With only an hour to go, I messaged them both at the same time.

Sophie: Mum. Dad. I'm playing in Battle of the Bands! You've got to come down.

I waited anxiously for the blue ticks to appear so I'd know they had read the message.

'What are you doing?' asked Powell.

'Texting my mum and dad,' I said.

'No – you've got to get ready,' she said. 'Give it here. I'll call them.'

I glanced at the screen one more time in hope.

'Okay,' I said, handing my phone over. 'But if they don't answer, please keep trying.'

'Course,' said Powell.

While she called my mum and dad, I joined the band on the stairs. They all stood around me – Rocco singing the lyrics, Kai and Mia playing their guitars, while I tapped the drumbeat on two stools

246

that Ty had dragged out from the ticket office. All the time I was watching the band, but also glancing towards the door waiting for Powell to come back in.

'It's good,' said Rocco, after we'd played 'Reasons'. 'This is how we'll do it onstage, Soph,' he said. 'We'll all watch you, and you'll be the one to count us in.'

'Okay,' I said, glancing anxiously at the door again.

Mum and Dad couldn't have answered yet because there was still no sign of Powell. As we played 'Girl in the Photograph', I couldn't stop thinking that even if Mum and Dad did answer now, they would never get to Rock City in time.

'I'll get my mum to video it,' said Mia after we'd finished rehearsing the set. 'Least your mum and dad will get to hear and see it.'

'It's not the same,' I said. 'I actually want them here. I wonder if we could ask to go—' I stopped talking as Powell burst through the door with a big grin on her face.

'They're on their way,' she said.

I smiled with relief. I was back in the band, and about to play in front of loads of people, but it would have been horrible if I hadn't got to perform in front of the two people I loved most. But they were on their way. Now all I had to do was get myself ready.

CHAPTER 38

THE BAND WITH A NAME

Everything had been such a rush that I hadn't had time to think about being nervous, but as we were called to go to the dressing room backstage, that was when I began to shake. And it didn't help that when we got there, Rocco was walking in circles, repeating the lyrics over and over while a band called the Purple Hearts were playing. Mrs Hopkirk sat down beside me as the bass thudded through the walls.

'You'll be fine,' she said. 'Just concentrate on what you're doing and block everything else out.'

I nodded, but just her mentioning 'everything else' made me think about the huge stage and the crowd all watching me.

'Just picture yourself in the shed,' she said. 'Or in the basement, playing drums with Tom.'

I took a deep breath, pictured myself in the basement with Tom, with the imaginary click track in my head, and then in the shed the day before, playing with nothing to help me at all. But there was no time to imagine any more, or feel scared, because a man wearing

248

a black T-shirt with STAGE CREW written on it, was waiting in the doorway. This was it. We were on our way.

Mia and Kai picked up their guitars, and Rocco helped Ty carry the keyboard as we walked out into the corridor towards the stage. The Purple Hearts had unplugged their instruments and were walking off the other side. Mrs Hopkirk had said to block them out, but I couldn't stop myself peering out at the crowd. When we were watching from the audience, all we could see was the backs of people's heads, but now we were about to step onstage, I could see all their faces. I searched for Mum's and Dad's, but then thought even if they were here, they wouldn't be in the mosh pit at the front. I tapped Mia on the shoulder.

'I'm so nervous,' I said. 'I can't stop shaking.'

'Me too,' she said. 'I think we all are.' She nodded ahead to the steps, where Rocco was bouncing up and down like a boxer getting ready to step into the ring.

'I'm glad you're here, Soph,' she said.

'Me too.' I squeezed Mia's hand.

The man from the stage crew waved us on.

'Here we go,' Mia said.

My heart thudded in my chest as I made my way across the stage to the drum kit. It was a seven-piece set just like mine in the shed back home. I adjusted the stool upward and centred the snare. The stage-crew member stood in front of me and said something I couldn't lip-read.

'I'm sorry,' I said. 'I can't hear you.'

He smiled and pointed at the cymbals.

'Did you _____?' He lifted a cymbal stand and started to slide it towards me.

'Yes.' I nodded, working out that he'd asked if I wanted them closer.

He moved them a few centimetres then went over to Ty, who was setting up his keyboard on a stand parallel to me. Beside him was Kai, and then there was Mia standing next to her amp, opposite them. It was like they had it all planned out. I was at the top of a horseshoe where they could see me and I could see them.

I checked the kit, kicked the bass, ran the sticks over the snares and cymbals. Mia came and stood beside me, playing the bass for the few seconds I was playing.

'It's good.' She stood closer. 'Soph,' she said. 'I know you can't hear it, but I think you should know, this place is buzzing.'

I smiled. 'It's okay,' I said. 'I can tell.'

I looked out into the audience.

The mosh pit was full of young people, some of whom I recognized from school, but mostly faces I'd never seen before. Behind them people had left a gap, and there were the judges sat up on a platform surrounded by older people. I spotted Rocco's mum and dad waving, then Ty nodding, slightly sheepish, at a couple who must have been his mum and dad. I scanned the room looking for mine, but the only other people I could make out were Mrs Hopkirk and Mia's mum, who were standing together towards the back.

I'd really wanted Mum and Dad to come, but it wasn't their fault I had given them less than an hour's warning.

I kept scanning – more faces, more faces – then Powell jumping up and down, waving her hands above her head. Tom was standing beside her, shaking his head like she was embarrassing him. I laughed to myself. They argued with each other a lot, but it was great seeing them in the audience together when Tom could have been with his band.

Rocco walked over to me.

'Think someone is trying to get your attention,' he said.

I looked down into the mosh pit and saw a tall, skinny figure waving at me.

'Liam!'

He grinned. I never thought there would be a time when I was glad to see him, but I was then. He hadn't told me he was coming.

'*What are you doing here?*' I mouthed.

'Later,' he said. Then he mouthed as wide as his mouth would open, '*MUM AND DAD, OVER THERE!*'

I stood up behind the drum kit. Dad was looking right at me, with Mum beside him, standing on tiptoe. My heart leaped. I was so happy they had made it in time that I wanted to jump down off the stage, push through the crowds and hug them. But Rocco was already walking up to the microphone.

The crowd started to inch forward in excitement. My stomach flipped with nerves. Mia smiled like hers was too. I glanced to my left as Ty turned some knobs on his keyboard and gave the thumbs-up while Kai put his fingers over the frets of his guitar.

Rocco took the microphone off the stand and stood side on so I could see his mouth.

'Okay, Soph?' he asked.

I nodded, resting my foot against the bass pedal, and set the drumsticks across my palms.

I took a huge breath. *I'm here*, I thought to myself. *I'm actually here.*

I thought of trying to find Mum and Dad again, but I felt like if I locked eyes with them, I would cry.

The main lights shone down on the stage. The audience disappeared into the dark.

Rocco turned slightly towards me and held the microphone up to his mouth. 'Hello, everyone,' he said, looking right at me. 'This is a song called "Girl in the Photograph", and we are the Noise.'

The Noise, I said to myself. Did Rocco really just say we were called the Noise? I wanted to check with him, but I could barely see him as tears built in my eyes. I wiped them on my sleeve. Rocco's face cracked into a grin.

'Cool?' he asked.

Yes, Rocco, I thought. *The Noise is very, very cool.*

I knocked my drumsticks together as Rocco counted us in.

'One, two, three!' he said.

I smashed my sticks down on to the snares, kicked the bass. We were called the Noise – now we had to make some.

Kai had his head down over his guitar, Mia was concentrating hard on her bassline, and Ty was rocking backwards and forward with his hair falling down over his keyboard. Rocco started to jump up and down.

Your smile lights up the page
Lights up my room
You made me happy
When I was feeling sad
Because everything looks fine
Everything looks great
When you're the smiling girl in the photograph.

Rocco put his arm in the air and spun round.

I smashed the cymbals and couldn't stop smiling. How could I ever have thought I wouldn't want to be here, when playing music with the band was the thing I loved doing the most? I wasn't on the outside any more; I was bang in the middle of it. Rocco was singing a song about a smiling girl in a photograph, and for the first time in ages, I might even have been as happy as her.

CHAPTER 39

CRACKED!

'Why now?' Rocco looked up at me. 'Why did it have to break *now*?'

'Maybe it wasn't that bad?' I said.

'But it was!' Rocco held his throat. 'See? It just did it again then. I squeaked like someone was letting air out of a balloon. Didn't I?' Rocco looked at the rest of the band as we sat outside in the foyer. 'See?' he said. 'No one's saying I didn't.'

'Well,' said Ty, wiping his face in a towel. 'It wasn't great, but . . .'

'There,' said Rocco. 'What did I say?'

'No,' said Ty, patting him gently on the shoulder, trying to calm him down. 'I was going to say at least we got the first song done okay. It was only after that your voice went a bit . . . you know.'

'Bad,' said Rocco. 'Just say it. I should have known; my voice has been cracking all week.' Rocco held his hand up to his throat again.

'Oh,' I said. 'I didn't know that's why you were doing that. You did it when we were looking at the poster on the noticeboard. I thought you had something in your throat or were upset.'

'No,' said Rocco. 'I've felt it going for two weeks, and then today it just went.' He sat down on the stairs and buried his head in his heads. Rocco could be dramatic, but I'd never seen him as distraught as this. I thought maybe he was doing what I'd done: criticizing himself and spotting mistakes others couldn't hear.

I looked at Mia and Ty.

'*Was it that bad?*' I mouthed.

They both nodded.

I looked down at Rocco. He'd wanted me so much to be back in the band. We'd spent so many lunch hours practising, writing lyrics or just dreaming of being rock stars that it was horrible to see him so upset. I hadn't noticed a thing while I was playing as he was having so much fun jumping around and singing. The people in the mosh pit had gone mad, and I hadn't been able to help smiling when I'd seen Powell doing her Octopussy next to Liam.

It was when we got to the chorus of the second song, I knew something had gone wrong. He'd pulled a weird face like he'd swallowed a bee when he sang the high note. I saw Kai squirming, like Rocco had stepped too far forward and had got feedback screech from the microphone. Even the people in the mosh pit came to a standstill. After that, Rocco had tried to keep singing, but he had panicked so much that he forgot the words. I knew what it was like to mess up, and even though Rocco hadn't been great to me when I had, I hated to see him like this.

I crouched down and put my hand on Rocco's shoulder.

'Rocco,' I said. 'I'm not going to tell you it doesn't matter, because I know how much it does to you. But we do all mess up.'

I waited for him to look up, but he just sat there, head down, mumbling something, because I could feel his voice rumbling through his shoulder. Perhaps one sentence, maybe seven syllables – but that wasn't enough clues to work it out.

'Rocco,' I said. 'I'm sorry, but I can't see your lips.'

He lifted up his head. Tears were building in his eyes.

'I said, I want to be left alone.'

'I know,' I said. 'That's what I felt like too, after I messed up in the semi-finals.'

'But that was the best place to do it, not here at Rock City.' Rocco wiped his nose on his sleeve, then nodded at Ty, who was heading towards the exit.

'I'll be out in a minute,' he said.

'We'll be at the back,' said Mia. 'Listening to the other bands.'

They all left, carrying their instruments. Rocco leaned back and knocked his head against the wall. 'That's it, Soph,' he said. 'We're out.'

'Maybe we are,' I said, searching for something to make him feel better. 'But we could be like HiFi Dad. We can all stick together and come back next year.'

Rocco looked away, like he didn't want me to see him cry. His Adam's apple moved up and down in his throat as he spoke.

'This way, Rocco,' I said.

'Oh, sorry, Soph,' he said. 'I don't know why I always do that. I said, maybe you're right. We might win next year ... if we stay together.'

The floor began to thud as the next band started to play.

'Why *if*?' I asked. 'I'm not going anywhere.'

'No.' Rocco grinned. 'Me neither. Besides, if we had won this year, we'd have found it hard to tour. But, hey, now this is out of the way, you can concentrate on your operation at the end of the week, then next year it'll be Paris, New York and Tokyo!'

I chuckled. Typical Rocco – he'd only been down for a few moments before he'd come bouncing back again. I was about to tell him how nervous I was about the operation, but Tom had come out of the main hall and was walking towards me. Rocco glanced at him, then at me.

'I'll wait outside, Soph,' he said.

'Okay,' I said.

Rocco walked away. It was like he was avoiding Tom, or maybe he didn't want him to see him upset.

'How was he?' asked Tom. 'I couldn't hear, of course, but Powell said he sounded like a cross between Donald Duck and Mickey Mouse, whatever they sound like.'

I laughed.

'Is that bad?'

'Yeah,' I said. 'It's bad. I feel sorry for him.'

'Yeah, me too,' said Tom. 'But, hey, you did great. Didn't miss a beat, and our guitarist said the bass was tight.'

'Thanks,' I said. I didn't tell him I'd missed a snare when Rocco was mid-wobble. 'Are you nervous?'

'Me?' Tom held up his drumsticks. They shook. 'Ha,' he said. 'Shouldn't have done that, should I?'

I laughed. 'You'll be fine,' I said. 'I bet there's not a day you haven't played.'

'True.' He picked at the plaster on his thumb. The thud of the bass suddenly stopped. 'I better get going,' he said, looking towards the hall. 'My lot reckon HiFi Dad were the best so far. But, hey, what do they know?'

'I just hope you beat them,' I said.

'Me too.' He smiled then nodded over my shoulder. 'I think someone wants to talk to you.'

I turned and saw Mum and Dad grinning at me by the doors.

'You were amazing,' said Mum, as they came over to join us.

'Brilliant.' Dad beamed.

I didn't know what to say. I'd been so wrapped up with performing and then looking out for Rocco that I'd forgotten what I had done. A lump grew in my throat. I was proud of myself too, and relieved, but I didn't want to cry, not in the middle of Rock City.

'Is this Tom?' Mum said, like she knew I might be getting upset and wanted to distract me.

'Yes,' I said.

'Pleased to meet you at last, Tom.'

'Yes,' said Dad. 'We've heard a lot about you.'

'Good things, I hope?' Tom said, smiling.

'Of course.' Mum beamed.

Tom knocked his drumsticks together.

'Sorry,' he said, 'but I better get going and find my band. I'll catch you after, Sophie.'

'Yes,' I said. 'Good luck.'

'Thanks.' Tom turned towards the hall.

'He seems nice,' said Mum.

'He is,' I replied as Tom made his way through the crowd.

Mum put her hand on my shoulder. 'I'm just so proud of you,' she said. 'We were going to get a drink. Do you want to come?'

'No,' I said, looking at the stage as the band unplugged their instruments. 'I'll stay here and watch Tom.'

'Okay,' said Mum, adjusting my headphones like I was five. 'We'll see you in a bit.'

I looked back at the stage. The Long Shadows had left, and Tom's band were walking on. Ahead of me I saw the back of Powell's head, bobbing up and down as she waved. Tom shook his head, like I did whenever Liam did anything to embarrass me, then sat down behind the drum kit. He looked so calm as he adjusted the snares, like he was in his own world. I felt myself smile. My band were unlikely to win after Rocco's voice had cracked, but watching Tom was like having a second chance, and I so wanted his band to win.

CHAPTER 40

HOT DOGS AT ROCCO'S

'Blimmin' fix!'

'Powell!' said Mrs Hopkirk. 'You can't say that.'

'I can,' said Powell. 'And I did. How could they win? The lead singer could hardly hold a note and she danced like a robot. I'd rather you lot won than them.'

'Thanks,' said the lead singer of HiFi Dad, walking away.

'You're welcome,' said Powell.

We were standing watching the Purple Hearts having their pictures taken with the judges on the steps outside Rock City. They were laughing and smiling as they held up a trophy of a rock star singing into a microphone. Mia had told me she thought they were the best because the singer had a great voice and their choruses were really catchy, which must have been true because while they were playing, I noticed a lot of the crowd nodding or even singing along.

I had dreamed of being the winner and having my photo in the paper, but as they all celebrated, I was just happy that I was there and not stuck in my room at home. At least I had got on the stage and played and we'd had loads of people dancing and jumping up and down to our songs. And, as I'd suspected, it hadn't taken Rocco long to get back to his old self. He must have said a hundred times that we would be back bigger and better next year.

We were all set to go to our homes when Rocco's dad suggested we all go back to his house for a barbecue.

'Nothing special,' he said. 'Just a few sausages and burgers.'

The band all looked at each other and nodded. I glanced at Powell and Tom. They didn't know any of the band apart from me. I wanted to be with them, but I also wanted to be with the band after what they had just done.

'You go,' said Powell, like she could see my indecision.

'No, no,' said Rocco's dad. 'You're welcome to come too. Rocco told us how Sophie's been playing drums with your brother, and we've got more than enough food.' He glanced at Powell's mum. 'Is that okay?'

'Cool,' said Powell, before her mum could answer.

'Well, I guess that's a yes, then.' Powell's mum smiled.

'Great,' said Rocco's dad, rubbing his hands. 'I'll go start up the barbie and I'll get Rocco to send you all the _____ in case we lose you.'

He turned and walked away and everyone else in the band followed with their mums and dads. Mrs Hopkirk walked with Mia, while Powell was on her own, until Liam suddenly appeared from nowhere. I couldn't tell what he said, only that Powell must have found it funny because she tilted her head back and laughed.

I looked at Tom.

'What? No! They're not ...?'

Tom laughed. 'No,' he said. 'But I guess you don't know.'

'Know what?' I said, still shocked.

'Powell's going to be lead singer in Liam's band.'

'What?' I chuckled. 'He can't even play.'

'That's okay.' Tom grinned. 'It's not like Powell can sing, either.'

We both put our hands over our mouths trying to stop our laughter. As we made our way to the cars, I thought about what a great friend Tom had become. All I hoped was that after the operation, even if I could hear a bit, we would still get together to play drums.

When Rocco's dad said the barbecue wasn't going to be special, he wasn't exactly telling the truth, because as we turned into his road, there was a huge banner hanging from the window of his house.

CONGRATULATIONS, ROCCO (AND THE NOISE)

Rocco was standing on the driveway, red with embarrassment as his mum and dad took photos on their phones.

I couldn't make out what he was saying at first, but as I got closer, he looked at me and said, 'I keep telling them, Soph, it wasn't just me, and we didn't even win!'

I laughed and spotted Mia by the garage door doing the same.

'He's loving it, really,' she said.

'Yeah,' I said, walking over to her. 'I think he is. But did you know –' I nodded in Liam and Powell's direction – 'they're in a band!'

'Yeah.' Mia laughed.

'After all the things he said about her.' I stopped when I saw Tom approaching.

'It's okay,' he said. 'She's said stacks about him, too.'

We all laughed, then followed Rocco's mum and dad as they'd finally stopped taking pictures of Rocco and were leading us round the side of the house.

For weeks I had avoided being in crowds because I wouldn't be able to keep track of all the conversations, but now it was just happening around me. I missed whatever made Rocco bend over with laughter. And I missed whatever Rocco's mum said that made Mia's mum go teary. And I only knew the food was ready when everyone else got up. But it didn't matter; I was just glad to be out enjoying myself.

As I ate, I watched all the adults sitting in their group. Rocco's dad seemed to be as animated as Rocco, but I couldn't help noticing Mum and Dad laughing like they were having their own little joke as Mum punched Dad on the arm. It was great to see them enjoying themselves after worrying about me for such a long time. Out of the corner of my eye I saw Liam laughing with Powell. The idea of them being in a band together was weird, but Powell had been brilliant to me and so had Liam; he could be a pain, but having me around for the past few weeks couldn't have been much fun. I was pleased for both of them.

I jumped out of my thoughts as Mia tapped my arm.

'We're going out to the garage,' she said, her eyes wide with excitement. 'We're all going to have a jam.'

'Oh, cool,' I said.

I looked for Tom, to check he was okay, but it was like he'd already made friends with the band, and Powell too, because they were walking with Liam across the garden towards the gate.

'We were going to just play air guitar and stuff,' said Mia, 'but Ty reckons playing air keyboards doesn't really work.'

Ty looked across at me.

'Well, it doesn't, does it, Soph?'

I shook my head and chuckled.

'No, Ty,' I said. 'It really doesn't.'

Rocco flipped up the garage door while Ty got his keyboard out of his mum's car and Kai and Mia got their guitars. Tom went to his mum's car too.

'We've only got two amps,' said Rocco, moving them out from behind a couple of bikes. 'But we could plug two guitars into one, then me and Ty will share the other.'

I looked into the garage. There was only just enough space when there were four of us in the band; there was no way we could fit seven. And what was I going to play anyway?

Tom stepped in front of me. 'Here, Soph,' he said. 'You and I can play on this.'

He rapped his drumsticks against a big plastic container that collected water from the roof of the garage.

I laughed.

'You think you can play anything, don't you?' I said.

'Yeah,' he said, reaching behind his back for his spare set of drumsticks. 'Pretty much.'

Rocco and Kai carried the amps to the front of the garage while Ty set his keyboard up on the stand.

I looked at Powell and Liam; everyone had something to play except them, but I needn't have worried because Powell had started to jig up and down on the spot like she was getting ready to dance. And Liam was watching her like she was going to teach him some moves.

'Okay,' said Rocco, turning round on the drive. 'You two lead and we'll follow.' He pointed at me and Tom. 'And I'll just make up some lyrics as I go.'

I glanced at Tom.

'You start –' he nodded – 'and I'll pick up.'

This is crazy, I thought, looking at the others.

I hit the water container with my left stick, then my right. Then again and again, getting quicker all the time. Tom watched me, sticks hovering over the water container. He nodded as I increased the rhythm, then grinned as he struck the water container and joined in. Mia, Ty and Kai listened, then one by one they too joined in.

I kept the same rhythm and looked up. Liam was doing a weird dance, thrusting his arms out in front of him like he was pushing someone over, and Powell was shaking her hair and flailing her arms. Rocco walked between and around them, singing into the microphone. I didn't know what he was saying, only that playing and watching everyone was better than being onstage, because instead of being nervous, the rhythm came easier now we were all relaxed.

Rocco reached into his pocket and pulled out his phone. For a moment I thought he was looking for song lyrics, or making a note of the ones he'd just sung, but then he spun round.

'Smile!' he said.

He pointed his phone at me and Tom, then Mia and Ty, but soon he was focusing on Powell and Liam, who were now both doing the Octopussy on the lawn beside the drive.

I shook my head and looked at Tom. He shrugged.

'Guess she's happy.' He grinned.

'Yes,' I said, looking around at the band. Powell wasn't the only one that was happy. Neither of our groups had won Battle of the Bands, but I wanted Rocco to pause this moment for ever, because even though they had won the finals, there was no way the Purple Hearts were having as much fun as us.

It was as the sun was going down that my noise started kicking in. I was tired, and it had been a long day, but that didn't mean I wanted it to end.

I sat at the bottom of Rocco's garden watching everyone talking in their groups – Mia's mum with my mum and Rocco's dad. My dad talking to Powell and her mum, while Rocco's mum was sitting with the rest of my band and Liam.

The noise had started as a gentle whoosh, like waves gently lapping on a beach. I closed my eyes, took deep breaths, but no matter how many I took, it was like a storm was gathering, and the waves were crashing in.

I felt a breeze, like somebody had walked by. I opened my eyes as Tom sat down beside me. He smiled, but it wasn't the same happy smile we'd shared when we were jamming.

'Your noise?' he asked.

'Yes,' I said. 'You got it too?'

He nodded. 'Always,' he said. 'Never really goes away, I just notice it more in the evenings. It's like everything else and everyone else slows down.' He nodded to everyone sat at the back of the house. 'But when they do, I'm left with this.' He pointed at his ears.

'Yeah.' I sighed. 'Exactly like that. But it's been fun.'

'Oh, yeah.' Tom grinned as he looked at Powell. 'It's definitely been fun.'

Earlier I'd thought of saying we should all do it again, or maybe get my band and his band together, but now everything had slowed down, all I could think of was the operation. It was like Battle of the Bands had stopped me thinking, but all the time I'd known it was coming.

In five days I was going to be in hospital having an operation to try to get my hearing back. I knew it wouldn't be exactly the same as it was; Dr Cowans must have told me twenty times not to expect that. But at least I had a chance of something.

'I hope it goes okay,' Tom said, like he'd read my mind. 'Your operation. I know you've been told not to get too excited. But I know I would.'

I smiled and wished he could have the chance too.

'But we'll still play drums,' I said. 'You could come to the shed.'

'I'll look forward to that.' Tom grinned. 'And of course you can always come to the basement.'

I smiled with relief.

'Thanks,' I said. 'I was wondering if we would still do that.'

'Why wouldn't we?' He smiled. 'It's been great fun.'

'Yes.' I nodded as I felt warm inside. 'It has.'

'After your operation,' he said. 'We'll do it then?' He looked at me like he was going to say something else, but then he nodded towards the other end of the garden where his mum was waving to get his attention. 'Seems like I've got to go.'

We both stood up.

'Message me,' he said. 'After you've had it done.'

'Okay,' I said. 'I will.'

I looked back at the house. Everyone was now stood up, some talking.

I couldn't hear any voices.

I couldn't hear the things that people say when they leave a party, like *thank you for having us* or *goodbye*.

And I couldn't hear Powell laughing at Liam or the scrape of the metal as Rocco and his dad pushed the barbecue back against the wall.

I couldn't hear any of that at all.

And I knew I wouldn't, even after the operation. But three weeks later, on activation day, I might.

CHAPTER 41

FIVE DAYS LATER

THE MOST SCARY DAY OF MY LIFE

It's seven a.m. and my whole body is shaking as I walk across the hospital car park with Mum and Dad. I'm holding Mum's hand while Dad carries my overnight bag. The cochlear implant leaflet said I needed to be prepared to stay over after the operation because people react differently to the anaesthetic. Mum said she'd been up and about after a couple of hours when she had her wisdom teeth out, whereas Dad had got sick from the anaesthetic when he'd had his appendix removed.

As we walk through the front entrance, I feel mum grip my hand tighter. It's like she's having the operation, not me. I'd tried my best to remain calm by reading the leaflet over and over last night. It said things like I was in safe hands with people who were well practised in what they were doing. I'd be asleep for the operation, and it would only take two or three hours. There'd be a small incision, and I'd wake up with a bandage around my head. And I may feel dizzy, but that should only last for a short while.

I feel like I need to go to the toilet, as I stand between Mum and Dad as we check into reception on the surgical ward. The receptionist smiles at me, like she knows I'm nervous, then points us towards the waiting room. I sit down next to Mum, and it's like she senses that I feel like turning back home, because she puts her arm across my shoulder and says, 'Don't worry, Soph, I'll be here. You'll be fine.' And I smile back, nervously.

It only feels like a few minutes before a nurse comes to fetch us and I go into a cubicle to change into a white gown. My heart is beating so fast with panic that all I want to do is cry. I tell myself that I must go through with it, and think about Tom, and how much he'd love just to be given the chance I have.

'So, this is what's going to happen, Sophie,' the surgeon says as I lie on a bed with Mum and Dad by my side, blue curtain surrounding us. 'You'll meet the anaesthetist in a moment. She'll run through how we'll prepare you for the operation, then we'll take you down at around nine. It's all pretty straightforward – we'll have to shave two small parts of your hair, just behind each ear, but we'll make them as small as we can.'

I nod then look at Mum, then Dad, who are nodding like they're trying to reassure me.

'Now, I'm sure you're a little nervous,' the surgeon continues. 'It's only natural, but if at any time you have any questions or concerns, you just tell us, and the same goes for your mum and dad.'

'We will.' Mum smiles. She's trying her best to stay calm, but her face is nearly as white as my gown.

The surgeon leaves and I sit with Mum and Dad. For a while we talk about anything but the operation – the band, school – and I laugh when Mum says, 'Yes, I know. Who'd have thought it? Powell and Liam.' Because no one had thought they'd be in a band, let alone start going out together.

We're still chuckling when my phone vibrates by my side.

'It's a message from Rocco,' I say.

'Good,' says Mum, like she's relieved we might have something else to talk about. 'Just don't let him wind you up.'

I open the message.

Rocco: Good luck, Soph ☺ Thought you might like this.

'What does it say?' asks Mum.

'He's sent me a YouTube video,' I reply.

Mum and Dad lean close to me as I press play and watch a video of a dog running across grass, then rocks, then jumping into the sea with a video camera strapped on its back. Mum and I put our hands over our mouths as Dad grins. We're in a hospital and it feels bad that we're laughing.

But that stops as soon as the curtain opens, and my stomach flips as the anaesthetist tells Mum and Dad that it's time for them to leave.

Mum leans over, gives me a hug and kisses me on the head. Dad does the same.

'We'll see you later, then.' Dad smiles, trying to be chirpy.

I don't want them to leave, but I also don't want them to know I'm so anxious, so I try to be chirpy too and say, 'Don't worry. I'll be okay.'

They both give me one more wave then the anaesthetist gently takes hold of my hand. 'Just a small injection,' she says. 'Might sting a bit, and afterwards you'll feel a little woozy. Then we'll take you down to the operating theatre. I'll be with you all the time.'

I smile, then look away as I feel a tiny sting, just like the nurse said. I relax back and wait for it to take effect. In seconds I will be on my way for my operation, but all I want to do is think about waking up.

My eyelids begin to drop.

'Will it grow back ... ? They said it would grow back ...'

A nurse smiles, then she smooths my hair.

'Yes, it will grow back,' she says.

Smiley face. Her blurred, smiley face.

'My friend Rocco said I should have a Mohican.'

'What's that, Sophie?'

'My friend ... Rocco ... He said you should shave both sides of my head so I have a Mohican.'

Another sting in my hand. *Was I supposed to feel that?*

'It's okay, Sophie. You're going to feel a little drowsy now. We're just going to take you down to the operating theatre.'

Dark shadow. A doorway, then a white corridor, with bright lights passing over my head.

My eyes start to flicker.

'My friend Rocco ...'

Smiling face. Warm, smiling face – lips moving, but too blurry to read.

I feel sleepy. I feel so sleepy. Warm hand on mine.

'Your mum said you like to play guitar?'

I smile.

'Yeah.' My eyes flicker again. 'My friend . . . Rocco said I should have a Mohican.' The nurse's face fades away. So sleepy. So sleepy. 'My friend Rocco . . . He said . . . He said . . . I should have . . . a . . . Mo . . . a . . . Mo . . . hi . . . can.'

CHAPTER 42

THREE WEEKS IS A LONG TIME

My head is sore when I wake up. Mum and Dad are sat either side of my bed, smiling, and asking if I'm okay. I tell them I'm fine. Even though I know it will be another three weeks until activation day, I still feel disappointed that I can only read their lips and not actually hear the words they say. It's like being given a Christmas present but then having to wait ages to unwrap it.

I'm half asleep as I scroll through my messages in the car on the way home.

Mia: Hope you're good, Soph, and that it went okay.

Ty: Me too 😊

Rocco: And me 😊 Hope you're not 🤮 from the anaesthetic.

Kai: I hope you're good too.

Rocco: Have you got a Mohican?

Although I was still dozy, I couldn't help smiling at Rocco's messages. Even when he was being considerate, he still had the habit of saying the wrong thing. I clicked on a message from Tom.

Tom: Hey, hope everything went well. Message me when you want, and we'll play 📺 soon.

I go to type, but my head is too fuzzy to reply. I tilt my head back gently against the car headrest as traffic passes by. A high-pitched whine pierces through my head. I sigh. The Noise. Dr Cowans had never said it would go away, and it hadn't, but I was hoping that when the implant was switched on, it might cover it up. I just want that moment to be now, not in three weeks. I put my hand up gently to the side of my head, feel the softness of the bandages and imagine my bald patches underneath and the implants under my skin.

Three weeks, I think to myself. *Three weeks until I find out if it works.*

Mum turns round, checks on me for what must be the tenth time since we left hospital. I nod. *Yes.* And as she turns away, my noise starts to fade, and I can't stop myself wishing we could switch the implants on now.

The bandages are still around my head when Mum comes into my room two days later.

'Sorry to disturb you, Soph,' she says. 'But Rocco's outside. He says he's been messaging you all morning.'

'All morning?' I say, picking up my phone.

'Yes,' says Mum. 'I told him you were still sleeping.'

I wipe the sleep out of my eyes. It feels like early morning, but as I look at the screen, it says it's half past eleven. There are five messages from Rocco.

Rocco: Soph, are you there?

Soph, are you up yet?

Soph. I'm outside, again.

Soph!

Soph, come on, even I don't sleep in till nearly midday!

'Shall I let him come up?' Mum asks after drawing back my curtains. 'Only he came round yesterday, but you were asleep.'

'I know,' I say, showing her my phone. 'He told me.' I rest my head back on the pillow.

'Maybe I'll just say you're still asleep,' she says.

I went to shake my head, but remembered it hurt whenever I moved it.

'He'll know I'm not,' I say. 'Because he'll see I've opened his messages now.'

'Okay,' says Mum. 'So what shall I tell him?'

I take a deep breath. I've been in my room for two days with my head sore and ringing, and the last thing I need is Rocco bouncing around me, but if I don't say yes, he'll only keep on messaging, and that would be almost as irritating.

'Okay.' I sigh. 'Let him in. But, Mum, can you tell him to keep still?'

'Are you sure?' Mum asks. 'Only asking Rocco to do that is like keeping a hamster in a paper bag.'

I laugh, then wince as a sharp pain shoots through my head. 'Yeah,' I say. 'It's okay, but tell him not to make me laugh either.'

Mum turns away. I ease myself up on my bed, then pull my red throw over me. It's weird enough that Rocco is going to come into my room, without him seeing me in my pyjamas.

'Actually, Mum.' I grimace as the stitches behind my ears pull tight.

Mum puts her head back round the door. 'Yes, love?'

'Change of plan,' I say, swinging my legs on to the floor. 'I'll get changed and come down.'

'Maybe grab one of Liam's hoodies,' she says. 'So there's more room to fit it over your head.'

'You must be joking,' I say.

Mum laughs.

As I get changed, I wonder what could be so urgent that Rocco has come round twice in two days. He lives over six kilometres away; it wasn't like it was a short walk down the road. Knowing him, it was just that he'd come up with a new song that he thought was absolutely brilliant and couldn't wait to share it. But if it was that, he could have just sent a message.

I put my slippers on and walk down the stairs. Mum's stood in the lounge doorway, nodding her head like she's talking. She steps aside when she sees me coming.

'Here she is,' she says, making sure I can see her face. 'Be gentle with her – especially you, Rocco.'

Especially you, Rocco, I think to myself. That must mean someone else is here.

'Thought maybe it might be less tiring if you all met at once, Soph,' says Mum.

I edge into the living room. Rocco's sitting on the edge of the sofa, holding his phone, while Mia and Tom are sat either side of him, watching the screen and laughing.

'Soph,' says Rocco, looking up. 'I've been messaging you for ages, but you've not replied.'

'I know, Rocco.' I roll my eyes. 'But I have had an operation, you know.' I point at the bandages on my head.

'We know,' says Mia, standing up. 'And we do hope you're okay. But really, Soph, you will love this when you see it.'

'You will.' Tom smiles. 'Believe me.' He moves along the sofa, making space for me.

I walk across the room and sit between him and Rocco, expecting Rocco to have found a funny YouTube video, like the one he'd sent me of the dog when I was in hospital. But as I look at the screen, there's no dog, just a picture of us all outside Rocco's house.

Rocco turns to me.

'Ready?'

'Yes,' I say. 'Just don't bounce around too much.'

Rocco smiles. 'I'll try not to.'

He looks at the others, then presses play.

We all huddle around the phone. On the screen is a close-up of

Rocco's face, then the camera spins round to reveal all of the band playing in the driveway of his house the evening after we'd played at Rock City. The camera zooms in on Kai playing his guitar, then Mia on her bass. Then there's me and Tom wearing our headphones as we smash out a rhythm on the water container.

I smile. We all look so happy, and I think how cool Tom and I look in our headphones, but I can't help wishing I could hear it too.

Rocco points at the screen then looks at me.

'Keep watching, Soph,' he says. 'This is the best bit.'

I look back at the screen as the camera zooms in on Powell, who's flailing her arms and shaking her head as she dances with Liam.

I put my hand up to my mouth. I want to laugh so much, but the cuts above my ears are so sore.

Rocco grins as he points at the writing underneath the video: *Octopussy discovered in suburban garden.*

'It's got over twenty thousand views,' he says.

'What?' I say, taking my hand down. 'You put it on YouTube?'

'Yeah,' says Rocco, looking pleased with himself. 'It's gone viral.'

'Oh my god, Rocco,' I say as Powell flails her arms on the screen. 'She'll go mad!'

Tom leans forward.

'No, Sophie,' he says. 'She loves it. Rocco says everyone at your school is doing the Octopussy – in the quad, the canteen. She's even signing autographs in the hall.'

I laugh, but then it's like everyone winces with me as my stitches pull tight.

'Sorry, Soph,' says Mia, looking like she's sharing my pain. 'But we thought you'd like to see it.'

'I do,' I say. 'It just hurts when I laugh.'

The video finishes, then everyone looks at each other like they don't know what to say next, and neither do I. I love it that they've come round, but it would have felt easier talking about my operation if I had met them one at a time.

'So, when do they come off?' Rocco says eventually, circling his hand around his head. 'The bandages?'

'Tomorrow, I think.'

'Then it's another three weeks until they switch the implants on?'

'Yeah,' I say. 'Another three weeks.'

Rocco glances at the others. It's like we all know what we're hoping will happen in three weeks, but are too scared to say. We look at Rocco's phone instead as the video automatically plays again.

'Is she really signing autographs?' I ask.

'Yeah.' Rocco chuckles. 'Well, she set up a table, but I'm not sure how many went.'

I shudder again as a pain shoots through my head.

'I think maybe we should go,' says Mia. 'It looks like it hurts.'

'Yeah,' I say, holding my hand up to my head. 'It does, but thanks for coming.'

'No worries,' Rocco says, standing up. 'Just hope, you know ...' He points at his ears.

I smile.

'Hey,' he says, looking at his phone. 'Twenty-one thousand, two hundred and forty-three now!'

Mia shakes her head.

'I'll get him out of your way, Soph,' she says, pushing Rocco out into the hallway. It was like she knew I wanted to talk to Tom by myself, but now we were alone, I felt more awkward than I ever had before. I was one step closer to getting some of my hearing back, but that felt like it was one step further away from the silence he would always have. From the nervous look on his face, it was like he was feeling the same.

'Three weeks, then?' he says evenutally. 'Until the bandages . . .' He circles his hand round his head, like Rocco did.

I smile. 'He was only trying his best,' I say.

'I know,' says Tom. 'Just messing. How do you feel?'

'Scared,' I say.

'Yeah.' Tom looks out of the window as Mia and Rocco lean against our front wall. 'But that's okay,' he says, turning back to me. 'I'd be scared too. But at least you're trying. Better to know you gave it a chance than not.'

'Yeah.' I nod.

'And don't stay in worrying about it,' says Tom. 'You're probably too sore to wear headphones, and best not play anyway, but we can still chat about it, after school.'

'Thanks,' I say. 'I would like that.'

Tom grins.

'Did I say something funny?' I ask.

'No. It's him.' Tom nods at the window, to where Rocco is holding up his phone.

'*Twenty-two thousand!*' Rocco mouths.

We both laugh until Tom says, 'I'd better be going. My band are already practising for Battle of the Bands next year.'

I follow him out into the hall. I loved how he was always looking ahead, like whatever was next was exciting and didn't fill him with fear. As I watch him walk down the road with Mia and Rocco, it's like the dark clouds in the sky suddenly make my noise grow loud. It feels like it will always be there, but if it is, I know I could cope with it, just like I could cope with whether the operation worked or not, because no matter what, I'd still have my friends.

I close the door and go up to my room. I pick up my songbook and flick through. 'Pictures of You', 'Girl in the Photograph', 'Roller-Coaster Ride' – it's like my songs are the story of the last few weeks.

I stop on the page where I've written the line about the pitter-patter of a storm when I was with Tom. I pick up my pen and start to write.

Sitting on a mountain top
Rain silently falling
Cars silently passing
In the valley below
And I see a girl on the other side
I want to shout
Can you hear me?
Can you hear me?
Because I want to hear you
And the rain keeps falling, gentle and warm

I can see the lightning
But only feel the thunder
All I want is a storm.

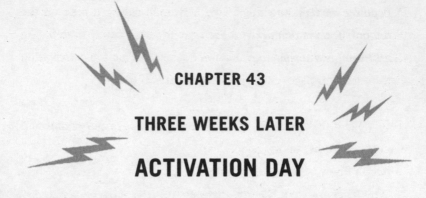

CHAPTER 43

THREE WEEKS LATER

ACTIVATION DAY

Mum always says it's wrong to wish time away, but during the last three weeks, I think even she has. Having the cochlear implants inserted wasn't like having a normal operation. And like Dad said after the bandages came off, it wasn't like when he broke his leg – I couldn't exercise and gradually make it better. All I could do was wait to go to hospital for Dr Cowans to turn the implants on.

When the bandages came off, a few days after the operation, the wounds felt sore if I ran my fingers over them. It felt like the bald patches were huge, as well as the lumps where the implants were, but they felt a lot smaller a week later, once I'd had the stiches taken out. I'd still been worried about the bald patches, though, but I'd felt a little better when Dad held up a mirror and showed me how the rest of my hair hung down and covered them up.

The car feels like its full of all our nerves as we drive to the hospital. Mum keeps tapping her fingers on the steering wheel, and

Dad points at random things, like a woman riding a bike on the pavement, or a man on a poster for a car advert. They're both trying to make out that it's just like any other day. But it isn't. It's activation day – the day I discover if I will ever hear sound again.

'How does it feel?' says Dr Cowans as he pushes back my hair and places the magnet on my head.

'Don't know,' I say. 'Just strange.'

'You'll get used to it,' he says, turning me to fix the second magnet.

'Yeah,' I say. 'I'm sure I will.' I nod, trying not to show my nerves, but my hands are sweating and my throat is dry. And it doesn't matter how much Mum and Dad smile, they can't hide the anxious looks on their faces.

'So, this is what's going to happen,' says Dr Cowans. 'First of all, we will do the beep test. I'll switch it on, but you won't hear anything at first. Okay?'

'Okay.'

'Then I'll just gradually turn it up, very slowly. I don't want to shock you, so don't be worried if you don't hear anything for some time.'

I look around at the monitors, the switches, and suddenly feel the weight of the magnets on my head.

I blow out my cheeks. Dr Cowans smiles then turns back to his computer screen.

My head begins to fill with noise, just like it did whenever Dr Cowans put me in the cubicle. I was glad I wasn't going in there now, but that doesn't stop me fidgeting in my seat.

'It's okay,' says Dr Cowans. 'Take your time. I know you've probably got a lot of other noises going on, but believe me, you'll know when it's the one.'

He turns the knob again. He's right, there are so many noises. Thousands of noises. Which one was the one being made by him?

He turns the knob again. I feel Mum's and Dad's eyes on me, like they are willing me to say, '*Yes! I can hear it!*' But I can't hear it at all . . .

But then there is something – a different noise. Is it real or is my head playing tricks?

I look at Dr Cowans.

'I think there's something,' I say. 'But it's just a *wow . . . wow . . .*'

'A swooshing?'

'Yes,' I say. 'A swooshing. That's it, a swooshing – but I think it might be in my head.'

'We'll see,' says Dr Cowans, turning the knob again. 'How about now?'

'Yes,' I say. 'Still there, but louder.'

Dr Cowans's face cracks into a smile.

'And still?'

'Yes.' I fidget in my seat. 'It's still there! Did you just make it go louder again?'

Dr Cowans nods then glances at Mum and Dad. It's only a *swoosh*, but Dad is wiping his eyes, and Mum's got tears running down her face.

'Okay,' says Dr Cowans. 'Now we'll turn the microphone on. Again, it will be slow, so don't worry. You won't hear anything at first. I'll just keep talking, telling you what I'm doing, until you say you think you hear something . . .'

I concentrate as hard as I can, searching my head for a sound, but not one of my own – anything that sounds like a voice.

I shake my head. Dr Cowans's lips are still moving, but I can't hear a thing.

'No,' I say. 'Nothing. I can't hear—'

Then a sharp, low sound.

I turn and look at Dad. His face is red, and he's got his hand over his mouth.

I point at him.

'There! There!' I put my hands up to my face. I try to speak because I think I heard something.

'Sophie,' said Dr Cowans. 'Did you just hear your dad cough?'

AUTHOR'S NOTE AND ACKNOWLEDGEMENTS

They say, 'write what you know', and there's much in this book that I know first-hand. But for the parts I needed help with, I'm hugely grateful to Zia Dredge, a nine-year-old girl from Brisbane, Australia. Her mum, Heidi, contacted me after I'd mentioned I was writing a story about a deaf girl during a Zoom call with a local school. Zia, I hope you continue to enjoy hearing in your new world.

As for the parts I do know, I was four years old when my parents first noticed I was hard of hearing. When they called out to my siblings that there were sweets in the kitchen, this greedy tyke stayed motionless in front of the TV. They repeated the 'experiment' over the next few days, just to be sure. Numerous hospital appointments followed, an operation, putty mould in my ear, and I was presented with a hearing aid when I was six. Dad told me it played music to encourage me to wear it. And when it didn't, I took it off one break time at school and stamped it into the ground.

I went through senior school without wearing one, not even telling my friends I was deaf. I was lucky that I was pretty gregarious, talking stacks without realizing I was doing so, because it meant I didn't have to listen. I more or less blagged my way through. I think mates found me coolly ignorant, and writing funny poems about them (and the teachers) helped me more than get by.

But it wasn't that way with everyone. At the age of twelve, an audiologist told my parents I was the rudest boy he'd ever known. That was after he'd played the sound of a 100 mph tornado through my headphones for half an hour! One French teacher asked my parents if I was simple, and a geography teacher couldn't hide his frustration when he had to ask me which way water flowed, ten times. 'Down, sir. It flows down,' I would have answered the first time if he hadn't whispered so quietly. It didn't help that he'd grown a beard too, making it impossible for me to read his lips.

This book came about one night when my tinnitus was so bad that I thought there was a bus idling outside my bedroom all night, but there are many upsides to being hard of hearing. The isolated feeling lent itself to inner thoughts and creativity. Mishearing song lyrics allowed me to come up with original lines for this book. And having to watch people's lips and body language has made me a very good listener. I've missed a lot, but I'm not always sure I'd swap it out.

So, enough about me, and more about you. If you're struggling to hear at school, or anywhere, speak up and tell someone. If you're worried about wearing a hearing aid, don't be – you'll get used to it, and the new sounds you discover will make up for that early pain. You'll realize, like me, that birds actually sing, and swans make a flapping noise when they move their wings. You'll also find people make a noise when they swallow, and that the cat you've had for ten years really does purr. ☺

Now's the time to thank my friends and my family – the ones who don't wave their hands in front of me, open their mouths wide like a goldfish when they pronounce each word and who seamlessly step in when I've missed something. You might have sore throats from talking up for me, feel frustrated when I've pretended I've heard what you said when I obviously haven't, or annoyed when you've stopped with a flat tyre and I've ridden off into the distance on my bike. Thank you all stacks.

In addition, I'd like to thank my editor, Amina Youssef, for her skill (and patience) in helping me make this story, my copyeditor, Veronica Lyons, and proofreader, Leena Lane, for their unfathomable help, and my agent, Clare Wallace, for our chats, which encourage me to keep at my laptop, typing my thoughts, every day.

Finally, thanks to all the teachers and librarians in schools that I've visited, who understood when my dog had chewed up my hearing aids. Or had to repeat a question a child asked, four or five times. Or had to run out into the car park shouting, 'Stew. Stew. I've been shouting down the corridor after you for ages. You've left your coat behind!'

The world can be a quiet place at times, but we've had some fun.

READ ALL OF STEWART FOSTER'S BRILLIANT BOOKS!

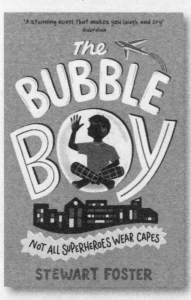

Turn the page for a sneak peek
of another fantastic book by **Stewart Foster.**

CHAPTER 1

ME AND ERIC

You might walk past me every day, when you're on your way to school, or going to town shopping with your mum. You've probably stood just down the road from me, talking to your friends, but I bet you've never even looked in my direction. Next time you're out, just stop for a second and look down the alley that runs along the back of the shops. The alley you never go down because it's dark and damp, with bags of rubbish strewn at the sides. The one full of silver bins and a big yellow recycling skip with a ladder leaning against it.

Can you see them?

If you creep down the alley, just a little, you'll see the skip has lots of writing on the side, such as:

CLEAN ME

DO NOT PUT HOT ASHES IN HERE

CITY RULE

ERC

I call the skip Eric and for the moment I want you to ignore all the things written on it and keep walking, just like I did the first time I came here, four months ago.

Oops, sorry, I forgot to tell you to duck under the line of Coke cans I've tied across the top of the skip. Now you've rattled them. This is my early warning system; it's how I can tell when people are coming, my alarm for when the bin collectors from the council arrive in their truck to empty the skip. Or sometimes it's just the wind blowing and the cans tinkling. But today, right now, it's not the wind, and it's not the workers from the council. It's you.

And I'm on full alert because you're past the cans and you've seen the ladder leaning against the skip. You're not sure you should climb it, but it's okay, you can. Just put two hands on the sixth rung and start to climb. That's it. Then, when you're on the tenth rung, peer over the yellow metal, into the skip. Inside, can you see the rope I use to lower myself in, and the pieces of cardboard propped up in the corner? The Samsung sixty-five-inch TV box lying across the top?

These are my walls and my roof that stop the sun baking me in summer, and the rain soaking me in winter.

Can you see me?

No?

Wait, I've just got to push myself up because the boxes have crumpled.

Ha, there I go.

'Hi! I'm Sam, little c, big C McCann. This is my home, and I'm pleased to meet you.'

CHAPTER 2

PLANES AND DREAMS

You might think it's weird that I call a skip my home, and not the house where I sleep and eat. But you see, a house and a home aren't the same thing. A house is the place you live in, made of bricks and cement with double-glazed windows and doors, with pipes and radiators inside. A home is only made by the things you put in the house, like sofas and chairs, beds and paintings, and pictures of you and your family at Santa's grotto or on your holidays. I live in a house with all those things, except the pictures are of Christmases I never had and holidays I didn't get to go on and the family isn't mine at all.

I've lived in nine houses over the last five years and they're all the same, with foster-parents who tell me I'm part of the family and that they'll treat me as if I was one of their own children. But they don't leave their own children out of a trip to the cinema, nor at a respite home in Keynsham while they all go away to Spain on holiday. It's like they think I won't notice, but it's obvious when they come back because I'm maggot-white and the family are tanned-brown. At the moment I live with Reilly and his mum, who gets paid for looking after me. I've been here for four months and twenty-two days, which is the fourth longest I've ever stayed anywhere. They haven't been on holiday without me yet, but they will.

I stay in Eric to escape from all that. It makes me feel better when I can lie back on the cardboard and look between the grey buildings at the sky. Yesterday when I was here, I saw a plane and imagined I was on it, flying to Disneyland. I pictured a big hotel, with Mickey Mouse and Donald Duck welcoming everyone in the foyer and saying, 'Have a great day!' every morning when I went out to ride on the roller coasters. I dream of going to Disneyland a lot, but today there are no planes in the sky to take me, just stacks of pigeons flying over the alley as the traffic rumbles by on the high street.

Reilly will be in his house, in his room, playing Ace Pilot on the Xbox he got for Christmas. I'd only been here for two weeks, so all I got was clothes, as usual. I sat on the sofa and watched Reilly open his box. I knew what it was before he even ripped off the paper. 'It's an Xbox One,' I said out loud when he stared at the box. He asked me how I knew. I just shrugged. I didn't tell him I'd watched James open one on his birthday, in the house I'd stayed in before. James had loads of friends who came for sleepovers and they'd eat pizza in his room and play Star Trooper until midnight. Reilly doesn't have many friends, and he doesn't have loads of sleepovers. I'm glad because it means I don't get left out when everyone else is shooting aliens on multiplayer.

I stare at the sky and wonder what it must be like to have just one family and live with them all your life. Well, not *all* your life, because you'd have to leave sometime, after you finished school and had to go to university or get a job. But if I had a family of my own, I don't think I'd ever want to leave them. Why would I want to leave the people I love? I'm not sure I loved Brad and Angie, my fourth foster-parents, but I did like them so much I didn't want to leave. They lived in a bungalow in Felton. It had a massive garden with a football net at the bottom. Brad used to go in goal, and I'd whack the ball at him while Angie watched from the patio. That was my record stay: nine months – three quarters of a whole year. So long that Brad even bought me a second-hand bike from eBay and we cycled together to town whenever he wanted to go to Forbidden Planet for comics. I thought I was going to make it until Christmas. I even started thinking about what presents I would like – not computer games or DVDs, just clothes and stuff. I really liked Brad and Angie, and I think they really liked me, but I could feel the end coming. I always can. The end is when people go quiet, and start having whispered conversations about me in the kitchen. That's what Brad and Angie did – whisper, whisper, whisper – every evening after they got home from work, every night when I was in bed. It was like listening to mice under the floorboards. I noticed Angie's belly was getting bigger. She started eating whole tubes of Pringles, while she showed Brad pictures of baby clothes and prams that she had searched on her laptop. And then she'd ask Brad if it was bad luck to paint the spare room before the baby came.

Yes. It was bad luck. It was bad luck for me.

'You can still visit, Sam,' they said. 'Still play football in the garden.'

But visiting isn't the same, I thought to myself. Even if they did let me keep the bike.